"Juliet Blackwell sits firmly on my list of must-read authors.... [Her] writing is like that of a master painter, placing a perfect splash of detail, drama, and whimsy in all the right places."
— Victoria Laurie, *New York Times* bestselling author of the Psychic Eye and Ghost Hunter Mysteries

"Cleverly plotted with a terrific sense of the history of the greater Bay Area, Blackwell's series has plenty of ghosts and supernatural happenings to keep readers entertained and off-balance." — *Library Journal*

"Smooth ... seductive.... Fans will want to see a lot more of the endearing Mel." — *Publishers Weekly*

"A winning combination of cozy mystery, architectural history, and DIY with a ghost story thrown in.... This well-written mystery has many different layers, offering something for everyone to enjoy."
— The Mystery Reader

"Amiable and realistic characters led by the endlessly appealing Mel Turner.... The author excels at blending historical scholarship, ghostly mythology, and architectural minutiae into a novel that is completely fascinating and perfectly balanced by a light tone and witty humor."
— Kings River Life Magazine

"One of the most exciting, smart, and funny heroines currently in any book series." — Fresh Fiction

GIVE UP THE GHOST

A HAUNTED HOME RENOVATION MYSTERY

Juliet Blackwell

AN OBSIDIAN MYSTERY

OBSIDIAN
Published by New American Library,
an imprint of Penguin Random House LLC
375 Hudson Street, New York, New York 10014

This book is an original publication of New American Library.

First Printing, December 2015

For more information about Penguin Random House, visit penguin.com.

ISBN 978-0-451-46581-8

Printed in the United States of America
10 9 8 7 6 5 4 3 2 1

Penguin
Random
House

To Jan Strout,

in laughter, joy, and social justice

Chapter One

It's hard to ruin a Pacific Heights mansion. After all, it's *Pacific Heights*.

One of San Francisco's nicest neighborhoods, Pacific Heights straddles the crest of one of the city's many hills and offers world-class views of the Golden Gate Bridge, the Bay, the Palace of Fine Arts, and Sausalito. In the late 1800s, following the Gold Rush and the acquisition of California, when robber barons were exploiting workers and stealing land to make their fortunes, this is where many of them chose to spend their ill-gotten gains: on the mansions studding this hill, one after the other, like a lineup of enormous ten-bedroom, five-bath, turreted, multistory, wood-and-stucco beauty queens—historic testaments to taste, craftsmanship, wealth, and ruthlessness.

But I had to hand it to Andrew Flynt, the fiftyish, plump, rather pallid man standing with me in the foyer. The mansion called Crosswinds now gleamed with the sleek, plastic-feeling newness of a really expensive, really modern, really wretched remodel.

A remodel plagued by ghosts, apparently.

"Cost me millions to bring this place into the twenty-first century," Flynt said, as I struggled to rein in my distaste. I've been told before that I don't have much of a poker face. "Wasn't easy to bring it up to snuff. Used to be nothing but acres of dark wood paneling in here. Can you say gloomy?" He nudged me with his elbow and pointed. "Take a look at that fireplace surround: blue Brazilian granite. Cost me beaucoup bucks, I don't mind telling you. Sleek, simple. Real class, something like that. You should have seen the original: carved limestone, with—get this—*cupids*." He shook his balding head. "So kitschy."

"*Mmm,*" I grunted, my go-to response when I was busy biting my tongue so as not to alienate an über-wealthy potential client.

My eyes cast around the space, searching for signs of history. Gone were the subtle dents and nicks a home acquires over the years. Nowhere did I see the soft edges or refined imperfections that characterized moldings hand-carved by long-departed master craftsmen. Victorian-era parlors and chambers, once discreetly separated by paneled walnut pocket doors, had been blasted open and merged into a single, echoing "great room" decorated in a blinding white-on-white color scheme. The original leaded windows had been sealed shut to allow the "smart" home to filter and recirculate the air at a perfect seventy-two degrees. Too-bright recessed can lights dotted the smooth, flat ceilings, now devoid of any trace of the original engraved plaster medallions and crystal chandeliers so common to buildings from the late 1800s. To my mind the formerly intimate space now resembled an oversize hospital operating room.

"Paid ten million for it, as it was," Flynt let out a rueful laugh. "Ten mill for a fixer-upper. But what can I say? I'm a visionary."

"And your Realtor said you were asking twenty-nine million?" Even in San Francisco, one of the nation's priciest real estate markets, that was a lot of money.

"Most expensive property on the market," Flynt boasted. "Well worth it, for the right buyer. It's a massive home, with ten bedrooms. *Ten.* And this location is priceless, of course. Have you checked out the views? Not enough money in the world for something like that. And then the remodel on top of it, everything totally updated, with the latest technology — what's not to love?"

"Yet you haven't been able to sell it," I pointed out.

"No. Obviously." A tic appeared over his right cheekbone. "That's where you come in."

I'm a general contractor, head of Turner Construction. We specialize in renovating historic buildings. But not like this. Never like this.

Besides, there was nothing left to redo. So far I had seen only the sparsely furnished main floor, but unless I missed my guess this place had been gutted, taken back to the studs, and rebuilt with all new materials. They had kept the home's classic exterior shell and built themselves a brand-new, *Sopranos*-style home within.

Still ... from the moment I stood at the foot of the front steps, looking up at the still-intact Victorian Rococo Revival facade, complete with a turret and carved garlands and gold-gilt shields, I had felt something.

Crosswinds needed someone to save it. And if the past few haunted home renovations I had completed were any indication, *I* was that someone. Whether I wanted the title or not. Just call me Mel Turner, historic home renovator and up-and-coming Ghost Negotiator.

"And what exactly do you want me to do?" I asked Flynt.

"Karla tells me you have experience with this sort of thing," Flynt hedged, referring to Karla Buhner, the no-doubt frustrated Realtor trying to off-load Crosswinds to some poor sucker for a sum equivalent to the gross national product of a small country.

"What sort of thing would that be?" I asked, all innocence.

I knew what he meant. But people like Andrew Flynt wanted underlings to read their minds, to relieve them of the burden of being explicit. It was a strangely childish habit that annoyed the heck out of me, prompting me to respond in an equally stubborn manner. If Flynt wanted something from me, he was going to have to ask for it.

"It's . . . all right, dammit, it's *haunted*," he said, the tic in his cheek accelerating. As he reached up to rub his face the two heavy gold rings weighing down his hand glinted in the sunshine streaming through the spotless—and modern—plate glass windows.

"Haunted, you say? *Really?*"

"The ghosts, or whatever it is, appear to be running off prospective buyers. Every time there are clients touring the house, something . . . happens. Last week, a physician and his wife—she's an heiress from New York, *very* old money—literally ran from the house screaming. Can you believe it? The man's a cardiologist!"

I wondered why Flynt thought being a cardiologist would render one immune from fear. Being scared by ghosts wasn't funny. I should know.

Flynt shook his head. "Karla says you're the go-to gal around here for this sort of thing. I need you to fix it."

Just then I heard a squeaking noise overhead and looked toward the ceiling.

"What's that?" I asked.

"That's what I'm talking about," Flynt groused. "That's the sound of the weathervane that used to be on the roof. Nasty old thing. It was the first thing to come down, let me tell you. But you can still hear it when the wind blows. What's *that* about?"

"And there's no other possible explanation? Is there anyone else in the house?"

"There's Egypt."

"Egypt? I assume we're not talking about the country?"

"No. A person. Egypt's the caretaker; lives up in one of the attic rooms. You know, when I bought Crosswinds my kids were still living at home, but the remodel took so long they're now off on their own. The wife and I don't need a huge house like this. Bought a beautiful place in Tiburon—a Bollinger."

"A Bollinger?"

"Young designer from Germany. Very exclusive. Place is right on the golf course, seventeenth hole."

"Ah."

"So anyway, I don't really believe in this ghost stuff but apparently buyers are now refusing to even look at the place, so last month my wife Stephanie called in a psychic Karla recommended. Name of Chantelle, you heard of her? Goes by just the one name, like Cher or Madonna. Very famous. Hard to get an appointment with her, much less get her to make a house call. She's . . . lovely. Cost me a pretty penny, let me tell you."

"And what did Chantelle make of Crosswinds?"

Again with the tic. He massaged his cheek. "She says the ghosts of the family that used to live here are angry about the remodel. She says the only way to appease them is to track down some of the original architectural stuff and put it back."

He glared at me. As though I had been egging on the Crosswinds spirits in some sort of supernatural bid to increase my client base.

"Do you *have* the original fixtures?" I asked.

"Nah. Who wants all that old stuff?" He threw his hands in the air. "I am so sick of this whole place I can't even tell you. Here's what I need from you: track down and reinstall whatever old crap you can find, starting with that damned weathervane. If you can't find the original, surely a reproduction will do—and then maybe these damned ghosts will shut up long enough for me to dump this place. Then it'll be someone else's problem."

A twenty-nine-million-dollar dump. Wow.

Andrew Flynt was a little much, but no big deal. I wasn't particularly compelled to help him out for his sake . . . but this house was calling out to me. Crosswinds had been done a cruel disservice. To restore it would take another big chunk of change, and to do it right would take at least a year, and I wasn't at all sure Flynt would sit still for either. But maybe I could help out a little. I suspected many of the recent "improvements" were purely cosmetic: Probably the contractor had put up wallboard over existing molding and nooks in some areas, cheating here and there. It was scandalous, given the amount of money Flynt had no doubt spent, but typical of overworked contractors, many of whom did the absolute minimum they could get away with—not bothering to clean up behind walls, for instance. Years later this kind of lick-and-a-promise construction could result in fun finds: I often came across decades-old newspapers or canned food or instruction manuals behind the walls, trash that the passage of time had rendered interesting and, occasionally, valuable.

Besides, the man had deep pockets. And he was desperate. Not to put too fine a point on it, but these are highly desirable qualities in a client. As a general contractor, I had a hefty payroll to make each and every month. If I couldn't keep my skilled crew busy I would lose them to contractors who would.

So yes, I was interested in taking on the challenge of Crosswinds, and whatever resident ghosts it might contain. However ... I glanced at Andrew Flynt, who was jangling his car keys—Lexus, of course—as though he could barely contain his agitation.

Number one rule for dealing with overprivileged clients? Imply that you're too busy. Drives them crazy.

I sucked air in between my teeth and shook my head slowly. "I don't know, Andrew, Turner Construction's pretty busy right now. We're working on a place in Cow Hollow and I've still got a crew on a retreat in Marin—"

"What if I double your usual rate? Seriously, track down some of those old fixtures, find a few new ones that look old, hold a séance, schedule an exorcism by the Pope—do what you have to, but whatever you do *get these ghosts off my back.*"

"Double my usual rate?" In neighborhoods like Pacific Heights, the more you charged people, the more they respected you. It was sort of like wine: The exact same bottle could be said to cost twelve bucks or twelve hundred—guess which one tasted better to someone like Andrew Flynt? Exclusivity was delicious.

I took a moment, looked around, then nodded slowly. "All right. I think I can help you out. I have to warn you, though, it won't be cheap and it's going to make a mess."

"Do whatever you have to do. This place has been a mess since I bought it."

"And it's going to take a while—"

I cut myself off as I saw something out of the corner of my eye.

It was a woman, creeping carefully down the stairs. She had dark eyes, olive skin, and an exotic aura—or maybe that was due to her white dress and the colorful batik scarf wrapped around her hair, as though she had just stepped off a Caribbean island.

Could this be the ghost of some long-dead servant, bound to toil in the Crosswinds mansion throughout eternity?

Chapter Two

"Egypt!" Andrew Flynt called out. "Let me introduce you. Egypt Davis, this is Mel Turner. Mel's going to be working on this place. You'll give her whatever she needs. Mel, Egypt lives upstairs. Caretaker for the interim."

Not a ghost, then. I relaxed. Ever since I had started seeing the spiritual remnants of those not-quite-passed, it had become increasingly difficult to tell reality from ... *my* reality.

Good thing I hadn't said anything embarrassing.

Egypt shook my hand and we exchanged pleasantries; then I gave her my business card.

"Please let me know if I can help with anything," said Egypt, casting a wary glance at Flynt. "Does this have to do with ... Chantelle's advice?"

"Precisely."

Egypt's cell phone beeped. "I'm sorry to rush off, but I'm late for an appointment."

"Turner here will be spending plenty of time at Crosswinds, so you two ladies will have a chance to catch up. In the meantime, could you find that list of items Skip removed from the house? And the blueprints? Turner will need to know what she's restoring."

"Of course." Egypt's phone beeped again, and she checked the screen. "I'm sorry. I really have to run. Nice to meet you, Mel. Give me a call if you need anything."

Another cautious glance in Andrew's direction, then she left through the front entrance, a beautiful paneled door with stained glass panels, topped by an elaborate fanlight, that was clearly original to the house. It had no doubt survived Flynt's renovation only because of pressure from the city to maintain the historic character of the neighborhood. I imagined if Flynt had had his way, the wood-and-stained-glass door would have been replaced by some sort of steel-and-glass monstrosity.

"Do you have time for a quick walk-through of the house?" I asked my new client.

He checked his expensive watch again, sighed, and then gave me a curt nod.

The home's owner might not have enjoyed the tour, but I did. Peeking through old homes was one of my favorite things in life. Still, it saddened me to see the renovations perpetrated on the rest of the four-story house. Happily the layout of the upper floors appeared to have been left largely unchanged—unlike on the main floor—though the original moldings, woodwork, and built-in cabinets and bookcases had been torn out, replaced by flat surfaces, hard stone, and vinyl windows.

As we walked along a sleek white corridor on the third floor I thought I heard music. I listened carefully: a Strauss waltz.

"Nice," I said. "Is Egypt a classical music fan?

Andrew gave me a sour look.

"What did I say?"

"That's ghost music."

"Ghost music?"

He nodded. "It's one of those things potential buyers always ask about. 'What pretty music—where's that coming from?' they say. I try to act like it's being piped in, but that doesn't work because it starts and stops randomly throughout the day. Drives me crazy."

"At least it's nice music."

"As if anybody waltzes anymore. Me, I'm a Grateful Dead fan."

I laughed.

"You have something against the Grateful Dead?" he demanded.

"Not at all," I said, wondering what Jerry Garcia would make of Andrew Flynt. " 'Every silver lining's got a touch of gray,' " I said, quoting a Grateful Dead song.

I have my moments of cool.

"Jerry's the man," Flynt said, nodding.

Once or twice I thought I heard—or felt—wisps of conversations just out of reach of hearing, but though I searched my peripheral vision no ghosts appeared. Still, I felt certain Chantelle was right: There were spirits in this house. Unhappy spirits. Perhaps they would try to communicate when Andrew Flynt wasn't by my side. A lot of times it happened that way.

A modern skylight at the top of the stairs lit the fourth floor. The landing opened onto a hallway with doors leading into several small chambers. These were probably the former servants' quarters, a little dormitory tucked under the eaves of the sloping roofline.

At the end of the hall was one closed door.

"That's Egypt's room," said Flynt, reaching for the doorknob. I opened my mouth to tell him not to bother, not wanting to intrude in her private space, but the door was locked. He rattled the knob. "Dammit! Why would she lock it?"

Maybe to keep her boundary-challenged employer from walking in on her private space? I thought.

Flynt looked dumbfounded, as though he couldn't imagine a door failing to open upon his command.

"It's all right," I said. "I'll ask Egypt if I can take a peek when I see her next. There are plenty of things to do first. We should go—I know you're a busy man."

"So, how soon can you start?" Flynt asked as we descended the stairs. He had offered to take the elevator, but I declined. This was earthquake country, after all. No way was I going to risk getting stuck in an elevator in a haunted house with Andrew Flynt. "The sooner, the better, as far as I'm concerned. Here's the code for the lockbox, and I'll let Egypt know you might be here, what? Tomorrow?"

"I'd like to stop by tomorrow to scope things out, but it will take a while to get started in earnest. Don't forget I'll need to pull some permits to renovate the renovations."

"Anything you need me to sign, just let me know. I've got connections at City Hall who can expedite things if you run into bureaucratic nonsense. The sooner this gets taken care of, the better. Every day this house sits on the market costs me money. If need be I'll pay you to put your other projects on hold until this one gets done."

"I don't leave projects half done, Andrew, but I understand your sense of urgency. I'll get on it as soon as humanly possible, I promise. I'll have my office manager, Stan Tomassi, fax a contract to your office. And in the meantime, I'd like to speak with Chantelle, and to the remodeler who did the work on Crosswinds. Who was that?"

"Skip Buhner."

"Buhner? Any relation to Karla Buhner, your Realtor?"

"Her husband."

"Ah."

It's not as though I know everybody in the Bay Area housing industry, but ever since I took over Turner Construction "temporarily" from my father a few years ago, I had made a point of meeting the major players—our competition, after all—in the high-end, historic homes business. So either Skip Buhner was brand-new to the area or restoring historic homes wasn't his primary area of expertise. Then again, I could have guessed that. Based upon what I'd seen at Crosswinds, Buhner was a rip-it-out-and-buy-something-new-at-the-big-box-store type of contractor. He would have lasted no more than five minutes, tops, trying to make a crooked doorframe function before tearing out the hand-carved wood and replacing it with a brand-new fiberglass set.

"Skip's moved on to a new project, an office building on Sansome," Flynt said. "You want to talk headaches? Every time they dig they uncover some old ship—did you know that area's landfill from back in the Barbary Coast days? And then they have to halt construction and file environmental reports, get some bleeding-heart academic out there to excavate and document the discovery. Like anybody really gives a damn. Waste of time and money, you ask me."

Just then I noticed a photograph at my feet. I picked it up: Sepia-toned and crumbling with age, it was of a young woman standing at a window. It was hard to tell, but it may have been the window right here in the hall—the view outside was the same of the Bay and Sausalito, but the iconic Golden Gate Bridge was missing.

"I hate those things," said Andrew.

"What, old photos?"

"They appear, here and there. It's like when my daughter Lacey was obsessed with glitter—once it's in your house you can never get rid of it."

"The photos just ... appear?"

He nodded. "I think there were a bunch of them be-hind a wall somewhere, and since we started construc-tion they just turn up now and then. Crummy old things. Just throw it away."

"May I keep it?" I asked.

"Why would you want it?"

I studied the photo in my hands. The young woman was lovely, with a cupid's bow mouth, her long hair pinned up in an elaborate bun. But the expression in her eyes was sad, and yearning, and ... it felt as though she had something to tell me.

"Not a history buff, I take it?" I finally said to Andrew, when I realized he was awaiting a response.

"Never have been," he said with a quick shake of his head. "It's the *future* that interests me. The past is gone; irrelevant."

Unless, of course, that past is quite literally haunting you, and keeping you from selling your obscenely priced home so you can golf in peace and retire to cocktails in your Bollinger. Whatever that was.

I felt almost triumphant that Andrew and I hadn't tripped over any bodies while walking through Crosswinds.

I know, I know, I'm getting stranger by the day. And certainly I worked on many houses where my biggest problem was a plumbing backflow issue or dry rot or earthquake bracing. But by and large, when I'm intro-duced to a house believed to be haunted, I tend to trip over bodies.

Maybe with *this* house, I would be able to deal with renovation issues and ancient ghosts, rather than any current homicides. Fingers crossed.

I lingered outside the property in my Scion, sizing up the home's beautiful Victorian exterior while I placed a few calls. First things first: I dialed a certain one-named psychic. Chantelle's husky voice burst into laughter when I mentioned Andrew Flynt and Crosswinds.

"He hasn't been able to sell it, has he? I told him so, over a month ago. He's stubborn. It'll be a thousand."

"Excuse me?"

"I charge one thousand dollars for a drop-in consultation. You're lucky, I just had a cancellation at three."

"But I'm not seeking a reading, or anything like that," I clarified. "I just wanted to talk to you about what you saw—and felt—at Crosswinds."

"I understand that, sweetheart. One K, that's my rate. Don't *you* pay it—charge it to Flynt. He'll pay. The man has more dollars than sense."

Luckily for me, clients with more dollars than sense were my specialty.

And heck, it wouldn't take the full hour to get Chantelle's take on Crosswinds. If she was as talented as people seemed to think, maybe I would make use of the rest of the session, since I was paying for it anyway. I wouldn't mind getting a psychic's take on what to do about my life.

It was a good life. But I had a few questions—in particular, I'd love some supernatural guidance on what to do about my boyfriend, Graham Donovan, green consultant to the rich and famous. We'd been seeing each other seriously ever since he was hospitalized at the scene of my last haunting. It was a nice relationship. Very comfortable.

He was the perfect boyfriend, and yet he wanted more. Though I loved him, I wasn't sure if we wanted the same things.

Give me a cracked foundation any day; romantic relationships aren't my strong suit.

I made the appointment with Chantelle at three

o'clock, then returned several calls and texts from fore-
men and suppliers. If the sheetrock contractor didn't get
his crew out to the Marin project soon I was pretty sure
I was going to have a cardiac episode. I then checked in
with my friend and office manager, Stan, and asked him
to draw up the contract for Andrew Flynt so we could go
over it tonight.

Next I drove over to the permit offices to harangue
and cajole the staff, in equal parts, and to expedite papers for a new project in the Sunset. Andrew Flynt wasn't
the only one with connections. In addition, I let them
know I would be doing work on Crosswinds.

After the permit office it was time to meet Chantelle.
I glanced at the address she had given me. Nob Hill
wasn't far, but traffic was a big question mark in San
Francisco—like any city with small streets, construction
or road repair would cause traffic snarls so bad it could
take twenty minutes to go two blocks. And don't even
get me started on parking. Luckily Chantelle had told
me to hand my keys to the doorman—her building had
valet service.

At a thousand bucks a pop for consultations, it was
little wonder Chantelle could afford a Nob Hill apartment with a doorman.

Nob Hill was the *other* San Francisco neighborhood
where wealthy robber barons had built their mansions.
Unlike in Pacific Heights, though, most of Nob Hill's
original structures had been destroyed in the fire sparked
by the 1906 earthquake. The burned-out shells had been
replaced by Grace Cathedral and expensive hotels such
as the Mark Hopkins and the Scarlet Huntington. Only
the Pacific-Union remained, its thick stone walls far too
stubborn to succumb to the flames; the exclusive men's
club still hunkered down atop Nob Hill like a sexist,
classist outpost.

Chantelle's apartment turned out to be in a disap-pointingly bland 1970s condo building. The doorman, Gabe, was expecting me and buzzed me right in. Gabe wore a formal valet's monkey suit but didn't otherwise look the part. Young and tattooed, his eyes were bleary and he had a serious five o'clock shadow. I feared my arrival might have interrupted his nap.

"How's it going?" I asked.

He shrugged. "You know how it is—late night. Chan-telle's on the ninth floor. Exit the elevator and down the hall to your right."

"Thanks."

Gabe took my keys and left the desk unattended while he went to park my vehicle. I assumed my old Scion would be safe with him but wasn't overly concerned— one of the perks of driving a slightly banged-up work ve-hicle. What was one more little scratch or dent?

The elevator whooshed up to the ninth floor. When the doors opened I exited and turned right. Down the hall I spied the door to nine sixteen, ajar.

A woman stood in the hall just outside the apartment. She was striking: tall, yet delicate and ethereal, with long honey-blond hair and big beautiful brown eyes. *Wow*. If this was Chantelle, it was no wonder people spent a thousand bucks to meet with her. Even from a distance she seemed to possess a striking demeanor. Perhaps she really *could* tell me something.

"Chantelle?" I asked. "I'm Mel. Mel Turner. We have an appointment at three o'clock."

She nodded, and without a word turned and went into the apartment. I followed.

And found her on the floor, in a pool of bright red blood.

Chapter Three

There was also a man in the apartment entryway, down on one knee, leaning over the body.

Upon seeing me he pulled a cell phone from his pocket, and announced, "She's . . . gone. I'm calling nine-one-one."

He looked pale and was probably suffering from shock. I assumed he wasn't the reason Chantelle lay dead on the floor in a pool of blood. Or, if he *was* the murderer, he was so overcome with guilt that he posed no threat to me. Either way, I decided to make a call of my own to Homicide Inspector Annette Crawford of the San Francisco Police Department.

"The dispatcher says the police are on their way," the man said, still holding the phone to his ear. There were tears in his eyes. His voice was gruff with emotion, the words clipped. He didn't have a foreign accent, exactly, but I couldn't quite place the oddness in his voice. "Who are *you* calling?"

"A, er . . . friend. Annette Crawford, homicide inspector." My eyes lit upon what looked like a butcher knife lying on the floor next to Chantelle. It was covered in blood. My stomach lurched. When I continued my voice dropped to a whisper: "We . . . Annette and I have a history."

Just then the inspector picked up.

"Again, Mel?" Annette answered. Clearly she had Caller ID.

"'Fraid so," I said, and gave her Chantelle's address.

"What's the situation? Anybody else there?"

"Yes." I turned away from the man, who remained beside the body.

"Friend of yours?"

"No," I whispered. "He was in the apartment when I got here."

"Are you in danger?"

"I don't think so. He called nine-one-one and he seems . . . stoic, but upset."

"Listen to me, Mel. I want you to go out in the hallway and wait until help arrives, do you hear me? No heroics."

"Don't worry. I'm not big on heroics."

"Allow me to rephrase: nothing stupid, understood?"

"Okay, good point."

"The officers should be there in a few minutes; give me about twenty. Don't touch anything and stay away from the body."

"I know, I know. I'm not *that* stupid."

"That's what they all say."

I did as the inspector said and went out to the hallway, but couldn't help but peer through the open door into the apartment. The man remained balanced on one knee beside Chantelle's body. The way he held himself reminded me of some of my father's former Marine buddies, making me wonder if he was in the military. He was handsome, with a trim beard and light brown hair worn long, sweeping his collar, reminding me of photographs of soldiers from long ago.

Aw, crap, I thought with a start. *Was he a ghost, too?*

When I'd first learned I could communicate with spirits, I saw them only in my peripheral vision. Recently, I had started to see some of them straight on, as I would anyone else. More than once, in fact, I had assumed a ghost was a living person, as I had with Chantelle a moment ago. Distinguishing between a spirit and a live human can be all the more challenging because ghosts often don't realize they're dead. Asking a few questions usually clarified the situation.

"Soooo," I said, feeling awkward. "Are you . . . from around here?"

Lame, Mel. You're not picking up a man in a bar.

"Just visiting."

Wait a minute—the man had called 911, I reminded myself. There's an awful lot I still had to learn about the supernatural world, but one thing I did know: Ghosts don't carry cell phones. Much less *use* them.

"Are you a friend of Chantelle's?"

"Her brother, Landon Demetrius III," he said.

"Oh, I . . . I'm so very sorry for your loss."

"Thank you." His eyes glistened with tears, but his voice showed little emotion. "And might I inquire as to who you are?"

His formal phrasing piqued my interest. Something about him made me suspect that he might have a mysterious past. Or was he just a theater major a little too committed to Shakespeare's English?

"I'm Mel Turner."

"How do you do?" Landon said with a nod, then looked toward the sound of distant sirens. "Let us hope those sirens are for us."

"Shouldn't be long now," I agreed.

We waited in silence for a few moments as the sirens drew closer.

"You had an appointment for a reading, then?" Landon asked.

"No, I was supposed to talk to your sister ab—" I realized with a start that I had not escaped *Mel's Dreaded Curse*: I had once again encountered a body associated with a haunted house. Chantelle's ghost wouldn't be haunting Crosswinds, but . . . could her death be linked to that haunted mansion, somehow?

"May I ask the nature of your reading?"

"A twenty-nine-million-dollar haunted house."

His elegant eyebrows rose, just a smidgen.

He was still kneeling, and despite the tragic circumstances I couldn't help but admire him for it. Last week my friend Luz finally convinced me to give yoga a try, and the balancing-on-the-knee thing just about did me in.

"Do you know Chantelle well?" he asked. "Any idea what could have happened? Who might have *done* such a thing?"

"I'm afraid I don't. We spoke for the first time a couple of hours ago, to make the appointment. We'd never met in person."

The elevator pinged and uniformed officers poured out. I automatically raised my hands and stepped away from the door to allow them to enter.

"Hands up! Back away from the body!"

I peered around the police to watch Landon Demetrius do as he was told, raising his hands in the air and rising smoothly from his kneeling position without tipping or falling over, or even using his hands to steady himself. He would do just fine in yoga class.

"I called Inspector Crawford," I said, my hands still in the air. "She's on her way."

"You in the apartment," one cop barked. "Come out here into the hallway."

"And *you* stay right here," the other police officer said to me. His colleague kneeled by Chantelle and placed two fingers on her neck, checking for signs of life. He shook his head and spoke softly into his radio.

Landon and I lined up against the wall, like kids waiting to meet with the principal, one officer in particular eyeing us suspiciously. Landon stood ramrod-straight, and I found myself checking my posture.

He looked at his phone, pursed his lips, and then glanced around the hallway as if to spot whatever was foiling his reception.

"Old buildings," Landon muttered, shaking his head.

"It's not that told. Probably from the 1970s, at the most." I dealt with truly old buildings—at least by local standards—and the 1970s didn't qualify. Besides, the architecture of that decade was so ugly that I didn't like it lumped in with historic buildings.

"Old enough not to have decent cell reception," he snapped.

"Probably reinforced concrete, or steel beams—earthquake stuff," said the young cop babysitting us. "And, uh, hands up."

A few more moments of silence ensued. I heard the sound of thumping from inside the apartment, as if the cops were searching the premises for evidence. The elevator pinged and opened once again, and another trio of uniformed officers arrived and crowded into the apartment.

"So, you don't care for old buildings?" I asked Landon.

He checked his phone once more, then shoved it into his pocket. "Not as much as I like connectivity."

Now that was a phrase I couldn't imagine uttering. As a contractor I live on the phone, and find it an indispensable tool for running several construction sites simultaneously. But to prefer connectivity over history? *No, thank you.*

His eyes slewed toward me. They were a light sherry, with a few specks of green.

"How does this sort of thing usually go?" he asked.

"What do you mean?"

"This . . . *homicide investigation* sort of thing."

"What makes you think *I* know?" For some reason I didn't want this man to believe I was the kind of woman who tripped over dead bodies with disturbing frequency. Even though I was.

"You're friends with a homicide inspector. I just assumed—"

Said inspector chose that moment to step off the elevator and fix me with her patented Interrogation 101 look: one raised eyebrow. Annette Crawford was tall for a woman, curvy yet muscular, a dedicated professional with a no-nonsense air. There was never any question as to who was in charge when Inspector Crawford was on the scene. She had climbed the ranks of the police department the old-fashioned way, through sheer hard work and talent, and had had to prove wrong more than a few who assumed a woman of color was not their peer. After working with her on a cold case recently, I knew she also had a wicked sense of humor and the imagination to think outside the box.

She nodded at the young officer, glanced at Landon, then zeroed in on me as she approached.

"Put your hands down," she said. "No one's under arrest. Yet."

"I had nothing to do with it this time," I said, relieved. Holding one's hands in the air is surprisingly hard work. "Nothing at all. I had an appointment, and when I arrived found her dead."

Landon looked at me. "*This* time?"

"And you are?" Crawford asked.

"Landon Demetrius III," he said. "I'm Chantelle's brother."

"Chantelle is ... ?"

"The victim," I said quietly.

"I see," said Annette, conveying a lot in a few words. "I'm sorry for your loss, Mr. Demetrius."

"Thank you."

"Were you the one who found her?"

He nodded.

"All right. Let me take a look at the scene, and then we'll have a little chat." She raised her chin in the direction of the young cop babysitting us. "Keep an eye on them, will you?"

"Yes sir! Um, Inspector," stuttered the officer.

She swept into the apartment.

Landon glanced at me. "I thought you said you two were friends. She didn't seem particularly friendly."

"'Friend' might have been a bit of a stretch. Acquaintance would be more accurate."

"Been involved with a murder investigation previously, have you?"

"A few. But my role was minimal."

"As in, not really your fault?"

"As in, I was an innocent witness."

He looked down his nose, and I sensed he didn't believe me. I sighed: first Andrew Flynt and now Landon Demetrius III. I'm from Oakland, so I'm accustomed to San Franciscans looking askance at me, but it doesn't mean I like it. I started to say something snide, but reconsidered. His sister had just been murdered, after all. Assuming he didn't do it, the least I could do was cut him a little slack. I thought about my own sisters, and what it would mean to find them like that, on the floor in a pool of their own blood.

I banished the thought; it was too painful to even contemplate.

I started to say something to Landon when black spots began to swim before my eyes and a wave of nausea took hold deep in my belly. I shook my head and breathed slowly, trying to hold it together. The temperature in the hallway plummeted; my breath came out in little clouds and hung in the frigid air.

Part of my brain knew what was happening, but the rest refused to acknowledge it.

Chantelle emerged from the apartment. She cupped Landon's face in her hands for a moment, then reached into the same jacket pocket where he had stowed his cell phone. She turned and gazed at me with those beautiful eyes, smiled beatifically, and nodded once. Then she drifted down the corridor and disappeared into the open elevator. The doors closed softly and the elevator started to ascend.

Landon frowned. "It's like ice in here. Another problem with these outdated buildings. Lousy HVAC systems."

"Got that right," said the young officer.

I didn't respond, still nauseated and breathless.

"Are you quite all right?" Landon asked me after a moment.

I nodded.

Not for the first time I felt exasperated after a supernatural encounter. Why couldn't the ghosts of murder victims just *tell* me what happened? If they weren't going to be of use, why subject me to funky feelings and such strangeness? I was a *contractor*, for heaven's sake. How come it was always up to *me* to solve these crimes?

Me, and Annette Crawford of the SFPD, of course.

I checked myself. It did no good to curse my fate. I'd tried that before, and it didn't get me anywhere.

"So," I said to Landon while we waited for Inspector Crawford to return. "Are—were you and your sister close?"

"Not recently."

"You live around here?"

"You already asked me that. Why are you obsessed with my residence? Are you with Homeland Security?"

I was going to bet that Landon Demetrius III here was the type to respond to tragedy with testiness. Either that, or he was an exceptionally cool murderer who didn't feel the need to be polite to anyone.

"Sorry," I said. "Just making conversation. How was it you were visiting the sister you aren't close to when . . ."

"When she was murdered?" He blew out a breath, as though trying to rein in his emotions. "I just flew in from England. I teach at Cambridge. We were quite close as children, but we . . . grew apart. Last time I saw Chantelle she still called herself Cheryl. Must have been ten years ago."

"I see."

"But I shall never forgive myself for not arriving an hour earlier. Or perhaps even fifteen minutes earlier . . . Whatever it would have taken to avoid this tragedy."

Landon's voice caught in his throat, and his emotions seemed genuine. Unless he was a first-class actor, which, for all I knew, he was. "I'm sorry, Landon. If it helps at all, I . . . I think she's okay."

"Pardon?"

"I mean, yes, she's passed on, but she's okay. What you felt a moment ago, when it got so cold? That was her putting her hands on your face."

The expression on Landon's face said plainly he

thought I was nuts. It didn't surprise me, I was accustomed to it by now, but it still annoyed me. I hadn't been in touch with the dead long enough to have figured out how to deliver the news—"Your loved one is gone, but not *gone* gone"—in a way that offers comfort instead of inspiring hostility or fear for my sanity. I wasn't sure it was even possible.

"Oh. I see. You're one of *those.*"

"Beg pardon?"

"A psychic." His tone was clipped. "As I said, my sister and I had grown apart, but I know she had . . . acquaintances who were as sketchy as her career implied. Is that why you dress in such an absurd fashion?"

I always wore my steel-toed work boots and carried coveralls in my vehicle for when I needed to crawl through dusty attics or basements, but most days I dressed in my friend Stephen's designs. His clothes were influenced by his childhood growing up in Las Vegas with a showgirl mother, and featured a lot of fringe and spangles. Usually when first meeting with clients I dressed more conservatively, but this morning's appointment with Andrew Flynt had been set at the last minute so he had to take me as he could get me. And, as Landon had just pointed out, my fashion sense wasn't all that disconcerting when I was in "ghost talker" mode; people seemed open to esoteric fashion choices from their supernatural connections.

"I dress this way because I can, not that it's any of your business," I responded. "And no, I'm not a psychic. I sometimes see dead people, that's all."

"That's . . . all?"

"It's not by choice, believe me. It just happens. I saw your sister a moment ago. She was smiling and looked . . . happy. She came out of the apartment, paused and touched your face, and then got on the elevator. Going up."

Landon's face darkened. "I must say, it is in very poor

taste to make fun of someone who has just suffered a terrible loss. My sister's body is still warm, for heaven's sake."

"I'm not making fun," I protested. "Honest, I'm not. I'm—"

"Winning friends and influencing people are we, Turner?" Inspector Crawford appeared in the apartment doorway. Without waiting for me to reply, she turned to Landon. "Follow me, please, Mr. Demetrius."

They disappeared into the apartment. I remained in the hall and watched the forensics team arrive, loaded down with bags of equipment. A few neighbors stuck their heads out of their apartments to check on the hubbub. I did my best to avoid their curious gazes.

I wondered if Chantelle would return. Why had she gotten onto the elevator? Where was she going? Had she ridden the lift all the way up, through the roof, and into the sky, Willy Wonka style?

The most pertinent question at the moment, for me at least, was if Chantelle's death had anything to do with Crosswinds. A psychic who made enough money to live at the top of Nob Hill might have had plenty of enemies. Certainly Landon had insinuated as much. Not to mention that, at a thousand bucks a pop for a consultation, Chantelle could have had money lying around her apartment that would attract interest. The building had a doorman, but Gabe didn't seem like a crack security guard. And even if he was, he was only one man and couldn't be everywhere at once. A determined and skilled thief could easily find a way in. Not to mention a neighbor who needed money for the rent, someone delivering takeout to any of the residents, or a repairman here to fix the plumbing. Chantelle's untimely death could as easily— no, *more* easily—have been due to being at the wrong place at the wrong time than to anything supernatural.

Probably it had nothing at all to do with Crosswinds and its ghostly weathervane.

"Turner!"

"Here!" I said, snapping-to without thinking. Then I regrouped. "You missed your calling as a drill sergeant, Inspector."

"Funny," Annette said, her notebook and pen ready. "Speaking of drills, you know this one by now. Tell me what you saw, what you did, and what you think. Add nothing in, and leave nothing out."

I told her my very short story, including my earlier visit to the haunted Crosswinds. Her patented cop look suggested she thought I was holding something back. Which, this time at least, I wasn't. But I didn't take it personally. I could only imagine how often she was lied to in the course of a single day.

"You know, it's downright eerie how often I find you at murder scenes," the Inspector said. "I'm going to assume we'll find some sort of connection between your latest haunted house and this situation."

"Well, there *is* a connection—that's why I'm here. Chantelle did a reading of the haunted house I've just been hired to renovate."

"Her brother says she did readings of a lot of places, has done so for years. But she didn't get dead until you arrived on the scene."

"When you put it like that, it really is eerie."

We both took a moment.

"Okay," she said with a sigh. "That about it?"

I nodded.

"You can go. I know where to find you for follow-up."

"Annette, do you have any idea when Chantelle was killed?"

"That's up to the medical examiner to determine. And it's none of your business. You be sure to let me know if anything comes up over at Crosswinds that might be related to this, you hear?"

"Will do."

She went back into the apartment, and I headed for the elevator.

"Turner."

I turned around and saw the inspector with Landon Demetrius. He was wiping his fingertips with a wet cloth, presumably to remove fingerprint ink.

"Take this one with you," Annette said. "Please."

"I won't stand for this," Landon protested. "Surely I can help. My bags—"

"Will stay right where they are. Everything in the apartment is potential evidence until further notice," Crawford said in her don't-even-think-of-arguing-with-me voice. "Forensics has to process everything, I'm sorry to say. You'll get your things back when they're finished. On behalf of the San Francisco Police Department, please accept our apologies for the inconvenience this may cause you, as well as our sincere condolences on the loss of your sister."

"But surely, Inspector—"

"C'mon, Landon," I said. "I'll give you a ride. There's no use arguing with the SFPD, I guarantee you."

As I guided Landon toward the elevator, I read the thanks in Annette's silent nod.

Chapter Four

On the way down in the elevator, I glanced at my watch: I was due home for dinner in an hour. Landon stumbled next to me and I reached out a hand to steady him. He looked stunned, almost bewildered. Grief was a strange thing. Everyone has their own way of processing it, and none of us knows what that will entail until we're faced with it.

"Where to?" I asked gently. "Were you . . . Were you planning to stay with your sister?"

"No, I have reservations at the Claremont Hotel in Berkeley. I'm a visiting professor at the university for the upcoming semester. I'll be subletting an apartment but can't move in until Monday. Until then, I'm in the hotel. But I dropped my suitcase and other things at Cheryl's — I mean, Chantelle's — apartment. We had planned to spend the evening together, and she was going to take me to the hotel after dinner."

"Listen, how about you come home with me for dinner?" We arrived at the lobby and the elevator doors slid open to reveal Gabe doing some sort of Tai-Chi.

"Hell of a thing," he mumbled. "Poor Chantelle. Did you see her?"

I nodded and asked him to retrieve my car, not wanting to engage further in this discussion.

I turned back to Landon. "Give yourself a chance to relax, have a drink and a good meal. I can scare up an extra toothbrush for tonight, and take you back to the hotel."

"I appreciate the offer, Ms., uh ..."

"Turner. Call me Mel."

"Mel, I certainly mean no offense when I say I'm ... I'm not really in the mood for a romantic dinner."

I burst out laughing as a discomfited Gabe ran to retrieve my Scion.

"No worries. It's not a *date*, professor. I'm inviting you to dinner with my dad, in our house in Oakland. Dad's making his special lasagna."

"Lasagna?"

"You know—big flat noodles, tomato sauce, lots of cheese bubbling up, special herbs. Dad serves it with a big salad and sourdough garlic bread...." My stomach growled so loud I thought he might hear it. "Don't you have lasagna in England?"

His eyes slewed over to me again. "Are you Italian?"

"Sure—that's why my family name is Turner. Seriously, no, I'm a hodgepodge of lots of things, but Italian isn't one of them. But remember, you're in the good ol' U.S. of A. We enjoy all sorts of cuisines: Italian, Ethiopian, Thai, Vietnamese, French, Indian. It's a veritable smorgasbord."

"You'll have to forgive me—I fear I'm a wee bit jet-lagged."

He swayed again.

"When's the last time you ate?"

He paused as if to consider. "It's been a good while,

I'm afraid. When the flight from London landed in New York there was a long wait to get through customs, and I had to run to catch my connection. There was no time to eat."

"You're gonna love my dad's lasagna," I said. "He's quite a cook."

"Really, I'd hate to trouble you. Why don't you just take me to the hotel, if you would be so kind? I think I need to be alone for a while."

"Suit yourself," I said. "But if you change your mind on the way over sing out."

Gabe screeched up to the curb and handed me my keys, and Landon and I climbed into the Scion. I had just started driving when my cell phone rang, so I put it on speakerphone. It was my foreman, Raul, wanting to discuss some rebar reinforcement at the retreat center in Marin.

Landon was looking at me funny as I finished up the call.

"Everything okay?" I asked as we headed for the Oakland Bay Bridge.

He nodded and checked his cell phone. A map on the phone's screen suggested he was following our route.

"You've had quite a shock," I said. "I'm so sorry about your sister. Have you ever seen a dead body before?"

He gave a humorless laugh and blew a long breath. His gaze shifted from the phone to the panoramic view: the Golden Gate Bridge over our shoulder, Alcatraz Island and Treasure Island on our left, the East Bay and Oakland hills ahead of us. "Nothing like this. It's all so very . . . unexpected."

"I understand. Are you British?"

"Pardon?"

"Your inflections are British, but you don't have an accent." I was trying to fit all this together with the fact that he was Chantelle's brother. "And your name's Demetrius—that sounds Greek?"

"Greek on my father's side, but I was born in Britain, then brought to upstate New York when I was still an infant. But I left the States many years ago. Perhaps British culture has had an effect I'm not aware of."

"I see. What do you teach?"

"Maths."

"We say math, here. Singular."

"Right-o."

I started to laugh. "You can't help it, can you?"

Landon seemed to relax a bit. "I guess not."

"I'm surprised to hear your specialty is math. I would have guessed English literature, or perhaps history."

"While I rather fancy that idea, what makes you think so?"

"You seem very . . . erudite."

"Wouldn't a maths—*math*—professor also be erudite?"

"I suppose so. It's just . . . never mind."

Traffic feeding onto the Bay Bridge did its usual rush hour stop-and-start tango, but once we made it onto the bridge itself we moved along at a good clip. Twenty minutes later we had arrived at the Claremont, a massive old hotel painted a pure white perched on the side of a hill in Oakland. Because it is located near the University of California many assume the Claremont is in Berkeley, but it is in fact a historic Oakland gem.

I pulled up in front of the main hotel entrance and turned off the engine, waving away a doorman who came to open my door.

"Do you want me to come in with you, help you get settled?" I cringed as the words left my mouth. Landon wasn't a young foreign exchange student; he was a grown-up college professor.

"I'll be quite fine," he said as he got out of the car. "Thank you for the ride."

"Landon," I called, and he ducked his head back in the open door. "If I were you I would stay away from room four twenty-two. Just in case."

"And why might that be?"

"Supposedly a ghost of a little girl hangs out in that room."

He looked incredulous. "And you know this how, exactly?"

I shrugged. "I can neither confirm nor deny the veracity of the haunting, but I hear things. Might make it hard to sleep, is all I'm saying. You've already had one shock today."

"Thank you, Ms. Turner. I shall take your words to heart. It has been . . . very interesting to meet you."

And with that, Professor Landon Demetrius III hurried into the hotel.

I headed across town to Oakland's Fruitvale neighborhood, where I live with my father, my ex-stepson Caleb, and our old family friend Stan Tomassi in a big old farmhouse. It was by far the largest home on the block, and at one time was surrounded by orchards until, one by one, the fruit trees were forced to yield to developers. Small houses sprung up, closely packed together. It was the kind of neighborhood, rare in urban areas, where working people raised their families and knew their neighbors. On weekends Fruitvale's old men—including my father, Bill Turner, the founder and erstwhile head of Turner Construction—hung out in their driveways fixing old cars and "shooting the breeze" with whoever passed by, while packs of kids played games in the street. People here hung their laundry out on clotheslines, mowed their own

lawns—such as they were, given California's drought—
and looked after their own kids.

Fruitvale was a stark contrast to the neighborhoods
Turner Construction typically worked in, where the only
people visible on the street were the ones who couldn't
afford to live there: the gardeners, the nannies, and the
housecleaners.

Living with my father hadn't exactly been part of my
life's plan, and moving out remained one item on my
very long to-do list. But there was no denying that this
neighborhood, and this old farmhouse, welcomed me
home with the warmth and comfort of a hug. Never was
this more appreciated than on the days I stumbled upon
dead bodies.

And most welcoming of all was the shaggy silhouette
of Dog's head in the living room window. I could hear
him barking through the glass, which was his way of
greeting his loved ones.

Dog was a stray I picked up from a jobsite, and in an
effort not to further complicate my life I had refused to
name him. As though that would help keep him from becoming a member of the family. That ship had long ago
sailed, and Dad had decided it was high time we give Dog
a real name. I had argued that since he now answered to
Dog, and had a profoundly limited vocabulary—*cookie,
walk, Dog*—it would be best not to confuse the poor canine any more than he already was.

So Dad alighted on the name Doug. "It's close enough
he won't get confused."

And in this Dad was right. The only ones confused by
the name change were the humans: None of us could get
used to the new name, so we started to say "Dog" and
shifted to "Doug," resulting in: "Come here, Daw-ugh."

The neighbors had begun to make fun of us, asking,
"How's Daw-ugh?"

Aw, life in the 'hood.

Standing around in the kitchen were Stan, my teenage ex-stepson Caleb, and my best friend, Luz. Visitors at the table were not uncommon for the Turner household: Dad liked nothing better than to cook for a big crowd, and anyone passing by was likely to be invited to stay for dinner. The air was redolent with the aroma of oregano and tomato sauce; on tonight's menu was something Dad liked to call "Turner special" lasagna, which included spinach for my sake—because according to him I'm a "health nut"—but also hamburger, because Dad is a big believer in beef.

I greeted the gang, petted Dog, poured myself a glass of the cheap red wine already open on the counter, and gave them the basic rundown of my day, including what happened when I showed up at Chantelle's apartment.

"Again?" Dad said, slathering butter and minced garlic onto a huge sourdough boule. "Again with the bodies? What goes on at these client meetings of yours?"

"It didn't happen at the client meeting," I said. "It was afterward. And there's absolutely no connection to Crosswinds. Probably."

"Wow, are you talking *Chantelle* Chantelle?" asked Luz. Luz was dark-haired and slender—but she ate like a linebacker, thereby ensuring her status as my dad's favorite. Though she worked like a fiend and was a well-published professor of social work at San Francisco State, she still managed to maintain a finger on the pulse of popular culture.

"Um, I guess so," I said. "She's a psychic . . . ? Or, *was* a psychic, on Nob Hill?"

"You've never heard of her?" asked Luz. "Chantelle's pretty well-known."

"Yeah," Caleb chimed in. Caleb had been only five years old when I married his father, and the only thing I regretted about the divorce was losing my status as his stepmother. Happily, Caleb was as loath to give me up, and we had stayed close. He was now almost a man, working on college applications and getting ready to graduate from high school. I was still stuck on how cute he used to be in his Batman underwear.

"Chantelle does these huge shows, like seminars?" Caleb continued. "People pay serious money to hear her talk, and hope she'll pick them out of the crowd and do a reading. There are billboards and commercials. Even *you* must have noticed them."

"I don't know anything," I said, unconsciously parroting my dad: *nobody tells me anything around here.* San Francisco—and the surrounding Bay Area—was the kind of place that hosted music/arts/food/wine festivals darn near every weekend, and Oakland had started a First Friday art walk that was hugely popular, with local restaurants offering canapés and happy hour drinks. There were museums galore: the DeYoung and the MOMA and the Legion of Honor. Cliffs enticed adventurous folks to hang glide, the waves were full of surfers, redwood glens beckoned hikers.

I took advantage of none of these things. All I did was my job. And talk to ghosts. One of these days I was really going to have to get a life.

Speaking of which, at that moment Graham Donovan walked in the door.

Graham was an attractive man, well muscled from years of working on construction sites. He now made his living as a green building consultant to rich people, and had recently become semifamous in the field due to his innovations at the Wakefield Retreat Center in Marin.

Over the past several months Graham and I had embarked on a full-fledged romance. It had gotten to the point where even I—who may have been a tad relationship-phobic after my marriage fell apart—had started referring to him as "my boyfriend" in public. Sure, we fought at times about certain green technologies—especially those that messed with my historic renovations—but on the whole it was a satisfying, comfortable relationship. Maybe *too* comfortable. My dad liked him, Stan liked him, Dog liked him (though, Dog liked most people, especially those who slipped him treats now and then), and Caleb liked him. Sometimes I wondered if I could extricate myself from this relationship even if I wanted to. It made me hyperventilate to think about it too much.

There were too many of us to fit at the small pine table in the kitchen, so we took our seats in the dining room. No sooner had we served ourselves generous hunks of steaming, gooey, fragrant lasagna, than Luz brought up what was on her mind.

"So Mel, I was hoping I could talk you into checking out an apartment—actually, it's a small cottage. The place seemed too good to be true, and I guess it is. Nice place, reasonable rent, walking distance to campus."

"I'm not really looking to move, Luz." I glanced self-consciously at my father and then at Graham, who had been making noises about our moving in together. "Not yet."

"That's not why I wanted you to look at it. It might need your special help."

"Uh-oh," groused Dad with a roll of his eyes. "Here we go."

"What's wrong with it?" I asked.

"The students say it's haunted. They're afraid to stay there."

"You want me to get rid of the spooks?"

"Exactly."

"I don't know, Luz, my schedule's pretty full these days. But there are people who do this professionally. Have the students call Olivier, see if he can help."

Olivier Galopin was my ghost guru. He knew things. Not long ago he had opened a store catering to the spirit needs of San Franciscans, and could barely keep up with demand.

"Olivier charges money," said Luz, taking another piece of garlic bread. "We're more in a pro bono situation."

"I already do construction work pro bono for good causes. I have to do ghost work for free, too?"

"Seriously? You're going to charge me?"

"I would never charge *you*. I would, however, charge a bunch of college students."

"These particular students are from my old neighborhood, Mel. East LA. They're already on Pell Grants and maxed out on student loans." Luz's head started to waggle, a sure sign she was peeved. "You know what it took for them to scrape together first and last month's rent, plus security deposit, in a city like San Francisco?"

"Aw, go on over there and check the place out," Dad said. "It won't take long."

"I thought you hated the idea of me 'mucking around with ghosts and whatnot,'" I said.

"I'm resigned," he said with a shrug. "You're gonna do it anyway, sooner or later. Can't keep your nose out of something like this."

"Yes, please, Mel, say you will," said Stan. "Quick, before Luz brings out the index finger of doom."

"All right." I had to smile. Luz's head waggle was one thing, but when she started waving her index finger in your face you were *really* in for it. "I am but your humble ghost-whispering servant, here to serve."

"Thank you," Luz said, shooting a pretend glare in

Stan's direction and helping herself to thirds of lasagna. My father beamed and pushed the bowl of parmesan cheese closer to her.

"What if you find *another* body?" asked Graham.

"Why would she find another body?" Dad demanded. "She already got her body for this go-round."

"Graham's got a point, though," said Stan, thoughtfully. "Different haunting, could mean a different body. Then you're gonna be running around after two entirely different murderers. Could get complicated."

"Maybe you should find the first murderer," said Caleb with a sage nod, "before you check out the college students' apartment."

"Come on, you guys. It's really not that bad," I protested. "I work on plenty of buildings without finding bodies."

"Yeah," said Caleb. "But the haunted ones lead to bodies, usually. And murderers, of course."

"It's settled, then. I can't wait," said Luz. "Semester starts next week, and in the meantime they're so scared they're sleeping on my floor."

I laughed. "No wonder you're so keen on justice for these kids. They're cramping your style."

"Better believe it," Luz said. "I live alone for a reason. I'm a mean old thing, plus I have only one bathroom. So, Mel: Meet me there tomorrow, noonish? I'll take you to lunch after."

"A fancy-pants sit-down restaurant?" I asked.

"Only the best for you," she confirmed, and winked.

Chapter Five

That evening, after doing the dishes—which was briefly interrupted by a dish towel fight with Caleb, during which the boy exhibited some truly impressive skills I'd like to believe were inherited from yours truly—Graham and I went into my home office and fired up the Internet to search for any references to Crosswinds mansion, as well as whatever we could find on the students' apartment.

The first thing to pop up was a Realtor Web site devoted to the Crosswinds sale, with a professional photograph of the mansion, complete with turret, on the front page. Asking price twenty-nine million dollars, boasting thirteen thousand, six hundred square feet of usable space. And there was also a photo of a beaming Karla Buhner, ready and oh so willing to hear offers from "qualified buyers."

"What kind of financial resources would someone need to be considered a 'qualified buyer' at that price?" I wondered aloud.

"Excellent question," said Graham. "I'm pretty sure I wouldn't make the cut, though."

He clicked on a local history Web site that mentioned

Crosswinds had been built by Peregrine Summerton in 1892. He scrolled through a few other sites, but there were no rumors of ghosts at the address. There wasn't much information at all about Crosswinds, actually.

"That seems odd," I said to Graham, as I closed yet another Web site that had been a dead end. "Doesn't that seem odd to you? It's a gorgeous old house, from a time period that San Franciscans typically take a lot of interest in."

"Lots of beautiful homes in the city; maybe it just got overlooked. If Crosswinds was owned by the same family for many years, there may not be a lot of public records for it."

"That's true, but still . . . All the local history buffs I've met have an almost obsessive interest in recording the minutiae of the city's past. Crosswinds is a pretty prominent Pacific Heights home, you'd think there'd be *something* about it available."

"Maybe a trip to the Historical Society is in order. You know, in all your free time. . . ."

We shared a smile.

"Are you saying I'm becoming obsessive, too?" I asked.

"But in a cute way. What about the apartment where Luz's students live?"

I typed in the street address Luz had given me for the Mermaid Cove apartment complex, and before long we were able to confirm that the Internet offered almost nothing on the students' apartment, or the complex as a whole, other than a building date of 1942.

"Now what?" Graham asked.

I typed in "Chantelle + Psychic," and the search engine spat out tens of thousands of hits.

"I guess Luz and Caleb were right. She was a big deal."

We started scrolling through them, one by one.

"This one is interesting," said Graham. "You said Chantelle's brother is named Landon Demetrius? Spelled like it sounds?"

"Yes. He's a mathematician."

"He's more than that: he's a computer whiz. He invented the Diogenes theorem."

"Really? That's quite something." I pretended I knew what we were talking about.

"Don't know what the Diogenes theorem is?"

"Um . . . not as such."

"Stephen Hawking, *The Theory of Everything*?"

"Him, I've heard of. Wasn't there a movie . . . ?"

"Well, this Demetrius fellow seems to be right up there with Hawking. But he found a practical application for one aspect of his work. The Diogenes theorem led to the Socrates chip. He's wildly rich from inventions related to it."

"Merely rich, or rich rich?"

"Think Bill Gates rich."

"Okay, *him* I've heard of, too. Wow. That explains how Landon was staying at the Claremont for a full week—that place is pricey." I pondered for a moment. "I guess that means he probably didn't kill his sister for the inheritance."

"You suspected he killed his sister? And you still gave him a ride to his hotel?"

"I did. And I don't. Think he killed his sister, that is. Besides, Annette asked me to give him a lift and she wouldn't have if she had the slightest suspicions about him. I'm just trying to keep an open mind. You know how bad I am at this."

He gave me a crooked smile and chucked me lightly on the chin. "Just because you accidentally befriend murderers from time to time doesn't mean you should start doubting yourself. You ghost buster, you."

"Ghosts, I can handle." Not so long ago I would never have imagined myself saying those words. My life had undergone some surprising changes. "It's the living, breathing murderers I have a hard time with."

"And did you make contact with any spirits at Crosswinds?"

"Not yet. But there's something there. I can feel it. Oh, and I heard music."

"What kind of music?"

"A waltz."

"Well, at least Crosswinds has classy ghosts."

"Mmm."

"By the way, I've been meaning to mention something to you."

I logged off the computer and turned my attention to Graham. "That sounds serious. Everything okay?"

"Yes, fine. A few months ago I received a phone call from an architect at a firm headquartered in New York that specializes in adapting green technology to high-end commercial buildings all around the world."

"That sounds flattering."

"It was. Anyhow, this firm has a project under way and wants to talk to me about doing some consulting work on it. It would be quite a feather in my cap—a high-profile project, an international firm, and a hefty consulting fee."

"That's great news, Graham. Congratulations."

"Nothing's certain yet, but they want to fly me out to meet with them. I don't suppose you could get a few days off and come with me to New York?"

"I don't think I can get away just now with so many projects in critical stages. We're still under the gun at the

Wakefield Retreat Center, I've got a couple other smaller projects that aren't completed, and now with Crosswinds . . ."

"I suspected as much."

"When do you leave?"

"If you're not coming with me, I'll fly out right away. Tomorrow."

"Need a ride to the airport?"

"No, I'll just leave my car in the lot. It's all on their dime."

"If you're sure."

"But another time," Graham said, holding my gaze, "I'd love for you to come with me."

I nodded. "That would be great."

The next morning, I stumbled downstairs to start another workday.

"Mornin', babe," Dad called out as he sipped coffee and read the paper at the kitchen table. "Sleep well?"

"I did, actually," I said, pouring coffee from the pot into my commuter cup. "I was thinking I'd take Dog with me to Crosswinds."

Dad fixed me with a look. "This is to track down ghosts, right? Not bodies, right?"

"Right. Our pooch is quite the ghost sniffer."

"Course he is," Dad said, leaning down and giving the canine a hearty thump. His voice was gentle, and he spoke in a tender tone I had only ever heard him use with animals. "People talk trash, but he's not without skills, are you, Daw-ugh?"

I smiled. "I think we may have to just go with Dog, Dad. This is getting ridiculous."

"We'll figure it out eventually. You sure I can't tempt you with an omelet before you go? With Cowgirl Creamery cheese and chives straight outta the garden, since you're so obsessed with organics."

"I am not 'obsessed with organics.' I just think they taste better, and I like supporting local farmers and producers."

"Never thought a daughter of mine would consider herself too good for Safeway," he grumped.

I smiled and kissed his whiskery cheek. "Bye, Dad. Say hi to Kobe and Etta for me."

A while back Dad had met Etta Lee and Kobe Sanders on a Neighbors Together community service project. I managed to volunteer Dad for a bit of extra work, and he'd taken the eleven-year-old Kobe under his wing. I had been hoping a romance might spark between Dad and Etta, but figured that was up to them; I'd done my part by throwing them together.

My mother had passed away a few years ago, and although my dad still missed her, and probably always would, he was an active, good-looking, and kind man with a big heart. Gruff, yes, but women brought out the best in him. Women and dogs and kids.

Dog stuck eagerly by my side as we headed out the door. He used to get carsick, but we had doggy Dramamine and our exposure therapy seemed to be helping, and he was always happy to jump in the car, nonetheless. I had given up hope that he'd ever become my construction dog—the kind that rode patiently onto every jobsite and stayed out of the way—but at least he was my ghost dog.

Dog and I spent the morning checking on the ancient monastery Turner Construction was reconstructing in Marin, where, in addition to actual work, I got to visit with Alicia Withers, the assistant to the wildly wealthy man spearheading the Wakefield project. Alicia and I had an inauspicious beginning to our friendship, but before long we had bonded over remodeling and ghosts. We took twenty enjoyable minutes to catch up over coffee.

Afterward, I headed south across the Golden Gate Bridge to San Francisco. Before meeting Luz at noon, I wanted to swing by Crosswinds. My crews were working steadily in Marin and on a house in Glen Park, and we still had a few unfinished tasks for renovations in the Castro and Piedmont, but a client with pockets as deep as Andrew Flynt was nothing to sneeze at. And besides, I was already itching to mitigate a little of the damage done to that once-beautiful Victorian—not that it would be an easy fix, in any sense of the word.

Unfortunately, I wasn't the only one checking out the manse. There were three gleaming luxury cars crowding the driveway. One straddled the sidewalk so pedestrians would have to go around. Not that anyone who considered themselves anyone walked in this neighborhood.

I had just raised my hand to knock when the door swung open.

Chapter Six

"**M**el!" Andrew gushed, as if we were long lost friends.

I had to admit, I had disliked Andrew Flynt on sight. Which was not a nice thing, not the *right* thing to do. First impressions can be wrong.

Except this time my first impressions were right. Andrew Flynt didn't converse, he pontificated. He talked *at* me instead of *to* me, and avoided eye contact as though to emphasize I was not of his social rank and therefore not worth acknowledging. I encountered this attitude from some of my more privileged clients, though thankfully, not all of them. It was strangely dehumanizing, and made me wonder how they interacted with those they cared about: Did they find true connection with their equally elite spouses, their pampered children? Or was the inability to connect with someone lower on the social ladder a reflection of a more general inability to find common ground with others? I gave a mental shrug. Andrew Flynt's emotional problems were none of my concern.

"Ah, Mel, great that you're here," said Andrew. "I'd

like you to meet my family. We were doing one final walk-through before you got in here and starting tearing things up. Whole family's lived through this endless renovation."

"Damned foolish notion," said an old man in a Greek fishing cap. "We're going to be late for our tee time."

"Mel Turner, this is my father, George Flynt. You'll know the name, of course."

"Of course," I lied, for I'd never heard of the man. "Nice to meet you, sir."

"And my wife, Stephanie, and our children Lacey and Mason."

"How do you do?" I said, and each nodded politely in return.

Stephanie Flynt was a slender woman in her fifties, who wore a long, flowing dress that I was sure cost more than I made in a month. She appeared to be an upscale hippie chick, in the way of wealthy Marin vegans. Stephanie had an airy, barely-there way about her, like someone who spent a lot of time meditating and concentrating on her breathing. Her hand was limp and cold in mine when we shook.

Lacey Flynt, Andrew and Stephanie's daughter, was very different from her mother. Tanned and athletic-looking, she wore a golf skirt and a pink polo shirt and seemed full of energy, like a young Katharine Hepburn. Her brother Mason was also coiffed and good-looking, though lanky rather than athletic. He had golden hair and a pleasant if bland demeanor. Smiling and Zen-like, he wore natural fibers and Birkenstocks.

"I'm sorry if I'm interrupting," I said. "I just wanted to stop in and—"

"No problem at all!" said Andrew. "We were just on our way to the golf course and thought we'd stop for a quick visit with the place, before you started in."

"Speaking of which, we should get going," said Lacey, ostentatiously looking her brother over. "Though, honestly, Mason, you know we're heading to the club the second we're done here. You couldn't maybe dress appropriately to play golf?"

"And that would consist of? You forced me to watch the Pebble Beach tournament and I gotta tell you, some of those lime green and plaid pants were pretty nauseating."

Lacey crossed her arms over her chest and fixed her brother with the look of impatient disdain that siblings excel at. My sister Cookie was a past master, and I must admit I'm no slouch myself. Mason rolled his eyes.

"Oh, please, you two." Stephanie looked shaken by their bickering. "Let's enjoy a nice afternoon as a family."

"Yes, kids," Andrew said, checking his cell phone messages. "Do as your mother says."

"No worries, Mom," Mason said, wrapping one arm around his mother's petite shoulders. "I've got my golf shoes in the car. We're all good."

"Did you get a chance to speak with Chantelle?" Andrew asked me.

"I—"

"The woman's a nut, you ask me," interrupted George. "She's a looker, I'll give her that. But I can't believe you're going to start tearing this place up, not after all the money you've sunk into it. You're like Sisyphus, son."

"Is that the one who flew too near the sun?" Andrew asked.

George rolled his eyes and snorted. "Damned public school education. The one who flew too near the sun was Icarus, son of Daedalus. Sisyphus has to roll the boulder up the hill every day, over and over again. Get the metaphor?"

Andrew blushed clear to the roots of his hair, which just went to show that even a pompous ass was vulnerable to a parent's scorn. Our adolescent selves ran deep.

"You might want to keep an open mind where Chantelle's concerned," said Mason. "She's really pretty amazing."

"You're saying you believe in ghosts, now?" George demanded in a loud voice. "I think she must be in cahoots with that Realtor and her husband, the contractor. *Somebody's* making money off this mess. It's like the damned Winchester Mystery House, never ending. Wasn't that because some crooked contractor had a gypsy fortune-teller convince a crazy old lady to keep building? It's a scam, I tell you."

"That's a beautiful place," Stephanie said.

"Which one's that?" Lacey asked.

"The Winchester Mystery House, in San Jose. You remember—I took you and your brother there when you were young."

"I would have thought that had been torn down by now. You mean it's still standing?" Andrew asked.

"As far as I know," Stephanie said.

"What does the Winchester place have to do with the price of eggs in Montreal?" George demanded. "We're talking about that psychic you hired."

"You brought it up, Grandpop," Mason pointed out.

"Time's a-wastin'," Lacey chimed in. "Let's get this show on the road."

I stood quietly, waiting for the right moment to extricate myself. It wasn't unusual for a family to involve the contractor in its squabbles since we were necessarily at the eye of the hurricane that was being visited upon their home. I'd learned long ago to never take sides and, once an argument had blown over, never to refer to it again. That didn't keep family members from trying to recruit me to their point of view, but I was good at remaining noncommittal.

Still, I didn't relish the idea of ol' Grandpop turning those beady eyes on *me*.

"As I was saying," continued Mason, apparently the only one not intimidated by George. "Chantelle ... She *knows* things. I don't understand it, but I think if you take the time to get to know her—"

"I'm not wasting my precious time with any damned witch."

"Psychic," Mason corrected.

"Whatever. You mark my words, Andrew, it's a scam of some sort." George gestured toward me with his head. "Probably this one here's in on it, too."

"I guess you haven't heard," I said, both to stop him from saying something I would have to respond to—which might result in me getting myself fired—and to avoid the awkwardness of speaking ill of the dead, who might very well be eavesdropping on us right now. Chantelle seemed more than capable of such. "It's really dreadful, actually. I went to meet with Chantelle yesterday to discuss what she sensed here—"

George snorted.

"And when I got to her apartment she was ... dead."

Stephanie gasped and clasped her hands over her mouth.

"*Dead?*" Andrew said, looking up from his cell phone.

"No way," said Lacey in a derisive tone.

"What ... What happened?" asked Mason, his arm still wrapped protectively around his mother.

George opened and closed his mouth without making a sound, his bluster at least momentarily gone. He looked a little green around the gills.

"She was killed. Stabbed to death, I think."

The family stared at me, dumbstruck.

"I . . . That's stunning," Andrew said. "What a terrible thing. You found her?"

I nodded. "Sort of. Her brother arrived right before me."

"What a shame. That must have been quite a shock for you both."

"It was, yes." No need to go into my history with dead bodies. Any time it happened was still shocking and sad, but as I'd told Landon last night, a person could become accustomed to most things given enough exposure. I had come to realize that the deaths I encountered signaled a beginning, like a starting pistol firing to signal the race to find the murderer had begun.

"Grandpop, we have a tee time at eleven," said Lacey, recovering from the news.

"Oh, yes, quite right," said George. He nodded at me. "Well then, sorry to hear about your friend."

"Thank you, but I'd actually never met her," I clarified.

"Oh, I just assumed . . . since you're in the same line of work."

"I'm not a psychic. I see spirits from time to time, that's all. It may sound related but is quite different."

"But that's wonderful," Stephanie murmured. "Why don't you talk to your friendly spirits and see if you can find out who did that to her?"

"Unfortunately, it doesn't work that way. Be nice if it did, wouldn't it? In my experience, ghosts don't remember their deaths. There's a kind of amnesia that sets in. It's a little frustrating, as you can imagine."

The extended Flynt family was staring at me, their expressions a mixture of awe and incredulity.

"But . . ." Andrew trailed off, blew out a breath. "I can't believe this. I spoke to her just the other day. Who would have done such a thing? And why? Have the police been called?"

"Yes, of course," I said.

"I suppose they'll be visiting us soon, then."

"Oh, my dear," said Stephanie to her husband. "You feel it, don't you?"

He cleared his throat.

"Well, well," said Stephanie, looking around as though summoning strength from the cosmos. "I imagine Chantelle's on a better plane of existence, now."

George harrumphed and rolled his eyes.

Stephanie ignored him. "Perhaps—perhaps she'll communicate with you now, Ms. Turner. Wouldn't that be wonderful?"

"Jim dandy," George said.

"Dad, please," Andrew replied.

"I'm gonna go start up the car," said Lacey, heading for the door. "Grandpop?" George shuffled out after her.

"They don't believe, you know, which is their prerogative," Mason said, clearly less keen on tee time than his sister. "But it must have been a shock for you. Please let us know if there's any way we can help."

"You're very kind," I said.

"You didn't have a chance to talk to her at all?" Andrew asked.

I shook my head. "I arrived after the . . . it had happened."

"Chantelle was practically a legend, really," Mason said with a sad shake of his head. "I mean, I know a lot of people don't believe in such things—witness my family. But . . ."

"But you do?"

"I'm not sure what I believe."

Andrew's face was ashen, and I saw tears in his eyes. He looked away and cleared his throat. "Me neither. The one thing I know is that Chantelle was a beautiful person, and I don't just mean physically. The world lost something very special when she passed."

"I didn't realize you knew her well," I said.

He glanced at his wife. "No, no, hardly at all. But . . . it's just such a shame."

"Come on, folks, we should go," Mason said. "Lacey and Grandpop are no doubt outside revving their engines and annoying the neighbors. You know how impatient they get."

"Well," Andrew said, blowing out a breath and standing straight, as though to shrug off his uncharacteristic show of emotion. "I don't know what's gotten into me. I think it's this place."

He gestured to the sterile, echoing room around us. It was off-putting, no doubt about it, thanks to his dreadful remodel.

"Good to meet you, Mel," Mason said as the Flynts headed for the door.

Stephanie paused, grasped my hand in both of hers, and gazed for a long, earnest moment in my eyes.

"If you are in touch with the spirits, please give Chantelle our best. I hope she goes with our blessing."

"Of course."

They finally swept out, leaving me in the stark foyer.

"They're a trip, aren't they?" came a sudden voice from behind me.

I turned to find Egypt coming down the stairs.

"Interesting family," I said with a nod. "But then, most families are interesting."

She laughed. "You can say that again. Only reason my family didn't argue over money was because there wasn't any."

"Do the Flynts argue about money?"

"It didn't come up? I'm surprised. It seems to be one of their favorite topics. But like I say, maybe it's because they have a lot of money to argue about."

"I may have diverted the discussion by telling them about Chantelle."

"What about her?"

"She was killed yesterday."

Egypt froze. "*Chantelle?* Why? How—I mean, what happened?"

"I really don't know. I had an appointment with her at three o'clock, but when I arrived she was already dead."

"Was she in an accident?"

"She had been stabbed."

Egypt looked stunned and gaped at me for a moment. "*Murdered?* Wow, that's just . . . *wow*. That's horrible. I don't know what to say."

"There's not much to say," I agreed with a nod. "It's a tragedy. Did you know her?"

"I . . . A little. I mean, I met her when she came to do a reading of the house. I basically acted as her secretary, following after her and jotting things down as she said them. She's . . . She was remarkable. Do they know who did it, or why?"

"Not that I know of." I glanced at the cardboard tube in her hands. "Are those the original blueprints?"

She nodded, still seeming distracted, and handed me the heavy tube. "These are the blueprints I was working from with Skip Buhner, though I have to warn you it doesn't include all the change orders. And there were plenty of change orders. Also, here's the list of items Chantelle—" Her voice wavered, and she cleared her throat. "Um, that she suggested we return to the house to appease the ghosts."

I read the list:

Weathervane
Widow's walk
Fireplace surrounds
Lead and stained glass windows throughout
Ceiling medallions
Chandeliers
Carved corbels
Gold gilt mirrors
Stage

My mind tripped over that last item. "Stage?"

"There used to be a stage in what is now the Pilates studio."

"You mean like a *stage*, stage? For plays?"

"More like a raised platform, but it had velvet curtains and some really cool carvings around it."

I nodded. "This is quite a list."

"It was such a shame they took everything out. I know they wanted to modernize the place, but I never understood why they had to just gut it."

"You were here throughout the renovation?"

"For most of it. Stephanie keeps busy with her spiritual work; we met on a retreat out at Green Gulch Farm, in fact. And Andrew is consumed with the business, and frankly I think he just didn't really have the heart to deal with Crosswinds after a while. So I agreed to act as an intermediary, fielding phone calls, keeping lists of things to discuss, and once a week Andrew and I would meet with the contractor, Skip Buhner, go over everything."

"And you lived on-site?"

"Not while the work was being done. I moved in once the construction was over. They were having trouble selling it so Karla suggested someone living here would make the place more welcoming. Do you know Karla Buhner, the Realtor?"

"Andrew mentioned her name."

"Karla says potential buyers can tell when a house is unoccupied, says it makes a home feel abandoned and unwanted. Gives out sad vibes or something. So Andrew asked if I would be willing to move in."

"Have you heard any of the strange sounds, or felt anything . . . odd?"

"I hate to admit it but I don't think I'm particularly sensitive. Everyone else seems to pick up on sensations, but I go on my merry way. And I'm a heavy sleeper, take a little nonaddicting sleep aid that puts me out like a light. You ever have insomnia, I recommend it highly."

"Thanks. I have plenty of problems, but so far that's not one of them." My schedule required me to get up at five a.m. every day, so falling asleep was rarely a problem. On the contrary, I was lucky to be conscious after nine at night, which put a little crimp in my social life.

"Anyway, sometimes I hear the weathervane squeaking — in fact, I think I'm the one who first mentioned it. Couldn't figure out what the noise was. Thought maybe it was a loose pipe or something that the workers forgot, so I asked Skip to look around. I don't know what happened next, but something scared him."

I nodded. "Anything else you can think of?"

Egypt hesitated.

"Anything at all, no matter how bizarre or silly it sounds?"

"I thought I heard a man's voice, calling out. Sort of like a moan, but more than that? For all I know it's the neighbors, but it's . . . eerie."

"Can you describe the moaning?"

She shrugged. "Just sort of . . . a ghostly moaning. Or what I assume a ghost sounds like moaning. I'm getting all my information from the haunted house fund-raiser we put on back in middle school. Haven't heard any rattling chains, though."

"So you hear the weathervane squeaking and a man moaning."

She nodded. "But like I said, the moaning might have been one of the neighbors or someone on the street, something not in the least bit supernatural."

"What else?" I felt like Annette Crawford, saying in her cop voice: *Even small things might be significant. Tell me everything.* To understand the world of spirits beyond the veil, small details that others didn't find significant often mattered.

"I guess you've heard about the music."

"Andrew mentioned that. Have you heard it?"

"I always sort of assumed it was a car passing by with a loud stereo system...."

"Blasting a waltz with a thumping three-quarter beat?"

Egypt shrugged. "Now that you mention it, I guess that seems kind of unlikely. I'm sorry, I guess I'm not the best witness. Chantelle never really believed me, either. What can I say? Crosswinds just doesn't seem creepy or haunted to me."

I smiled. A little obtuseness was a handy quality in a haunted-house sitter. "Do any parts of the house seem unusually cold or drafty? Any lights that go on and off, or doors that open and close for no apparent reason? Maybe the smell of pipe smoke or flowers or perfume—anything unusual?"

She shook her head.

"Have you noticed objects being moved around?"

"It'd be kind of hard to tell—there's not much in here to move. Andrew won't pay to stage the house, so Karla and I brought in a few items, but ..." She waved one hand. I had assumed it was a style choice, but she was right: The home was virtually empty. "The only place that's lived-in is my room on the fourth floor, and the bathroom up there, of course. I don't cook so I barely use the kitchen. Just the fridge and the microwave. Oh, I do find old photographs from time to time. I've got a little collection going."

"What kind of old photos?"

"Very old, sepia. Always of the same young woman, but in different costumes."

"Could I see them?"

"They're upstairs."

"That reminds me, would it be all right if I took a peek in your room?"

She hesitated.

"It's no big deal," I said. "I'm just trying to get a feel for the place, see if there really is anything to this haunting."

I *knew* there was something to it, since I could feel the vibrations, like an alarm clanging so far in the distance it was scarcely perceptible. But for the moment it was best to leave things open-ended.

"Could we do it another time?" Egypt asked, checking her phone. "Right now I have to run, and I'd like to tidy up first."

"Oh Lord, you should see the places I've been," I said, hoping to put her at ease. It didn't work.

"Tomorrow, if you don't mind."

I decided Egypt excelled at dealing with difficult clients like Andrew Flynt and family: She was unfailingly pleasant and polite, and yet revealed very little.

"Sure. If you think of anything else, let me know, okay? And, this is probably going to sound weird, but would you mind if I brought my dog in, and we poked around a little?"

"Your dog?"

"He won't hurt anything, though he might leave a few brown hairs. . . ."

She smiled, but the humor didn't reach her troubled eyes. "It's not a problem. Karla would probably say it would add to the lived-in look."

"Until tomorrow, then."

She nodded, opened her mouth as though to say something further, then shook her head and slipped out the front door.

Chapter Seven

Dog and I did some quick scouting through the lower floor, where the massive "Pilates studio"—still awaiting exercise equipment—must once have hosted stage-worthy events for the Summerton clan. There was also a Jacuzzi room, sauna, and bedroom with en suite bath. Two equipment rooms felt overheated and stuffy with a mechanical smell; they were full of big gray boxes featuring multicolored lights and hummed with the high-tech improvements Andrew Flynt had spent so much money to install.

Dog trotted along at my side, checking out corners, sniffing here and there. I imagined he was disappointed not to find anything putrid or disgusting in the underfurnished building, but as was his wont he was good-natured about it all. He did not, however, bark or mewl or crouch as he often did when in the presence of ghosts.

But as we passed from the Pilates room to the sauna, something caught my eye.

The wall seemed awfully thick. I prowled around looking for a closet door or something that would account for the missing space, but couldn't find anything.

Every house has hidden chases, channels that hold heating vents, air returns, pipes, and electrical wires. Old buildings often had large voids between the walls that had once been filled with stovepipes or chimneys that were no longer necessary.

But a void in this location struck me as odd. There are reasons old houses were laid out a certain way, and this layout wasn't making sense.

"Is it just me, or is this weird?" I asked Dog. He cocked his head, and I could tell he agreed with me. "Let's go find those blueprints."

We climbed the stairs to the main floor and I unrolled the heavy blueprints atop a shiny black granite kitchen counter.

Yep. There were areas left empty for no apparent reason. They did not contain electrical grids or vents, at least not according to the drawings. They were simply dead space. Worse, I realized as I examined the drawings closely, the blueprints did not match the actual building in some places. For instance, the blueprints called for a twenty-five-foot-long foyer, but the actual foyer wasn't a full twenty-five feet. I would bet my steel-toed boots on it.

"The game is afoot, Dog," I said. Dog, for his part, looked ready to figure things out. Or maybe he was hoping for a snack, it was hard to tell.

I unclipped a heavy tape measure from my belt. It was my favorite, the one I had nabbed from my dad when it became clear that his "temporary" hiatus as general director of Turner Construction had morphed into full-blown retirement, leaving me in charge. The tape was made of heavy metal and never crimped like the new ones tended to.

I took a few quick measurements, then consulted the drawings. It wasn't my imagination: The blueprints did not match up with my measurements. Where was the missing square footage? It was one thing to cover up existing moldings, quite another to hide entire rooms or hallways.

That couldn't be what had happened. Must be my measurements. So I went out to my Scion and rummaged around until I found my latest gadget: a tool that measured with a beam of light instead of a tape.

Same result. There were definitely hidden spaces in this house.

And then, as I was trying to figure out what was going on, I heard the faraway strains of classical music. Without thinking, I started humming along: *Ta da tan, tan, tan . . .*

Another waltz.

The music sounded as if it was coming from the foyer, but when I got there I realized the strains were coming from behind the wall, in the dead space. I put my ear up to the new wallboard.

Ta da tan, tan, tan . . . ta da tan, tan, toooon . . .

Whispers.

Giggles.

And overhead, the loud squeaking of the weathervane.

Then from very far away, a man's anguished voice, calling out: *"Oooooooor!"*

Dog started barking, and raced up the broad sweep of stairs before I could stop him.

I ran after him, past the second floor, then the third-floor landing. I was gasping for breath, but kept going, all the way up to the fourth floor where I could hear the clicking of Dog's nails on the wood floor, then down the hall past Egypt's room.

I found Dog at the end of the corridor, simultaneously barking and mewling and crouching, his attention fixed on a large window overlooking part of the roof.

Still trying to catch my breath, I approached slowly, listening, taking in deep breaths to try to catch any odd odors, trying to "feel" what I was dealing with, if something was off. I kept casting compulsive glances over my shoulders and searching my peripheral vision, where I habitually first saw ghosts.

Except I didn't see or sense anything here. But Dog certainly did. And in this area, at least, he was the expert.

It was bright daylight, but contrary to ghost mythology the time of day was irrelevant to spectral activity. Nighttime made everything spookier, and it was easier for spirits to manifest more fully at night, but in my experience ghosts didn't care much about the clock. When they wanted to reach out—and were *able* to—they did.

I reached around Dog and pushed up the sash window. Wonder of wonders, it was an original wood frame, not one of Andrew's vinyl replacements. I stuck my head out the window and craned my neck, but saw nothing except the roof a few feet away.

"What is it, Dog? Do you see something?" I asked, sounding like a character from an old Lassie movie. Still, it made me feel better to talk to him. One of the many reasons Dog had become part of our family was because his ability to see ghosts made me feel less like a nut. And because he had saved my life more than once. And because he was just plain adorable.

"I'm not seeing anything," I continued. Dog wagged his tail at the sound of my voice, but his hackles were up and he was growling, a deep, rumbling growl that he made only in the presence of ghosts.

"It's like that, is it?" I don't know what Dog was seeing or sensing, but if he said something was there, then something *was* there. "All righty, then. Looks like it's the roof for me. Maybe that weathervane is trying to tell me something?"

At the far end of the hall was a rather rickety-looking set of metal spiral stairs that led to the roof of the turret, accessed through a skylight window.

"You stay here, okay? Stay." It wasn't as though Dog was big on English. But he would understand my tone, and I didn't want him trying to follow me up those little metal stairs. "I'll see you on the flip side."

Then I mounted the spiral stairs, my boots clanging on the thin metal risers. Why in the world had Skip Buhner left the wooden window in the hall but yanked out the antique stairs to the roof, I wondered. The original spiral had no doubt been substantial, either wrought iron or wood, not cheap and rickety like these.

Still grumbling, I released the latches on the skylight and pushed it open.

One thing I'll say for modern skylights: they're easier to operate than the old hand-crank versions. I climbed through, and found myself on the roof of the turret.

Dog stuck his fool head out of the window below me and started to bark. Like a crazy canine.

I caught a whiff of something noxious and chemical-smelling, but couldn't place it and it was soon replaced by the salt air breezes.

I took a moment to reassure Dog and to get my bearings. At the top of the cupola was a pole where the weather vane should have been, and encircling the turret was a blank space where the widow's walk had once been. A ladder on the far side of the turret led to the rest of the roof.

The view was phenomenal, and while I didn't agree with Flynt's assessment that it was worth twenty-nine million dollars—was *any* private residence worth that much?—it was, indeed, impressive. I had a panoramic view of the Golden Gate Bridge, the Presidio, Sausalito, the islands in the bay, and all of downtown. As much as

I loved Oakland, it was clear why tourists from around the globe sought out San Francisco and why folks were willing to pay so much to live here. It was simply gorgeous.

Maybe not twenty-nine million dollars' worth of gorgeous, but still.

A bit of moisture blew in off the bay and nearby Pacific Ocean. A couple of big black birds glided by as though seeking their erstwhile perch on the widow's walk, which now probably sat in the corner of some salvage yard or adorned some upscale urban garden, or had long ago been melted down at the scrap yard. Which was a depressing thought.

The day was sunny and bright, not what one would think of the right weather for a haunting.

And yet.

The wind shifted suddenly, and I sensed the weathervane spinning wildly.

The weathervane that didn't exist. I *felt* it as much as heard it, the vibrations of its creaking and squeaking reverberating through the roof tiles. I turned to see where it would have once been.

A man was glowering at me through the skylight window.

Chapter Eight

The person in the window appeared angry. Furious, actually.

Apoplectic, an old-fashioned word, came to mind next, and it took me a moment to realize why: The man was wearing a waistcoat over a brocade vest, and his florid cheeks sported thick muttonchops.

And in his eyes was a rage that chilled me to the core.

Dog went wild. Startled, I reached behind me to grab onto an eave and steady myself.

When I looked back at the skylight, the angry visage was gone.

In the old days, before I understood what I was seeing, I would have tried to explain away what I had just witnessed: It must have been a trick of light, strange reflections in the too-shiny glass. Surely it couldn't have been what it looked like. Surely not an angry man out of time and place. Surely ... not.

And yet that was exactly what it was.

Now that I was more experienced I didn't waste time in denial. I yelled.

"Hello?" I said, my voice sounding scratchy and weak.

I cleared my throat and tried again, in a stronger voice this time. "*Hello?* Can you hear me?"

Nothing. I approached the skylight slowly. I reached up to feel my grandmother's ring, which hung around my neck, and took a moment to center myself.

"Is anyone there? Do you want to speak to me? Do you . . . Do you have something to tell me?"

I had learned through my classes and reading and ghost-busting friend Olivier that ghosts were humans who had passed on. They were no better or worse than anyone else, and they were frightening only because they were dead. Usually.

Except I was willing to bet this guy had been frightening back when he was *alive*, too.

Still, if he was hanging around this house he had a reason. And if he appeared to me here, in broad daylight, then he probably wanted—*needed*—to tell me what that reason was.

The wind shifted again. This time the squeaking was so loud I wheeled around to look at the spot where the weathervane should be, wondering if the man would appear there.

As I twisted I lost my footing on the steep tiles, slick with moisture off the sea, and lunged for the dormer eave.

"*Get back in here!*" the man bellowed.

At least, I thought it was him. I could no longer see him, so I couldn't be sure. But it was a man's voice, gruff and low, which certainly seemed to suit him.

I'm not good at following orders—just ask my dad. But this time I did as I was told.

If I was going to deal with this ghost, best to do it where I wasn't in danger of tumbling four stories to a messy death on a Pacific Heights sidewalk.

The only flaw in this plan was that I had to go back in the way I'd come out: through the skylight, where I'd last seen the man. What if he was still there, brows beetled, furious with me for going out on the roof?

Or . . . perhaps he was only concerned for my welfare. Could that be?

Taking another moment to slow my breathing, I rubbed the ring I wore around my neck, and summoned my courage.

I heard another grumpy old man's voice, this time in my head: *All you can do is get it done.*

My father, Bill Turner, retired general contractor and sage.

I crawled back toward the skylight. Slowly, looking for the apparition.

"Hello? I'm getting off the roof, just like you said. Okay? No fair scaring the crap out of me, deal?"

But as I crawled through the skylight, I felt nothing. I smelled the faint stench of chemicals again, but it dissipated so quickly I might have imagined it. No cold air, no breath on the back of my neck, no outward sign of anything supernatural. Just Dog, whipping his tail wildly, doing that thing where he curls his butt around so far it practically reaches his snout and then whaps himself in the face with his tail in his frenetic display of delight in seeing me.

I reached the little platform at the bottom of the stairs and collapsed on the floor, cradling Dog for a few minutes. Ostensibly this was to reassure him, to show him he was loved and to thank him for his concern. In reality, burying my face in his soft brown fur and hugging his warm wiggly canine body grounded me, and helped to bring me back from the odd sensations of ghosts appearing before me.

Olivier Galopin frequently took me to task when I called a ghost a ghost. He preferred "former humans," and insisted *we* were the ones intruding on *their* peace and quiet, not the other way around.

In public, I nodded. In private, I disagreed. Vehemently. Ghosts, I explained to Olivier, are creepy precisely because they are "former humans"—the key word being "former." Their very former-ness weirds me out.

And yet . . . I felt compelled to help.

What could old grumpy-pants want? Besides having his house put back in order, of course. Was it that straightforward? Could I assume he was the Peregrine Summerton who had built the house? If so, would he be satisfied if I reinstalled the widow's walk and weathervane, uncovered a little original paneling, and added some plaster medallions? Voilà, no more ghosts?

Somehow I didn't think it was going to be that simple.

Especially if Chantelle's untimely demise was somehow connected to the goings-on within these walls. I wondered what Inspector Crawford had uncovered about her murder, if anything.

Since Olivier was on my mind, I texted him, asking for advice.

Dog and I took some time to poke around a little more—looking through the ten bedrooms and various "plus" rooms, with the exception of Egypt's locked chamber—but I heard no more ghostly music, no more squeaky weathervane. I was doubly convinced, however, that this already huge house was even bigger than it appeared. If I was reading the original blueprints correctly—and I was; Dad and Stan had schooled me thoroughly in the art of reading blueprints—then Skip the remodeler had put up false walls.

But why? Because it was simpler and faster to block off a space than to reconfigure the entire floor? Or could there be another explanation?

Only one way to find out. I had gotten an early start

today, so I could probably manage to swing downtown before meeting with Luz and the students. I would text her to let her know I might be late.

It was time for a little chat with Skip Buhner, remodeler to the stars.

It was easy to find the construction site on Sansome and Washington. What was difficult was finding a place to park. The security guard controlling the entrance to the working lot refused to believe I was a contractor, no matter what my business card said. Today probably hadn't been the best day to wear sparkly attire.

"I assure you," I said patiently. "I am Mel Turner, and I'm a general contractor. I need to speak with Skip Buhner."

"You know, I might let you in just to give him a good laugh. Construction workers don't wear dresses."

"They do when they're the ones in charge."

He grinned. "Sure ya are, hon."

"Tell you what. Why don't you call Skip? Use that little radio there. Otherwise I'll happily demonstrate that these are steel-toed boots I'm wearing."

The security guard winced and waved me in.

My little Scion nearly disappeared when sandwiched between two full-sized trucks: one dusty white Ford, one gleaming white Chevy.

I put Dog's leash on, and we went to find Skip Buhner.

A bearded man with a clipboard, I assumed, was the man in charge. He did not, in fact, look amused to see me. He looked downright angry.

"Who the hell let a civilian on-site? And a dog?" he yelled to no one in particular. A few men glanced our way before shaking their heads and getting back to welding or carrying their building supplies. They projected the lackadaisical attitude of workers being paid by the hour by a general they didn't respect.

"Skip Buhner?" I asked.

"Who wants to know?"

"Mel Turner. I'm working for Andrew Flynt."

His eyes looked guarded, but he backed down. "Oh yeah, sure. What do you need? I'm a little busy."

"Sorry. I'll be quick. I—"

"I don't know anything about the so-called haunting at Crosswinds. You ask me, it's that woman making things up."

"You mean Chantelle?"

"No. I mean yes, but she's probably working in concert with the other one."

"Which other one?"

"That . . . What's her name? Israel?"

"Egypt?" According to Egypt, she and Skip had met weekly with Andrew Flynt to discuss the renovation. Yet Skip couldn't remember her name?

"Right. That one."

"Why would Egypt make up something like that?"

"She's got herself a pretty nice setup, doesn't she? Place is a showcase. Gorgeous. Lives like a queen and doesn't pay rent. Not a bad gig, especially when she's got nowhere else to go."

"How do you mean?"

"She's down on her luck, is what I mean. That Mrs. Flynt is a lovely woman, but she's got too big a heart, it gets her in trouble. I've seen it happen lots of times with these wealthy women. They're gentle souls, don't realize they're being taken advantage of."

That hadn't been my experience, I thought. Most of the wealthy women I'd worked for were wealthy for a reason.

"So you're saying Egypt was in need of a job, or . . . ?"

"She'd be homeless, living on the streets, if it weren't for the Flynts letting her stay in that place. She's good with computers, or so I hear, but have you seen the rents in the city lately? And it's not like she contributed much to the renovation. I pretty much took care of everything."

"I see."

"Hey, don't get me wrong—I got no problem with Egypt. If she can get someone else to pay her bills, more power to her, you know what I'm saying? But I think she might have put ideas into Mrs. Flynt's head. Funny noises here, spooky music there, and next thing you know nobody'll buy the place and she don't have to move out. For someone from the wrong side of the tracks, she never had it so good."

"Uh-huh. Where would that side of the tracks be, do you know?"

"Oakland."

His tone told me all I needed to know. To me Oakland was home, a diverse town of working people and taco trucks and Vietnamese restaurants and famous jazz clubs and the elegant Lake Merritt. We were also home to the Black Panthers and the Oakland Raiders and the Hell's Angels and Jack London and Gertrude Stein and rap legend Tupac Shakur. It was anything but boring.

But a lot of San Franciscans were afraid of Oakland, as were the folks from the bedroom communities over the hills. There was no denying that my hometown had a vivid reputation.

"Other than the fact that she wasn't born to money, anything else make you suspicious about Egypt?"

He shrugged. "*I* never heard anything in that house."

"Nothing at all?" According to Egypt, Skip said he heard something and got scared. Which one of them was lying?

He shook his head. "That about it?"

"Actually, I was just starting."

"Look, I'd like nothing better than to stand here all day and chat, but I've got work to do. Good luck with your ghost hunting."

"Just a minute there, Skippy." I had tried being nice, and was out of patience. Time to speak the language men like Skip understood best. I reached into my bag for my cell phone. "Andrew Flynt said you'd be happy to answer any questions I had about Crosswinds. Shall I give him a call to confirm?"

Skip swore softly, caught himself, and slapped a fake smile on his face. "No need. Ask away."

"Did you take before-and-after pictures of the renovation?"

He shrugged. "Some. I can send you digital copies. Karla has more, took them to show clients all the work that was done."

"This is your wife, Karla, the Realtor? Could you give me her contact info?"

He did so and I dutifully wrote it down.

"Thank you. Now, what happened to the historic items you removed from Crosswinds?"

His eyes shifted, looking around at the jobsite, following workers. *He's about to lie,* I realized, again feeling like Annette Crawford. Good heavens, was I beginning to take cues from Annette? The image of Inspector Crawford as some sort of justice-wielding Johnny Appleseed made me smile.

"What's funny?" Skip demanded.

"Nothing. Sorry. Thinking about something else. So where's the stuff from Crosswinds?"

"What stuff?"

"Let's see, I have a list in my bag. . . . Let's start with the weathervane."

"The one that's supposed to be haunted?" He sneered.

"The very one. Mr. Flynt wants me to put it back."

"How you going to do that?"

"That would be why I'm asking you about it. What did you do with it?"

"Prob'ly threw it away."

My stomach clenched.

"In the trash?"

He shrugged.

"You threw what was no doubt a pure copper antique weathervane in the *trash*?"

"What about it?"

He was lying to me again. I don't care how out of touch the man might be with the beauty and glory of historic architectural features, nobody who works in construction doesn't know how valuable copper is, in any form.

"Any chance it found its way to a salvage yard or eBay?"

Right above the bushy hair on Skip's cheeks I saw the pink of a blush. He was still looking anywhere but at me.

"'Fess up, Skip. Andrew Flynt doesn't care about whatever you got for it, he just wants me to put it back. I can probably track it down with a few phone calls, but if you save me the time Flynt will never hear about it."

He mumbled something.

"I'm sorry?"

"Urban Ore, or Griega Salvage, maybe."

"Which one?"

"I can't remember, honest. But I'm telling you, that stuff won't still be there. That was, like, months ago."

"When, exactly?"

Another shrug. "I guess, about . . . five months ago. Everything was sitting in the garage, and then Flynt told me to clean the place out, so I cleaned it out. Hey, at least I didn't just take it to the dump! I, uh, recycled it."

Sure he did. Right into his pocket. "Okay, let's move on to the actual remodel: Did you use all the available space?"

"How do you mean?"

"I was looking over the blueprints and taking some measurements, and it looks like there are some voids in the walls, things like that."

He gave me an odd look. "That house is over thirteen thousand square feet. What, do they need *more* closets?"

"What homeowners do with their square footage is none of my business. What *is* my business is why the blueprints and the measurements don't match up. Did you frame off portions of the house, or maybe seal up entire rooms . . . ?"

He looked uncomfortable and yelled at a young man carrying welding equipment.

"Skip?" I continued, channeling Inspector Crawford. "We haven't known each other very long, but trust me when I say: I'll figure it out. And you can either be my friend and help me figure it out, or you can *not* be my friend and make things more difficult for me, in which case I will find a way to make your life unpleasant."

His look of anger was tinged with respect. "Nobody else even noticed that."

"What can I say? I was taught by the best in the business. So what's the story?"

"There were a coupla old closets, old servants' halls or stairs, it would have taken days to take everything out and redo it, moving walls and everything, and all Flynt cared about was keeping on schedule and on budget. He was pretty unreasonable. The pressure . . . It got to be too much."

I had no trouble believing Andrew Flynt could be unreasonable. But more likely what had happened was that ol' Skip Buhner here, with his lack of experience in historic renovations, had underbid the job with regard to both the budget and the timeline. That happened a lot with amateurs, and typically resulted in shoddy renovations. Turner Construction often lost bids because we were honest and realistic about renovation costs and schedules. Many's the time a potential client who had gone with another construction company called to ask me for help. Just the other day a woman called out of the goodness of her heart, to tell me she should have gone with Turner Construction rather than the company whose low bid turned out to be too good to be true.

"So I take it you didn't keep records of where these spaces are, or what might be in them?"

He shook his head and glanced at his watch again.

"Anything else you can tell me about Crosswinds? Anything odd?"

"Nope. Just glad to have that damned monkey off my back. Went on forever." His radio crackled and he answered: "Be right there. Hold on." Then he turned back to me. "I don't know anything else. Is that it?"

"For now. Thanks for talking with me." I handed him my business card. "Call me if you think of anything else, will you?"

"Sure," he said, sticking my card in his jeans pocket where, I was pretty sure, it would be forgotten and run through the next wash.

Chapter Nine

I returned a couple of calls with my hands-free set while driving across town to meet Luz and her students near the campus of San Francisco State.

Sandwiched between nice examples of the sort of Victorian town houses for which San Francisco was justly famous, the Mermaid Cove apartment complex had been built in the mid-1940s, a time when pragmatism ruled. I imagined that inside each cottage were simple boxy rooms: two bedroom, one bath apartments with a living room and small dining room/kitchen. The best feature of the complex, by far, was that the cottages had been built in a square around a central courtyard, forming a tiny little neighborhood within a neighborhood. Several of the residents had brightened up their cottages with little pots of geraniums and impatiens on their small front porches.

"And here she is now," said Luz as Dog and I approached, as though they had just been talking about me. She was standing at the mouth of the apartment complex with five young adults: three girls, two boys.

"No way," said one young woman with long dark

hair, her generous mouth sporting retro deep-red lip-stick. "That's not her."

"Way," Luz said.

"Way," I seconded.

"You're not even wearing scarves, or anything," the student pointed out.

I looked down at my sparkly dress. "This isn't enough for you? What am I, Scheherazade? Hey, who likes dogs and wants to pet-sit?"

"I will," said one young woman, taking Dog's leash and petting him.

"His name's Dog," I said as she talked in a high voice to him.

"Dog?"

"Yep."

"Isn't that sort of . . . obvious?"

I nodded. "You can call him Doug, if you prefer. He's not fussy that way. All right, let's get to work, shall we?" I slapped my hands together and rubbed them vigorously. "I'm a busy person, things to see, people to do."

"I think you mean the other way around," another of the students said. "*People* to see, *things* to do."

"Whatever."

"Mel, this is Sinsi, Carmen, Diego, Eddie, and Venus," said Luz. "Everybody, this is Mel Turner. Despite her lack of scarves, she apparently talks to ghosts."

"Nice to meet you all," I said, doubting I would be able to keep their names straight. "How about no one tells me anything about what's been going on yet. Let me do a walk-through first, so I can feel what I feel."

"I'm not going back in there," said Carmen . . . or maybe Venus. "Hey, could you get my toothbrush? Actually, just grab my toilet bag, will you? It's the one with the pink flowers."

"I need my hair gel, too," said another one of the girls. "It's the blue tube on the shelf above the toilet."

"My iPod," said one of the boys. "I think it's on the coffee table in the living room."

"Tell you what," I said. "Why don't I do some reconnaissance first, try to see what we're dealing with, and if need be we'll get your stuff out after. Okay?"

I stepped onto the front porch and reached for the doorknob.

"Hey," said Diego or Eddie. "This is serious. Are you sure you should go in there, just like that? You don't have, like, a crucifix or anything?"

Luz crossed her arms over her chest and raised one eyebrow. I knew she was grateful to me for coming, but the whole business of ghosts made her nervous.

"Don't worry," I said. "I got this. I'm a professional."

Despite my bluster, I was sort of making this up as I went along because there was no one-size-fits-all approach to ghosts. Other than my grandmother's ring around my neck, I didn't have any ghost-busting equipment with me. Nothing to capture spirits, or to protect myself from ghosts. No EMF detector, no camera, nothing to detect their presence. But truth to tell while it's always disconcerting to encounter a spirit, I'd never been attacked by one. Frightened by them, yes. Made uncomfortable by them, most certainly. But by and large my experiences proved what my ghost-busting mentor, Olivier, taught: Ghosts are remnants of the humans they once were, no better or worse than when they walked this earth in living form.

I lingered on the doorstep a moment, took a few deep breaths, stroked the ring at my neck, and reminded myself of that.

Then I pushed in the plain, unadorned door and stepped into a living room with a large window looking onto the courtyard. To one side were a small dining area and a kitchen. The lines were plain, with no moldings or built-ins except in the kitchen, which had beautifully crafted original wood cabinets. I spied one tall, narrow cabinet, which probably housed a built-in ironing board, an old-fashioned convenience I wished houses still had. It was so much easier than getting out the screechy foldable ironing board. But that was back when a good housewife did things like iron on a daily basis.

The kitchen was sparkling clean and neat, the bright yellow tiled counters empty, the linoleum floor freshly mopped. The ancient refrigerator was an ugly avocado green, but otherwise appeared spotless and hummed quietly to itself.

Other than the kitchen, however, the apartment was a pigsty. The students had fled in the middle of the night so the apartment was still full of their stuff, arranged willy-nilly as in so many student apartments: a hodge-podge of salvaged furniture and expensive electronics. There was an old couch with the stuffing peeking out from one arm; a simple pine table with two mismatched straight chairs; a folding beach chair in front of a large, bulky TV, the old-fashioned kind, that was hooked up to what looked like a gaming system.

They'd been here all of three days, were full-time students, hadn't arranged their furniture but had found time to hook up their gaming system? I could see Caleb fitting right in at college.

I held my hands out at my sides, palms up, then took a moment to breathe deeply and tried to feel for vibrations, as I'd seen Olivier do when I trailed him around haunted locales, but in this regard I was a bust as a ghost buster. I couldn't really make anything happen. Instead, I usually just hung around—or clambered over roofs—until some ghost took pity and contacted me.

As far as methodologies go, it left a lot to be desired.

So I wasn't surprised that this time, like most times, I didn't feel anything.

A simple arch in the living room opened onto a short hallway that led to two bedrooms and a bathroom. The bathroom counter was littered with toiletries, two hair dryers, and several towels hanging listlessly from a rack. The bedrooms were disheveled: Sheets hung off the twin beds, and clothes were strewn everywhere.

Either this gang had been visited by a poltergeist, or they were typical students.

I lingered for a few more minutes, but didn't see or feel anything unusual. Finally, I went outside to join an anxious-looking Luz, still standing outside with the students.

I took a moment to greet an ecstatic Dog.

"You see anything?" asked Sinsi. I think. Maybe it was Carmen.

I shook my head. "Not much, except that you guys are slobs. Except for the kitchen. Somebody gets props for that."

The students exchanged wary glances.

"What did I say?"

"That's the weirdest part," said the student I thought was Eddie, and the others nodded.

"What do you mean?"

"*We* didn't clean the kitchen. The ghost did."

"Excuse me?"

"We've never cleaned the kitchen. It gets cleaned at night. We're sleeping and we hear something, and when we get up we see this . . . thing, or whatever it is, in the kitchen. Cleaning."

"Doesn't matter how messy it is when we go to bed," said Sinsi. "We wake up and that place is spotless."

"Have you seen it happening?"

One of the girls shook her head. "Not, like, as a person, or anything. Just—you can see stuff getting done, moving around and stuff."

"Mops the floor and everything," said Venus.

"Doesn't touch the rest of the apartment, just the kitchen," Diego chimed in.

"Is that normal? I mean, have you ever heard of something like that?" asked Carmen.

"No, can't say that I have." I studied the students for a moment, then looked at Luz, who had a *hoo boy* expression on her face.

"Just out of curiosity: Are you sure this isn't something you can live with?" I asked. "I mean, a lot of people would pay extra for that kind of service."

They gaped at me, and Carmen made the sign of the cross.

"It's not right," Sinsi muttered.

"They're scared, Mel," Luz weighed in.

Venus nodded. "Last time, she started yelling at us to keep it clean, to get out of her house."

That wasn't good, I thought. Sometimes harmless hauntings ratcheted up over time, grew more intense or more threatening. Even if this spirit didn't mean to hurt anyone, it could be difficult to live with something like that. Nothing like sharing your living space with someone who was unpredictable, intimidating—and dead.

"Gotcha," I said. "All right, here's what we're going to do. We're going inside as a group, and you're going to grab whatever you'll need for the next few days. I don't want anyone going back in until I figure out how to resolve this, and while I'll do my best to be quick about it, I can't guarantee how long that will take."

"Let's hope not long," Luz said. "Okay, gang, let's hustle. Inside, grab your stuff, and out. Quick like bunnies."

Dog and I stood in the doorway to the kitchen like a

security detail while the students hurried into the bathroom and bedrooms and brought out their things. Diego unhooked his gaming system and Eddie cradled his iPod to his chest like a lost child.

Finally, as they carried their things out to Luz's car I asked her, "What do you know about the history of the apartment?"

"Nothing really. I was hoping you could just go in there and tell that thing to go toward the light, or whatever. I gotta say, I'm a little disappointed in your abilities."

"Get in line. I'm not the one who claimed to be good at this, remember?" I said with a smile. "So have you talked to the landlord?"

"Not yet. Get this: The kids haven't even met her, they just have a PO box to send their rent check, and she mailed them the keys."

"Hmm."

"I guess I should try to track her down."

"Don't you have classes to teach?"

"Classes don't start until next week. There are incessant faculty meetings, of course, but as for my own prep work, as you know, I am the soul of efficiency." This was true. Luz was hyperorganized, and so on top of things that I wondered if it was some really effective form of OCD. Probably, though, it was just the hard-won habits that led a girl with a less than privileged background in East LA to win a scholarship to an Ivy League college and then to graduate school.

Across the little courtyard, I saw movement behind a curtain.

"Maybe there's an easier way. These neighbors must all know one another."

I knocked on the door of the apartment facing the students' rental.

An unsmiling woman, likely in her seventies, answered. Her gray hair was in a twist atop her head, and she was wearing what looked like a polyester jogging suit, red with a white stripe. Perfect for running a marathon in 1982.

"Hello," I said. "My name's Mel Turner."

"I don't want any," she said.

"Any what?"

"Whatever it is you're selling."

"Oh, no—sorry—I'm not selling anything. I promise. I just wondered if I could ask you about Unit B."

She shrugged. "You thinking of moving in?"

"No."

"Good."

I wasn't sure if I should take that personally, so I let it slide.

"Could you tell me anything about it? Anything at all?"

"All I know is it never rents for long. People move in, then move out within a couple of days."

"Really. Do you know the landlady?"

She shook her head. "The units are all owned by different people."

"But the owner of Unit B just keeps renting it out? Has she ever arranged for a cleansing, or anything?"

"I don't keep track of housecleaning services."

"I meant a spiritual cleansing . . . ?"

"A what, now?"

"It's like a spiritual sweep of the place, meant to get rid of . . . spirits."

She looked at me much the way I would have, a few years ago. Not unkindly, but with sympathy, tinged with worry. As though I'd gone off my meds.

That was back when I thought the little boy I'd seen when I was a child was an imaginary friend. Back when

I would have sworn that when people were dead they were gone, end of story. Back when I thought my mother was just plain weird when she refused to allow my father to buy and flip certain houses because they had a bad aura.

Now that I had, apparently, inherited my mother's sixth sense, I had been forced to eat a certain amount of crow.

"Do you happen to know anything about the history of these apartments? You haven't had any trouble in your unit?"

"The plumbing keeps backing up, I'll tell you that much. And the hot water runs out after about five minutes."

"What about odd noises? Things moving around . . . ?"

She shook her head and went back into her place, slamming the door. Friendly.

I knocked on a few more cottages, but no one answered. It was the middle of the day; most folks would be at work.

Finally, I turned back to the students, who had finished loading their stuff and were now picking at their nails and looking at their phones.

"This blows," said Sinsi. The others nodded in agreement.

"So, this place is cheaper than the other units?" I asked.

"I don't know exactly, but probably," said Diego. "It's well under market value, I can tell you that much. Have you seen what places rent for in the city these days? We've got no shot against the Google techies."

"You can say that again," said Venus.

"So, what do we do now, chief?" Luz asked.

Good question.

"Okay, it's a ghost who's a neat freak. What say I go mess things up, see if I can annoy her?"

The students looked shocked.

"Are you sure that's a good idea?" Luz asked.

"It's worth a try, right?"

I went into the kitchen and started to throw things around. Luz hovered in the doorway of the apartment, clearly worried.

"Helloooo?" I yelled as I flung open cabinets and tossed a dish towel to the floor. "Anyone home?"

I started to smell fresh baked apple pie.

"Anybody?"

The canned goods in one cabinet were lined up in straight rows. I rearranged them.

Suddenly, the aromas of cinnamon and fresh dough enveloped me. The scents might be coming from another unit, I supposed. Maybe Friendly from across the way had been in a hurry to take a pie out of the oven. But scent was often my first indication of a spiritual presence; cigar smoke or citrus or perfume sometimes lingered from days past.

"Is anybody here?" I tried again. "Is this your kitchen?"

I opened a drawer. Inside, mismatched cutlery was arranged in neat stacks. I pulled the drawer all the way out, shook it so the silverware was one big jumble, then pushed it back in.

I waited.

Nothing.

I gave up and headed toward the door. "Sorry, Luz. I guess she's not in the mood. Maybe I should try at night. Sometimes it's easier to make con—"

Behind me, there was a deafening crash.

The silverware drawer had been pulled out and

thrown to the floor, sending the spoons, forks, and serving utensils skittering across the linoleum.

Luz screamed and ran out the door.

"It's all right, Luz," I said as I urged her to have a seat on the half wall, the students milling about her.

"Is she okay?" Carmen asked.

"You okay, Luz? *Estás bien?*"

"Of course," Luz said with a frown, gruff with embarrassment at having lost her composure in front of the students.

"What happened in there?" asked Eddie, putting a comforting hand on her shoulder. "Did she come after you with the egg beaters? Dude, she did that to me once, I was freaked."

"She attacked you?" I asked.

"You trippin'," said Diego. "She did not. You dreamed that."

Eddie shrugged. "Seemed real. I was trying to get the cupboard over the fridge open. It's, like, painted shut? And I practically fell, I was so freaked-out."

"All right," I said, blowing out a breath. "I'll try to figure this out, but it might take a few days."

"Okay, guys, you can unload your stuff from my car back at my place tonight. I'll see you all later." Luz turned to me. "I know I said I would take you wherever you wanted for lunch, but I am in desperate need of lemongrass chicken and a beer. Maybe the other way around."

"Beer and Thai food, it is."

Chapter Ten

On the way to the restaurant I dropped Dog off with my foreman Raul, who loved dogs and whose own beloved pup had recently passed away. The pup would be well taken care of while I was at lunch. Raul still carried Milk-Bones in his truck.

"You okay?" I asked Luz.

We were seated at Lers Ros Thai restaurant and had ordered egg rolls, pad Thai, lemongrass chicken; beer for Luz and Thai iced tea for me.

Luz nodded, but she seemed distracted, as though she had something on her mind—something beyond her troubled students. And I had a sneaking suspicion I knew what it was. Luz was fierce and proud, and wasn't afraid of anything except ghosts and clowns. The clown part was self-explanatory—they gave me the willies, too—but for some time now I'd had the sense that Luz had had some kind of experience with the unexplainable, something that had left a scar. And if she wouldn't tell me, I imagined she hadn't shared it with anyone.

"Sooner or later you're going to have to tell me," I said as I dug into the egg rolls.

"And why is that?"

"Because I'm your best friend. And I won't make fun of you or think you're crazy for having seen ghosts. Or ... whatever it was you saw, or experienced. Not that I'm saying you have, you know. Just in case you did."

She shrugged.

I watched as she toyed with her food. Luz always played her cards close to her chest. Though she taught social work, she was much more comfortable with theory than practice and didn't believe in a lot of self-disclosure. She knew far more about my issues and concerns than I did about hers, but she was fiercely loyal and dependable and about the best friend a person could have. I wanted to be that for her, too.

I forced myself to remain silent. Finally, she opened her mouth as though to say something.

My phone rang.

Dammit. The screen read: Annette Crawford. I try to avoid answering the phone while dining with friends, but the SFPD was hard to ignore.

"Take it," Luz urged.

"I'm sorry. It's Annette Crawford, so I probably should. I'll be right back."

I went outside and ducked down a little alley, away from the noise on Larkin Street.

"I thought you were babysitting Landon Demetrius?" Inspector Crawford asked without preamble.

"I, um ... didn't realize babysitting was in order." Had the Inspector picked up on Landon's lost puppy vibrations? Or was he just getting in her way? "I dropped him off at his hotel yesterday. I figured he'd be all right since he is, after all, a grown man, and ..." I paused. "You're just messing with me, aren't you?"

I heard her deep, pleasant chuckle. "He thinks you're very ... interesting, I believe was the word he used."

"Isn't that polite Brit-speak for 'kind of weird'?"

"That'd be my guess."

"Yeah, well, tell him to take a number. So what can I do for you, Inspector?"

"According to Demetrius, you saw his sister. His *dead* sister. In a didn't-seem-dead state, if you catch my drift."

"Well, now, I suppose that is true...."

"Any reason you didn't think to mention that to me? You know, when I asked you if there was anything else, anything at all you needed to tell me?"

"No.... She didn't tell me anything pertinent."

"Did she say anything at all?"

The fact that Annette would ask me this, that she even *knew* to ask me this, was proof of how much our relationship had changed over the past couple of years. When I first met Inspector Crawford on a crime scene, neither of us was sure we believed in ghosts. Since then, we'd both learned a lot.

This was why Annette was my go-to homicide inspector whenever I tripped over bodies. It was refreshing not to have to explain myself each and every time.

"No," I said. "She didn't speak. She came out of the apartment, and sort of smiled, as though trying to signal she was okay. She ran her hand over her brother's face, and then she went down the hall, got in the elevator, and went up."

"Is that a metaphor?"

"No. Or ... yes, I suppose it is. But it's also what I saw."

"What about Crosswinds?" Annette asked. "Anything further on that possible connection?"

"I went by there this morning, and spoke with the caretaker and the extended Flynt family, who all seem pretty eager to sell the place. They seemed genuinely shocked by the news of Chantelle's death. I can't imagine what they would be holding against Chantelle, but then as we both know I'm not very good at this sort of thing."

"I don't know about that. You tend to stumble on murderers."

"I guess 'stumble on' is the part I'm referring to. I rarely seem able to suss out the killer before they try to kill me. I should probably work on that."

"Personal growth. It's important never to stop learning."

"You're funny today," I said. Annette was in a positively jocular mood. It was rare for her. "What's up?"

"Can't a woman enjoy her work?"

"Of course . . . although considering you work in homicide, that gets into a creepy zone pretty quickly."

She chuckled. "Anyway, what else have you learned about Crosswinds?"

"I can confirm the presence of at least one ghost. An older man, late fifties or early sixties, dressed as though from the late 1800s. I don't know what his story is yet, much less what he has to do with Chantelle's death, if anything. He yelled at me to get off the roof. He startled me, and I nearly fell."

"What were you doing on the roof?"

"Looking for a ghost."

Annette paused. "You do have an interesting time of it, don't you?"

"Anyway, after my ghost encounter, I went to speak with the contractor who did the remodel. Before Chantelle was murdered, she told the Flynts to appease the ghost by undoing some of the renovations on Crosswinds. So now I'm trying to track down some of items that were ripped out. The contractor, Skip Buhner, is supposed to be getting me some before-and-after photos. But there's no obvious connection between Crosswinds and Chantelle's death that I can see so far. Is there?"

"I have no idea. She worked out of her condo and had a lot of clients going in and out, which annoyed some of the neighbors. Didn't seem like the problem was sufficient to provoke murder, but I've seen murders committed for less reason. She also appears to have been juggling more than one boyfriend, which may be a promising lead. There are plenty of ways to get in and out of the building undetected, so the murderer could also have been a stranger. But I'll be talking to the Flynts today. Just wanted to touch base with you first for any insights you might have."

"Oh, Skip says the Crosswinds caretaker, named Egypt Davis, probably killed Chantelle so she doesn't have to move out."

"Excuse me?"

"I'm just telling you what he told me. Seems like a bit of a long shot, but as you always say, tell you everything."

"True."

"Sorry I can't be more help."

"Just keep me up to speed, if you don't mind."

"Annette, is Landon Demetrius a suspect?"

"We don't have anything in particular to make us think so—other than you."

"Me?"

"You saw him kneeling over the body."

"Well, yeah—but he wasn't stabbing her, just kneeling there looking like he was about to cry. Is there anything else to suggest he did it?"

"Not so far. Forensics took photos and swabbed his hands and clothes, but didn't find anything incriminating such as defensive wounds or blood spatter. We released his luggage to him today. But family often seems to drive people to thoughts of murder."

"I suppose that's true enough. Hey, while I've got you on the phone, does this address mean anything to you?"

I read off the address of the Mermaid Cove apartment complex.

"No. Should it?"

"Just wondering. Seems to be haunted. A group of students going to San Francisco State rented it, and were run out by a spirit or spirits unknown. According to the neighbor, no one stays very long."

"I'll run it and see if anything pops up, crime-wise. But you haven't found any dead bodies there, so far?"

"Dead-body free at the moment," I said.

"Good. Let's keep it that way. Gotta go."

"Bye." I hung up and turned to go back into the restaurant. One of the chefs had come outside for a smoke break, and was staring at me with a look of horror on his face. Either that or he'd eaten some bad lemongrass.

"Sorry," I said. "Talking to my friend, the homicide inspector."

This explanation did not help the situation.

I ducked back into the restaurant and joined Luz, who was scrolling through her phone.

"Googled the address, but nothing came up," she said, before shutting it down. "How's Annette? Find the killer yet?"

A waitress chose that moment to approach the table with steaming plates of noodles and chicken. Again with the look of dismay. I wondered if she and the chef would trade notes and ban us from their restaurant, which worried me. Lers Ros was my favorite Thai food in the city.

"Not yet," I said after the waitress left. "In fact, the investigation is just starting. And we don't even know that it's connected to the Crosswinds mansion."

"Probably is."

"Why do you say that?"

"Because you're involved. No offense, *amiga mia*, but you do attract this kind of disaster."

"Hey, weren't you the one asking for pro bono ghost-busting services? Speaking of which—what were you about to tell me when Annette called?"

She gave a quick, tight shake of her head, which meant: off-limits. *Dammit.* She had been ready to spill, but had changed her mind while I was on the phone. No point pushing her now. If there was one thing I knew for certain about Luz Cabrera, she wouldn't tell me—or anyone—anything until she was good and ready.

Instead, she changed the subject.

"So, you were saying last night that there was a weathervane on Crosswinds? Makes me think of the opening scene in Mary Poppins. You remember that one?"

"Remind me."

"The wind changes, and down comes Mary Poppins with her umbrella."

"Strangely enough, that thought doesn't actually comfort me. I always found Mary Poppins sort of creepy."

Luz nodded. "Anybody who holds her feet like that shouldn't be permitted around small children without supervision."

"She scared the heck out of me when she floated down like that. I'll bet that movie wouldn't even be made in today's day and age."

"Me too, to tell the truth." She helped herself to more pad Thai. "So any idea how we track down this land-lady?"

"There must be a record of who owns the property at the city," I said. "I'll check out the paperwork, you check out anything you can think of."

"The students send their rent to a PO box, but maybe I can get some information from the post office, or Goo-

gle her name for an address. And then we'll go talk to her
together, try to figure out what she knows, shake her
down if need be. But in the meantime, could you look
into arranging for a spiritual cleansing so the kids can
move back?"

I nodded as I dug into my lemongrass chicken. "Usually, though, if a ghost is hanging around there's a reason.
And as loath as I am to admit it, I seem destined to help
them out. This ghost reached out to me. I'd like to see if
I can figure out what it wants."

"She reached out to you by throwing silverware all
over the floor?"

"It's a ghost thing," I said with a shrug. "They can only
communicate in very particular fashions. Sometimes
they scare by accident, even when they don't mean to.
It's not easy to get through the veil."

"An accidental haunting?" Luz finished off her beer.
"I gotta hand it to you, *chica*. You do have an interesting
take on things."

Chapter Eleven

Before I left the house the following morning, I met with Stan and went over the Crosswinds contract which, due to its unusual content—ghost ridding and remodel dismantling—required more thought than the usual boilerplate. Then we chatted about where some of the Crosswinds items might have wound up. Yesterday Stan had called around to salvage yards, but so far he hadn't gotten any hits. The folks answering the phone were usually underpaid workers who didn't keep records of where items came from. And they surely didn't keep track of what they sold. It was a cash business, easy in, easy out.

A lot of their inventory came from off the back of some contractor's truck, but items also came in from homeowners and junk dealers, or were picked up off the street. I myself once had caused a major traffic snarl when I stopped my vehicle in the middle of International Boulevard to pick up a slightly distressed stained glass window.

I hated to admit it, but finding the items torn out of

the Flynt residence was a long shot. According to what he'd told me, Skip had dumped them five months ago, and many would have been snatched up by savvy antiques store dealers. A solid copper antique weathervane wouldn't have lasted two days in a well-patronized salvage yard.

On the other hand, there were enough nooks and crannies in some of those places that some items could be overlooked. I decided to check a few out in person later this morning. But first, I had made arrangements by e-mail to meet the Crosswinds Realtor, Skip's wife, Karla.

"Bye, Dad," I said as I breezed through the kitchen. "No coffee for me this morning, I'm meeting Karla Buhner at the Royal."

He fixed me with a look. "You're gonna pay perfect strangers to make you breakfast but turn up your nose at mine?"

"I'll just have coffee, like I do here. No more, no less. No worries."

"And who is this Karla Buhner person?"

"She's the Realtor for Crosswinds; her husband did the remodel. Brittany Humm gave her my name as the ghost buster of choice on this project."

He grunted. Brittany Humm was a bright, wonderful woman who had been the first Realtor I'd ever met who specialized in haunted houses—which, to my surprise, was a thing. There were actually people who *wanted* to live with ghosts. Just like those folks who requested the haunted room at the Claremont Hotel.

This was precisely why my father didn't care for her. While he was slowly coming around to *my* seeing ghosts, the understanding did not extend to Brittany or Olivier or any other of the other "ghost professionals" who were now in my supernatural social circle.

I kissed his whiskery cheek, petted Dog good-bye, and headed to Mama's Royal Café on Broadway in Oakland.

Karla was waiting for me at a table; I recognized her from the Crosswinds Web site. She was a well–put together, somewhat tight-lipped woman. Fortyish, reddish-brown hair. Attractive in that bland way of business professionals who weren't lucky enough to be able to wear sparkles to work.

"Hi," I said as I approached. Her eyes slid up and down my outfit. "Karla? I'm Mel. Good to meet you."

"You're Mel Turner? The contractor?"

"Yes, nice to meet you."

"I thought you were a man. By your name, I mean."

"I get that a lot."

The eyes flickered over my ensemble one more time. It was annoying, but this was on me. The guys I worked with were used to my personal style, and since I signed their checks and got the job done it wasn't an issue. For everyone else it came as a surprise. But Turner Construction was doing just fine lately—I still had a full-time crew on the Wakefield Retreat Center up in Marin County, and several other smaller remodels—and frankly, I was getting the feeling that if I wanted to work full-time as a ghost consultant, there was plenty of demand in San Francisco. So I figured my combined talents of historic reconstruction and spirit talker gave me a little sartorial leeway.

We ordered coffee, and I launched into what I wanted to know.

"So, what can you tell me about Crosswinds?"

"Probably nothing you haven't already heard," she said as she stirred cream and two packets of Sweet'N Low into her cup. "Gorgeous property, incomparable views, so spacious! And an address to *die* for."

I cringed at her pun, and wondered if she was even aware she'd made it. Had Karla heard about Chantelle's death? She must have. It had been splashed over the papers; apparently, everyone but me was familiar with Chantelle-the-psychic.

"Did you hear about what happened to Chantelle?" I asked.

"Oh! Oh yes, I did. I could scarce believe it when Skip told me! And then the police came to talk with me, because I had left a message on her answering machine *right as she was killed.* What a thing!" Her blue eyes settled on me. "Oh, wait. Are you thinking there was a connection between what Chantelle said about Crosswinds, and her death?"

"It's possible. I imagine the police will want to rule it out, anyway."

"Oh, good heavens." Karla sighed and began shaking another packet of sweetener in the air. "Scandal does seem to follow this house, doesn't it? First the haunting, then the association with Chantelle's murder?"

"No one knows yet if there is a connection. It's probably wholly unrelated."

Karla poured the third packet of sweetener into her mug and stirred vigorously while I sipped my unadulterated coffee and thought about what Graham and I had discovered on the Internet about Landon Demetrius. A world-famous mathematician with a well-known psychic sister. If he was wealthy it was doubtful money would have been a motive for murder, but could she have been an embarrassment to him? He said they used to be close but had grown apart. Had his logical mind suddenly snapped for some reason, and he took her out there and then?

While I was pondering, Karla took a gulp of her sweet coffee, set the mug down on the table, and pulled a file out of her leather satchel. Crosswinds was written at the top in a round, loopy script.

"I brought the before-and-after photos you asked for," she said. As she opened the file, a couple of very old photographs fell out. Similar to the photo I had found while touring the house with Andrew, these were sepia-toned and appeared fragile, with several of the corners broken off.

Leaning across the table, I picked one up. It was of the same young woman: pretty, clearly pampered, and yet with a sad expression on her face. In this photo, though, her long hair fell to her waist, she wore gauzy white robes, and she held a small leafy tree branch, as though costumed as a nymph or some other character from mythology. In the second photo, she carried a parasol and wore a hoop skirt and stood in profile, gazing over her shoulder at the photographer.

"They're sort of . . . wistful, aren't they?" asked Karla. "When they were doing the construction they found scads of these old photos behind the walls, under the floorboards, just everywhere. Skip threw most of them out, of course, but I kept a few. I thought they'd look amazing in the right frames, don't you think? For staging houses? Like when you buy old photos in antiques stores and pretend they're your relatives?"

"Um . . . yes, they *are* amazing." It felt unseemly to pretend the young woman was some sort of ancestor. She gazed so directly—yet so mournfully—at the camera that I longed to know who she was, what had become of her. I saw intelligence in her eyes, an almost palpable sense of simmering urgency, as though she were willing the photographer to put down the camera so she could get on with her life.

Why were her photos found at Crosswinds? Had she lived there? Perhaps died there?

I had seen only the spirit of an older man at the house, but I hadn't spent much time there yet, so perhaps she would appear as well. On the other hand . . . the young woman was dressed in different costumes, so perhaps she wasn't the lady of the house after all, but an artist's muse. A working-class woman, or an actress, who posed for money. This must have been early days for photography, when the early adaptors applied the artistic conventions of fine painting to their subjects.

"Do you know if one of the former owners was into photography?" I asked.

Karla looked surprised. "I really have no idea."

"Skip didn't find anything related to photography at the house? Just the photos?"

"He didn't mention anything to me. So anyway, here are the before-and-after pics. And here's the promo shot we're using for the sale. We have an entire Web site devoted to Crosswinds."

"I saw that," I said. The eight-by-ten glossy she handed me was the same photo featured on the Web site.

Except, now that I was looking at it more closely, it looked like a figure was standing atop the turret, where the widow's walk should have been. A ghostly, barely-there figure, hard to make out against the cloudy backdrop.

"What's this?" I asked, pointing to the turret.

"That? It's a tower," Karla said. "Common to Queen Anne Victorians. Mostly for decoration, it's largely unusable space but it does make for a distinctive roofline."

"No, I meant—" I looked at the photo again, and saw nothing but the turret. Were my eyes playing tricks on me? I took another sip of coffee. "Sorry. I could have sworn . . ." I trailed off as the image returned. There was a figure standing on the tower. A woman in a dress. And it looked an awful lot like the young woman in the sepia-toned pictures.

Great. Just great. I was now being haunted through *photographs*? Seriously?

"Are you all right?" Karla asked. "Let me get you a glass of water."

"No, thanks. I'm fine. Really."

She gasped and her blue eyes widened. "Wait a minute. . . . Did you see something? As in, *see* something?"

"I thought I did, but . . . never mind. Let's look at the before and afters."

The before photos showed that Crosswinds had originally featured the kind of architectural details I would have expected: gorgeous finishes and moldings and built-ins. True, it looked a bit run-down and rooms such as the kitchen, especially, had been in need of updating. People live and entertain differently these days, and want their houses wired and energy efficient. Old is not necessarily better, I really do get that. But still.

And then I saw one photo that caught my attention: It was a weathervane shaped like a ship. But unlike modern mass-produced versions, this was full-bodied, the details ornate and beautiful. A green oxide patina heightened the relief and the detail on the ship, and below it was an arrow and the four directions: North, South, East, West.

"Could you e-mail me those photos?" I asked. "They'll be very helpful when I look for items to replace in the house."

"I can do you one better," she said, handing me a memory stick. "I loaded them on the memory thingee for you. Along with several listings I thought you might enjoy perusing."

At my questioning look, she continued: "Andrew mentioned you live with your father, so I took the liberty. . . . A woman like you must want privacy." She winked.

I didn't quite know how to react to that.

"I, well . . . Thank you," I said. "Karla, may I ask you something? Please don't take this the wrong way, but your office is in Walnut Creek, and I know that Realtors tend to specialize in certain localities. Why didn't the Flynts hire a San Francisco Realtor for Crosswinds?"

Karla laughed, clearly unoffended. "Skip introduced me to Andrew and Stephanie at the Hearts after Dark Ball last Valentine's Day—it's a fund-raiser for San Francisco General, do you know it? Skip and I are *huge* supporters of charitable causes, so we have that in common with the Flynts. The minute Stephanie and I met we hit it off! It's important clients feel comfortable with their Realtors, and, well, Stephanie and I became as close as sorority sisters. And while it's true I'm not as familiar with the city as others might be, what matters most is to have the *best* no matter her office address, don't you think?"

"I suppose so," I nodded. Still, it seemed odd, and I wasn't willing to take Karla's word for it. She seemed open and friendly enough, but she was married to Skip, who I would trust about as far as I could throw my table saw. I decided to call Brittany later and do a little fact-checking on Karla.

"I see your husband is working on an office building downtown," I said.

"Oh, yes, his business is really taking off."

"How did Skip get the Crosswinds remodel?"

"The Flynts had several bids, and Skip's won. He's really very good, as I'm sure you noticed when you visited the house." She checked her phone. "Transformed the place; really brought it into the twenty-first century."

"But how—" I broke off when I saw none other than Landon Demetrius III walk into Mama's Royal Café, and come straight over to where we were sitting.

"Excuse me for intruding," he said in that stiffly polite, deep voice.

"What are you doing here?" I asked him.

"I called your office, and a man named Stan told me I could find you here. And it just so happens I was hoping to talk to Ms. Buhner, as well." He nodded at the Realtor sitting across from me. "You are Karla Buhner, are you not?"

"Yes," she said, rather breathlessly. "I am."

"You left a message on the answering machine at my sister's flat. I heard your voice when I . . . just as I came in and found her."

"Oh, how awful! I was *so* sorry to hear about what happened," Karla said with a little gasp. I watched, fascinated, as she keyed into Landon: preening ever so slightly, sticking out her chest, playing with her hair. "What a shock. What a tragedy! And to hear me leaving a silly message when you were finding her . . . How *terrible*!"

I had been so focused on the shocking events that evening at Chantelle's apartment that I hadn't really noticed, but now it hit me: Landon Demetrius was an extremely good-looking man. He and his sister must have made quite the gorgeous pair. Despite his rigid posture and formality—or because of it?—Landon really was captivating.

"Thank you," said Landon with a little nod. "I wanted to ask you why you had called, and if you knew anything about her schedule that day?"

Karla shook her head. "The police contacted me about that already. It was nothing, really. A professional colleague, Brittany Humm—she's a friend of Mel's, by the way, I see you two know each other!—has a certain expertise in . . . in psychics and whatnot. So when I told her of my difficulties selling Crosswinds because of the ghosts, she recommended the Flynts ask Chantelle to do a reading."

"So you are the one who arranged for the reading?"

"Yes, I was. Although I must say, I was a wee bit disappointed that she recommended tearing out all of Skip's hard work. That's what I was calling Chantelle to discuss that day. I think it's an atrocity. No offense, Mel, but it just makes no sense at all. Skip has been working there for *years*, managed to turn it into a showpiece. It's going to be a hodgepodge of styles if you bring back that old garbage."

I counted to ten.

"It remains to be seen how far we'll go with everything," I said finally. Much as I hated to admit it, Crosswinds had been too butchered to easily restore. I had dreamt about it last night: smooth expanses of white walls, sleek lines, clean open spaces. To bring it back to its former glory would take far more than a couple of trips to the salvage yard. "I think I may have made initial contact with the ghost, though. I thought I'd try to track down the weathervane and widow's walk, at least start with those, and see what happens."

"That's absurd," Karla said.

"It's a place to start, and neither of those will interfere with any of Skip's interior work."

She shrugged.

I became uncomfortably aware of Landon's intense gaze. Finally, he said, "Contacted by the ghost?"

"It's a thing. We can talk later." I turned back to Karla. "So, do you know what happened to that old weathervane? Or any of the other stuff Skip pulled from the house?"

She blushed and looked away. Very much like her husband. And also like him, she didn't volunteer any information.

"Karla?" I urged. "Do you still have it?"

"Don't be absurd." She checked her phone again, in what I was beginning to think was a nervous habit. Either that or she was desperate for it to ring so she could extricate herself from this discussion. "It's . . . This whole discussion is absurd."

That seemed to be her favorite word of the day.

"Could you tell me what you experienced at Crosswinds?" I asked. "In as much detail as possible."

"It's . . ." Again with the phone. "It's embarrassing, really, and I have to say I don't really believe in any of this. But . . ."

"But?"

"I had a very exclusive client in from Dubai. He was very interested, absolutely loved the place. Very qualified buyer—oil money. You know, they're buying up all the truly exclusive places these days. Even the more exclusive computer folks aren't as interested in these big old mansions anymore—they're all buying islands. It takes a foreigner to truly appreciate an old-style mansion."

Landon was sitting straight and attentive, as though hanging on every word. Karla kept looking up at him through her lashes.

"Don't you want something?" I asked Landon. "Coffee or tea? You have to order up at the counter."

"I'm fine. Thank you."

"Would you mind getting me a refill?" I persisted. I wanted Karla to be able to speak plainly without worrying about what Landon might think. "I would so appreciate it."

After a beat, he said, "Of course. Anything else?" His

words had a subtle edge, as though he knew I was send-ing him away.

"That's it. Thank you."

Karla's eyes watched him as he went up to the counter. Then she turned back to me and blushed pret-tily, and shrugged. "Nice view from here."

I gave her a tight smile.

"What is it they say: Just because I'm on a diet doesn't mean I can't look at the menu?" She leaned forward, and her voice dropped. "Besides, a person can cheat on a diet once in a while and still be okay, am I right?"

Karla was a trim woman, but she wasn't talking about her calorie intake. As someone who only recently had waded back into the romance department after a diffi-cult divorce from a man who frequently cheated on his diet—*me*—I wasn't about to voice my thoughts on this topic. In fact, one of the reasons I wasn't ready to commit wholeheartedly to Graham was because I wasn't sure about the whole one-person-for-the-rest-of-my-life thing, which, it seemed to me, was implied when a person said "I do." But then Karla and Skip seemed an odd pair, especially if her idea of a good time was going to the Hearts after Dark Ball and landing multimillion-dollar real estate deals; he seemed more the drown-my-sorrows-in-beer-down-at-the-corner-bar type. But I was making assumptions.

Besides, maybe if I'd been married to someone with flat, emotionless eyes like Skip I'd be ordering from the dessert menu myself.

"Where in the world is he *from*?" Karla continued, eyes still on Landon, apparently not ready to move on from this topic.

"Upstate New York, I think he said. But he's been living in England for several years."

"Oooh, I love England. I'm a bit of an anglophile."

"I have a thing for France myself. Anyway, back to the topic: What did you see at Crosswinds?"

"That place has become an albatross around my neck." Her lips pressed back together and I wondered whether her displeasure was related to the ghosts or the delayed commission, or both. "When I signed Andrew and Stephanie Flynt I thought I had it made, you know? They are so charming, so cultured. Very exclusive."

"And the ghosts?" I was feeling like a broken record, but either Karla was avoiding talking about this or she had a scattered mind.

Just then Landon returned to our table. Perfect timing.

"Well, there's the squeaking of the weathervane overhead, of course. And the strains of an orchestra. But I was able to explain those away until Abdellah Hammoudi's wife, Iftikar, claimed she heard a man's voice crying out. She hit the floor, and her husband had to coax her out of the place."

"She hit the floor?"

"She said the man was yelling at her to get on the floor. What can I tell you? Her English wasn't so hot, she might have misheard."

"But you didn't hear it?"

She shook her head. "I really don't know what she heard, but it was *something*. And it freaked her out, and her husband later called to pull his bid. Do you have any idea what a three percent commission on twenty-nine million amounts to?"

I shook my head, not even willing to try the math in my head. I measure things on jobsites so I'm pretty good at adding five-sevenths of an inch, but otherwise arithmetic wasn't my strong suit.

"Eight hundred seventy thousand dollars," said Landon without a pause.

"Human calculator," I said at Karla's questioning look. "Math*s* professor."

"Ah," she said.

"That's quite a commission," I said. "I can see why you're anxious to seal a deal."

She made a grunting sound of agreement. "Anyway, after that fiasco I managed to find another likely buyer, this one from India, and something similar happened. The woman heard a man yelling at her, berating her. Someone, or something, is running people off. It's absurd."

"But you yourself haven't seen anything?"

"I've heard the music, that's all. Do you think . . . ? Could that Egypt person have anything to do with this?"

"Why would you think that?"

"She lives there, and claims she doesn't hear anything. Doesn't seem bothered by it at all. I was thinking, as soon as the place is under contract she'll have to move out. She's going to lose a pretty cushy situation there."

Sounded to me like Skip and Karla had discussed this possibility. And they could be right. Skip had mentioned Egypt was good at computers. Maybe she was a technological whiz who'd figured out how to pipe random noises into the house, and to tell poor Iftikar Hammoudi to hit the floor.

But if she was that gifted, why wasn't she using her powers to make a comfortable living somewhere? The Bay Area was the high-tech hub of California, after all. Why go through all that trouble to stay in a former servant's room in a house where you barely even used the kitchen?

"And Chantelle's reading said the ghosts were unhappy?" asked Landon.

"Yes, apparently. I wasn't actually there; it was just family, and Egypt was there to take notes. But Stephanie told me they went through the whole house, every room, and even up on to the *roof*. And then afterward Chantelle met with each and every one of the Flynts privately. At her rate? *Very* expensive."

"Why did Chantelle meet with each of them privately?"

"Stephanie said that it was quite a coup to get an entire evening with Chantelle. So while they had her there, she wanted the whole family to receive guidance from the spirits."

"And did they?" asked Landon. At our questioning looks, he continued: "Was she able to give them guidance from 'beyond'?"

"Of course. I mean, I suspect so—your sister was so very talented. Very exclusive!"

Karla went on to confirm what the Flynts already had told me: that during the séance Chantelle made contact with spirits who told her to undo all the work Skip had done, or at the very least to replace some of the architectural features of the house.

"But all of this still begs the question," Landon said in a harsh whisper. "How in the world would any of this relate to someone killing my sister?"

Karla checked her phone. I tried to think how to answer him.

"I spoke with the inspector on the case earlier today, Landon, and she says they're following up on several leads. It's possible Chantelle was reading for someone unstable, who became so agitated they attacked her. Or it could be a disgruntled boyfriend. At this point there's really no reason to think it has to do with Crosswinds."

He remained silent, staring at the table.

Karla checked her phone once again. "I'm sorry, but I really have to run. I don't feel like I was able to answer your questions very well, and I apologize for that. But believe me when I say there is no one—with the exception of the Flynt family—who more wants to complete the sale of Crosswinds than I do. So if you need to install a few antique fixtures, it seems rather absurd to me, but it's fine. Whatever you need to do."

And with that Karla excused herself, leaving Landon and me staring across the table at each other.

Chapter Twelve

"You said you were looking for me?" I asked.

"Yes. I want to understand how Crosswinds relates to my sister's death."

"As I was just saying, we don't know that it *is* related," I repeated. "And fair warning, Landon: Inspector Crawford isn't fond of people 'mucking around in her crimes,' as she would say."

I would have thought it impossible, but he sat even straighter. "I am not 'mucking around.' I never muck."

"It's an expression. Not an insult. It's just . . . She's a homicide inspector. It's a pretty rough gig, and she likes to be in control of all the possible issues."

"From what I gather, *you* have interfered in quite a few of her cases."

"Where did you hear that?"

"I looked you up, Mel Turner. You're all over the Internet. On some rather sketchy Web sites and blogs, sorry to say. I also read an article on you in *Haunted Home Quarterly*. And then I spoke to your father, I believe. And Stan. And a young man named Caleb."

"What, did they pass the phone around?"

"Indeed."

Mental head slap.

"Anyway," I continued, tamping down the impulse to disavow my chatty family. "Inspector Crawford is the best—if your sister's murderer is out there, she'll find him. Or her."

"And what if all of this has to do with the supposed ... haunting of Crosswinds?"

"Even then. Inspector Crawford and I have worked on some unusual cases together."

He lifted his eyebrows but did not speak.

"Seriously, Landon. I know it's hard, but try to get your mind off this. Don't you have classes to teach?"

"Not for another two weeks. I came early to get settled and to"—his voice cracked slightly—"to spend time with my sister. And now I suppose I need the time to plan her funeral. To tell you the truth I have no idea where she would have wanted to be buried. Who thinks about such things?"

"What about your hometown?"

He gave a quick shake of his head. "We both left years ago. There's not much sentimental attachment."

"I didn't know your sister, but here in Oakland there's Mountain View cemetery. It's not far from here, as a matter of fact. Hands down the best views of San Francisco. It's a really magical place."

"Do you say that as a magical expert?"

I smiled and finished the dregs of my coffee. "More as someone who loves to walk there. It's so beautiful the locals use it as a park. That might sound macabre, but when you check it out I think you'll agree that it's really lovely. It was designed by Frederick Law Olmsted, who also planned New York City's Central Park. He was part of the landscape school of park designers. And next door is the Chapel of the Chimes, an incredible columbarium designed by Julia Morgan, the architect who built Hearst's Castle, sort of Gothic Revival meets Italianate. . . ."

I trailed off. Sometimes my love of architecture and design could veer right on over into crazy-making territory, as my sister Cookie took pains to remind me.

"Sorry," I said with a shrug. "It's none of my business, I know."

"I appreciate the suggestion. Thank you. I will look into it."

"So, what was it you wanted to talk to me about?"

"I'm just . . . trying to figure this out. I'm about at my wit's end. I was up until three in the morning pondering the cardinality of the continuum—sorry, that's a mathematical equation. I suppose it's jet lag, combined with the shock. Cheryl—Chantelle and I were orphaned early on in life. I'm afraid there will be no one to mourn her."

"Chantelle's death was reported in the local papers yesterday. I think you might underestimate the effect she has had on the lives of people she's read for, all those she's helped."

"*Bollocks.*" He seemed to catch himself. "Pardon me. Nonsense."

"It's not nonsense. If she really could speak and see beyond the veil, her insight would have provided consolation, and resolution for her clients. I imagine your sister was popular for a reason."

He seemed to be debating something in his mind.

"And I know whereof I speak," I said, trying to lighten the mood. "I mean, I don't want to brag, but *Haunted Home Quarterly* doesn't anoint just anybody as their most promising up-and-coming ghost buster."

One side of his mouth kicked up in a reluctant half smile. "That article was over a year old. Have you fulfilled your promise?"

"You have no idea."

When my phone beeped, I answered a text about plumbing issues for one of the numerous guest suites at the job in Marin, and then confirmed an order with Economy Lumber.

"Sorry about that," I said as I stashed my phone. "Rude, I know. Anyway, I really should get back to work."

" 'Uneasy lies the head that wears a crown,' " he said with a ghost of a smile.

"Shakespeare?"

"*Henry IV.* Say, if you're going to Crosswinds, I'd like to accompany you."

"Actually, I'm not. I'm headed out to some salvage yards."

"Whatever for?"

"It's probably a wild-goose chase, but I'm hoping to find items that were stripped from Crosswinds so I can put them back. Or, failing that, to find something similar. Also because my client is paying me to troll salvage yards, which is one of my favorite things to do."

His eyebrows lifted. "Aren't salvage yards, by definition, full of other people's rubbish?"

" 'One man's trash is another man's treasure,' " I said. "Shakespeare wrote that, too."

"No, he didn't."

"Well, he should have. Think about it, Landon: It's not trash, it's remnants of other lives. You never know what you might find, so it's kind of like a treasure hunt. Sometimes I comb through salvage yards when I'm at a loss or was up until three a.m. trying to figure out the continuing cardinal equation."

"The cardinality of continuum."

"Right. That's what I meant."

Another reluctant smile. "It sounds fascinating. Might I accompany you?"

I hesitated.

"Please," he said softly. "I'm sorry if I am making a pest of myself, but I'm truly at my wit's end. I need to do something, anything constructive, and quite frankly you're the only person I've met since I moved here. Besides, if Chantelle's reading of Crosswinds was in any way connected to her demise . . ."

I started to remind Landon once more that there was no evidence, none, that his sister's murder was related to Crosswinds. But he was a smart man; he already knew that. As he said, he was at his wit's end. Once he moved into his apartment and the semester got under way he would meet people, but until then he was cast adrift. He didn't strike me as the type to drink himself senseless and dance up a storm on the club scene or lose himself in the latest marathon of *Hoarders* while ordering room service.

"Sure," I said, gathering my things. "It'll be fun. Allow me to introduce you to the magical world of other people's rubbish."

First on the list: two Oakland junkyards, which yielded precisely nothing. I hadn't expected much; they were sketchy places specializing in stolen hubcaps, kidnapped garden statuary, and purloined copper pipe, but they were close by and I figured it was worth handing out a few business cards. If nothing else, word would pass down through the junkyard grapevine that I was interested in items from Skip Buhner, in particular a weathervane shaped like a ship.

"Well, that was interesting," Landon said as we climbed back into my Scion. "I may now die happily, having seen firsthand the veritable underbelly of Oakland's rubbish."

"Stick with me, professor, and I'll show you the world," I said, firing up the engine. As we set out for one of my favorites, Griega Salvage, I could have sworn I heard Landon chuckle.

Most builders knew Griega well. Salvage yards in the Bay Area ran the gamut from true junkyards specializing in rusty car parts and broken plastic toys, to businesses that could pass as antiques stores. Griega Salvage's owner was devoted to true architectural salvage, such as marble columns and tumbled cherubs and huge stained glass windows. Griega also carried such basics as crystal doorknobs and carved and stamped hardware that was hard to find elsewhere. Mingled among the more precious items was just enough junk to make the search exciting.

The open yard was chock-full of treasures and rife with possibility: fountains and carved fireplace surrounds, slipper tubs and ornamental metal, plumbing fixtures and cool old wooden doors. I felt like a kid in a candy store.

Some people go for spa treatments or fancy dinners when they want to treat themselves. I poke around funky places like this.

Landon didn't look quite as thrilled. True, items left out of doors got a bit grungy, adding to the accumulated grime of the basements and attics where the pieces previously had been stored. I wondered if he might be afraid to muss his black jacket, which to me looked old-fashioned but which was no doubt on the cutting edge of fashion in London.

After several minutes of watching me pick through a pile of old metal pieces, Landon leaned toward me and whispered, "What are we looking for?"

I looked around: There was no one in sight. "Why are you whispering? I told you, I'm looking for some things removed from Crosswinds."

"Two questions."

"Shoot."

"First, do you honestly think anything will still be here, after all these months? Second, even if something is still here, will you be able to find it amidst all this ... treasure?"

"Check out those andirons," I said, pointing to a pair of iron and brass andirons wedged under an old brass bed frame. I squatted down and reached one arm through the metal bars, but could just barely touch them with my fingertips.

"Are those on the list?" Landon asked, squatting next to me and sounding moderately more interested.

"No, but aren't they cool?"

Landon frowned.

"Here's the thing," I explained. "Shopping salvage yards is a lot like looking for a romantic partner. You only find them when you aren't looking. And when you do find one, you have to strike while the iron is hot."

Landon mulled that over. "So, then, if I follow your logic we won't find what we're looking for precisely because we're looking for it. Then why are we here?"

I was regretting bringing him along.

"Because you just never know." I abandoned the andirons. "Let me see if Nancy's here. If she can't help us, we'll move on to the next one on the list."

Salvage yard proprietors were as varied as salvage yards themselves: Some were toothless guys in overalls and ripped T-shirts who moonlighted as trash haulers, and others were like Nancy, who knew the difference between Art Deco and Art Nouveau, and had a knack for acquiring some true gems. Nancy was a large woman with a short, spiky haircut and a pleasant but no-nonsense attitude. I sometimes wondered if she had formal training in architecture, though we weren't close enough for me to ask.

Landon and I found her sitting behind her desk in the small office, a phone to her ear. There was a shrine to some sort of goddess in one corner, covered in little cards and figurines and pieces of fruit. But the rest of the office was jammed with treasures too fragile to be exposed to the elements: wooden carvings and paintings and photographs. As I flipped through a few of the pictures I was reminded of the photos from Crosswinds, and thought of what Karla said about pretend ancestors hanging on the walls.

"Hi, Mel. Long time no see," Nancy said as she hung up the phone. "Help you?"

"I hope so. Do you know a builder named Skip Buhner, of Buhner Builders?"

"Doesn't ring a bell. Not one of our regulars."

"I'm looking for some things he might have sold from a Pacific Heights remodel a few months ago. In particular, there was a weathervane, all copper, shaped like a ship. Antique, from the late eighteen hundreds? Nice green patina?"

The phone rang. She answered, had a brief conversation, and hung up.

"Sorry. Weathervane, you said? I love weathervanes. They're special. Powerful."

"Powerful? How so?" Landon asked.

"They represent the four directions: North, South, East, West. And they're said to capture some of the energy of the elements, responsive as they are to the wind, and, because they're usually on the highest point of a roof, they soak up the vibrations from the home."

"Huh," I said. I grew up in the Bay Area, and used to be dismissive of what we Oaklanders called "Berkeley types": New Age-y, health-food-eating, spiritual nuts. But ever since I started seeing ghosts . . . Let's just say I'd become more open-minded.

"Frankly," Nancy continued. "We don't get a lot of weathervanes, and most get snatched up by antiques dealers. But something might have come in when I wasn't here—did you check the metal corner outside?"

I nodded. "No luck. Do you keep records of who buys what?"

"Only when we think something might have been stolen."

"Do you frequently acquire stolen goods?" Landon asked.

"We're a salvage yard, and buy things other people don't want. Sometimes this means the criminal element tries to use us a way to fence stolen goods they can't off-load elsewhere. I'm pretty good at spotting them and sending them packing, but my employees occasionally let something pass," said Nancy. "If someone wants to buy an item I think is fishy, I keep track just in case. It's sort of middle-of-the-road karma: I still make money off it, but if someone comes looking for it later I have a direction to point them in."

"So, nothing from the Flynt job, by Buhner? A place called Crosswinds?"

She cocked her head. "You don't mean the Crosswinds Collection?"

"Excuse me?"

"Are you talking about the Crosswinds Collection? That's right—now that I think about it, there was a weathervane on the cover. Shaped like a ship."

The phone rang again, she answered and chatted for a moment, then hung up and turned back to us. "Sorry. I'm the only one covering the phones today."

"So you were saying about the Crosswinds Collection?"

"Yeah, I think it was at Uncle Joe's. You know them?"

I nodded. I knew Uncle Joe's Salvage Yard only too

well. I had been trapped there once, a couple of years ago, on a case related to the first ghost I had knowingly seen and heard. I hadn't been back, and had been hoping to skip it this go-round. Bad memories.

"A couple of months ago, they send out this big announcement, like they're suddenly an auction house. I mean, who do they think they're fooling? I don't mean to cast aspersions but ..." She trailed off with shrug. "Anyway, they claimed to be running an auction for an anonymous client. Sent out an e-mail blast and everything."

"Who was their client, do you know?"

She shrugged. "I didn't go. For all I knew that stuff was stolen, which is *really* bad karma."

In another part of the world Nancy might have crossed herself. But we were in Berkeley, so it was all down to karma. I imagined she might leave an extra something out for her goddess after we left.

"Do you happen to still have the catalog?" I asked.

She shook her head slowly. "It's possible I kept it, but no idea where it would be."

I took in the desk, laden with piles of papers and folders. I wasn't casting judgment—it looked a lot like my office at home.

"Probably I threw it in the recycling. The whole thing sounded fishy to me."

"Okay. Thanks for all the info. Hey, about those andirons out there, under the brass bed...."

We haggled a little, and in the end I bought the andirons, a few other decorative metal pieces that caught my eye, and three plaster ceiling medallions. Also a toilet lid for the downstairs bathroom in my dad's house, which was a never-ending renovation project. Turner Construction's home base proved that old adage about the cobbler's child having no shoes.

Landon carried the toilet lid out to the car, but I had already made arrangements for my moving guy, Nico, with his big truck to pick up all the other items from the various salvage yards when I had finished shopping. Much easier that way.

Back in the car, we headed north on 580 toward Richmond.

To the salvage yard where I was once kidnapped.

Chapter Thirteen

"You seem rather hesitant to go to 'Uncle Joe's,'" Landon said. "Is it too grimy even for you?"

"Oh no, of course not. I'll dive into a Dumpster for the right set of shutters."

He stared at me.

"I'm not kidding."

"I fear you're not. That's what worries me."

I laughed. "You can't be afraid to get your hands dirty in my business. Or anything else, for that matter. No, it's just that I . . . had a bad experience at Uncle Joe's a couple of years ago. *But* it's right across the street from a great barbecue place. You like barbecue?"

"Of course. It's been a while, though."

"I'm guessing they don't have a lot of barbecue in England."

"They have kidney pie, and fish and chips. Excellent scones, and marvelous Indian and Pakistani food. Everything else is pretty much up in the air. The English *do*, however, brew great tea. I had a ten-dollar cup of tea at the hotel this morning and it was atrocious. A stale tea bag plopped into a pot of hot water."

Isn't that the way you make *tea?* I wondered. Maybe that's why I was a coffee drinker. Maybe I would change my mind in England.

"When you say you had a bad experience at Uncle Joe's," Landon said, "what do you mean?"

"I was sort of, um, detained there."

"Were you shoplifting?"

"Of course not! It's a little complicated, but basically someone didn't want me involved in something so he tied me up and locked me in after closing."

Landon stared at me, appalled.

"As it turns out, he didn't really mean anything by it. And Zach's become a good friend, so all's well that ends well."

"You are a most extraordinary person."

"Thank you," I said, though judging by his tone it wasn't at all clear this was a compliment.

He gazed out the window, though the scenery along the freeway toward Richmond was not the type to appear on tourist brochures. It was a pretty ugly, nondescript drive, featuring big box stores, carpet warehouses, fast-food restaurants, and the like.

"Can you think of any unfinished business your sister might have had? Maybe something she always meant to tell you, or wanted you to know?" I thought back on my vision of Chantelle in the hallway, when she paused in front of us. I couldn't shake the feeling that she was trying to tell Landon something. "Could she have written you a letter, or maybe left a note . . . ?"

Landon looked startled. "How did you know that?"

"She did?" I said, at least as shocked as he that I'd gotten it right. "What did it say?"

He looked uncomfortable. "It's . . . complicated."

"Families are always complicated. Did it have anything to do with what happened?"

"It's hard to say."

"Do you have it with you?"

He nodded. "I received it just before leaving England, and brought it with my papers. I wanted very much to have a conversation with my sister about its contents."

"Landon, you don't have to show it to me but if it might have anything to do with Chantelle's death, you really need to tell Inspector Crawford."

"I already called the inspector and read it to her over the phone. She'll be dropping by to pick it up and 'have another talk,' I believe is how she put it."

"When?"

"She said she was looking into something, and that she would be in touch this afternoon."

We drove the rest of the way in silence. I got off the freeway in Richmond, headed down Macdonald Avenue, and pulled into Uncle Joe's gravel parking lot. The salvage yard was in a less than desirable part of town. The massive hangarlike structure, junk-filled yard, and pot-holed parking lot were all surrounded by a tall chain-link fence topped by a roll of barbed wire.

I lingered in the car for a moment, studying the salvage yard. On the one hand, I had managed to extricate myself last time I was here, which made me feel rather badass. On the other hand, just looking at the place made me feel a little claustrophobic. But it was the middle of the day, and I had a man with me who would not, I felt reasonably certain, try to trap me within the salvage yard. And I had my cell phone, and an attitude.

"Are you quite all right?" Landon asked. "Would it be better if we just left?"

"I'm fine," I said, grabbing the door handle. "Let's go."

The attendant behind the register in the open warehouse was paid minimum wage, and was not as invested in the yard as Nancy and her employees were. I had never seen a manager, much less the owner, Uncle Joe, who was reportedly an old man who liked to fish.

So I was almost sure the pimply kid sitting at the counter wouldn't be able to tell me much. But I was going to give it the old college try.

While Landon flicked through a rack of "vintage"— read: old—clothing, distaste registering on his face, I approached the register with a big smile.

"Hi! I'm here about the Crosswinds Collection?"

"The what?"

"The Crosswinds Collection. You guys were hosting it here, I guess, doing some sort of auction?"

"We're not an auction house, lady. Try Clars in Oakland, on Telegraph."

"Someone told me that a couple of months ago, Uncle Joe's put out the word that you had the Crosswinds Collection, even did up a little brochure and sent out an e-mail." As the words left my mouth I realized just how ludicrous they sounded. This wasn't the kind of place where it would ever even occur to management to stage an upscale auction; still less likely that they would know how to go about such a thing. Uncle Joe's was a just barely legal, cash-only business that didn't bother with records or receipts that the IRS might want to audit. The idea that Uncle Joe's maintained a mailing list was ridiculous.

Could Nancy's memory be faulty? She seemed as surprised as I that the auction was at Uncle Joe's.

"Dunno." The young man shrugged and turned back to his iPad.

"Any chance I could speak with your boss?"

"He's fishing."

"Anybody else I could talk to, a manager, maybe?"

"You want to leave him a note, I'll pass it along. But I can't guarantee anything. He's not what you'd call hands-on."

I was getting that feeling.

I wrote a note asking the manager to call me, and pushed it across the counter. He put it in a drawer under the counter, where I imagined it would remain, along with the Chinese takeout menu and the mélange of soy sauce packets, paper clips, plastic spoons, and old napkins.

"Hey, is the barbecue at CJ's still good?" I asked.

A glimmer of interest. "The best."

"Want me to bring you some?" I offered in a blatant attempt to win the young man over.

"Nah. I had Chinese. Thanks, though."

"Do you know Skip Buhner? Or Andrew Flynt?"

He shook his head.

"How about Chantelle?"

"Chantelle? The psychic lady? She was awesome! Dude, she got killed though. Did you hear?"

"I did, yes. Did her name ever come up in relation to anything here at the salvage yard?"

He looked confused. "Nah, Dude. She's like a famous lady, lives in the city, I think. Not likely to hang out at a dump like this, right? I mean, what kind of people would hang out here?"

I refrained from pointing out that *we* were hanging out here, and thanked him for his help. I saw Landon examining a card table loaded with old electronic equipment: stereo receivers from the 1970s, a CB radio, and the like. He was leaning over from the waist and holding his hands clasped behind his back, as though afraid to touch anything.

"Wait. One more thing: Do you have any weathervanes?" I asked the young man.

"Weather what?"

"Do you keep decorative metal someplace special?"

He gestured to the far corner, past long aisles of doors. This was where I had been trapped that one time. I hurried through, hoping to put those demons to rest.

No weathervane, but I did find a heating grate that might fit well in an Art Nouveau house Turner Construction was finishing up in Bernal Heights. Then I noticed larger metal pieces piled up against the chain-link fence next to one of the open warehouse doors.

Several lengths of wrought iron seemed to be from the right time period. I knew a metal artist who could probably fashion them into a widow's walk for Crosswinds. I hadn't measured the exact length needed, but after years in this business I was pretty good at guesstimating, and I thought there would be enough.

Landon joined me, and I pointed out the scrollwork.

"See the workmanship here?" I asked. "You can tell it was soldered by hand because there are no marks of joinery the way there would be if it were cast from a mold. And the patina's great. There's almost never a maker's mark on old wrought iron, unfortunately, but this is still a lovely piece."

"What would you use it for?"

"I was thinking of the widow's walk."

"Why do they call it that?"

"Women used to stand up there to look for their husbands coming back from sea."

"And they so often didn't come back," he said with a pensive nod. "So even though this scrollwork wasn't original to Crosswinds, you think it might do?"

"It might." Our gaze met and held as we crouched over the metal. "I hate to disillusion you, but I don't know what the Crosswinds ghost wants, and at the moment am only operating from Chantelle's directions. I wish I could talk to her, get a little more detail."

Only then did it dawn on me: This was Landon's recently deceased sister I was talking about. *Idiot.*

"I'm so sorry, Landon. Sometimes I get so focused on my job I forget . . ."

"No, no." Landon waved me off. "That's quite all right. I understand. The important thing is to try to figure this out. Perhaps putting the house to rights will allow the ghost to communicate with us and tell us what it knows."

"Like I was saying, though, we don't know that Chantelle's death had anything at all to do with Crosswinds, much less with the haunting of Crosswinds."

"True, but . . . it's the only thing I can think of to do at the mo—"

He was cut off by a shout.

"Watch out! *Car!*" the young man behind the counter yelled.

I was still trying to process his words when Landon sprang up and grabbed me, half carrying and half throwing me to the ground ten feet away. A terrible screech of metal on metal rang out as a big black truck veered off the road and smashed into the fence. The metal pieces crashed and scattered, and a column and various sections of lumber smashed onto the very spot where we had been standing a moment ago.

We had barely rolled over to see what had happened when the truck was thrown into reverse and, tires screeching, raced down the street.

Landon and I stared at each other in shock.

"It's official," I said finally. "Uncle Joe's is, hands down, my least favorite salvage yard *ever.*"

Chapter Fourteen

"There's an old saying," Landon said in a quiet voice. "If someone's trying to kill you it's a good sign you're onto something."

"It could have been an accident," I suggested. "This part of town is a little dicey."

The young salvage yard attendant had run toward us, swearing a blue streak. But no one managed to get a license number or a description of the driver.

"It was a nice truck, though," said the young man. "I know trucks, and that was a shiny, late model."

"What make?" Landon asked.

"Dunno."

So much for his expertise.

Only then did I realize Landon was favoring his right leg. His pants were torn at the knee, and the fabric was stained with blood. "Landon, are you hurt?"

"Nothing serious."

"Come on, I'll take you to the hospital."

"*No.* Listen to me, Mel, it's not serious. My ribs, on the other hand . . ."

"At least let me look at it—I've got a first-aid kit in the car."

"I have a better idea," he said, glancing at the young man who was holding his head and staring at the mess of iron and lumber and twisted fence. "Let's put some distance between us and Uncle Joe's. Why don't you take me back to the Claremont, and we can clean up there."

"Good idea," I said. "I'm just going to tag those iron pieces for Crosswinds, and then we'll get you fixed up, right as rain."

As I had told Landon, at salvage yards you have to strike while the iron's hot. Even when people are trying to kill you.

The elegant old hotel sat white and beaconlike on the side of the hill. I had been to the bar there a few times because it offered a spectacular view, but I had never seen the guestrooms.

When Landon opened his door and waved me in, I decided I hadn't been missing much. The room was nice enough but underwhelming, as if someone had tried to take this historic building and make it look like a standard Hilton: There were ugly bedspreads and ugly blackout draperies and ugly lamps. But then I was often disappointed by the attempts to bring historic buildings into the modern world.

"So, did you check out room four twenty-two yet?" I asked.

"Not yet," Landon said. "But I did ask the staff at the front desk. I was told you're quite right, a little girl's ghost is said to linger there. Some guests actually request that room, hoping to interact with spirits from the beyond."

"Well, as my father would say, there's a lid for every pot. Why don't you take a seat, and either, um, take your pants off or rip them the rest of the way."

"They're a dead loss anyway," he said, slowly lowering himself to sit on the edge of the bed and grimacing. He ripped the right pants leg open as I went to the bathroom to get soap and a damp washcloth.

Good. I wasn't sure I was ready to be alone in a hotel room with a pantsless Landon Demetrius III.

"So," I said as I knelt before him and organized my first-aid kit, setting out the gauze and cotton balls, hydrogen peroxide and Neosporin. "Besides a little-girl ghost, the Claremont holds another distinction. They used to have fire silos on the outside of the building. There were entrances on each floor and this long spiral slide that would deposit you out on the ground."

"Is that so?"

"This might sting a little," I warned him.

"I believe I am man enough to handle it," he replied. "Ignore any screams, and should I faint, well, that will be all for the best, won't it?"

At my expression he added, "I'm kidding, Mel. Do your worst, I'll be fine."

I carefully washed away the dirt and blood on his leg with soap and water, though his shirttail kept intruding. "You should probably take your shirt off, or at least pull it away from the wound."

"Yes, ma'am," he said, and unbuttoned his shirt, baring a torso that was . . . just lovely. I kept my focus on his wounds, but I was by now a pro at seeing things in my peripheral vision, and his chest was hard not to notice. Either he was naturally ripped or he spent a lot of time thinking about the cardinal equation while working out at the gym on the Cambridge campus.

I blew out a breath.

"Are you all right?" he asked me. "The sight of blood make you queasy?"

"No, not at all," I said, and started to clean the gash

on his knee. No way was I going to admit what was really bothering me. I wished he'd button his shirt back up, but he was looking at his side, gently probing his ribs, where a large area was red and already purpling.

"I should be the one asking you: Are you all right?" I said.

"I enjoy starting the day with a broken rib or two. Makes me feel manly."

I smiled. Once I had cleaned the wound, it was clear it wasn't too serious. Still, he wouldn't be balancing on that knee anytime soon.

"So anyway, as you might imagine, kids made it a sport to evade hotel security and slide down the fire escapes as often as possible. The silos were torn down a while ago, unfortunately. Those were good times."

"You Oaklanders make your own fun, don't you? Using the cemetery as a park, sliding down emergency fire chutes . . ."

"And running from drive-by shootings. Sure. We know how to have a good time."

He smiled. I applied salve and a small bandage to his knee. As it turned out, his ribs were the biggest casualty of the day. But if he hadn't thrown me to the side, I might well have landed in the hospital.

"Listen, Landon, thank you. I think you may have saved my life."

"Nah, you're tough. You probably would have survived."

"Well, in any case. Thank you."

"You are most welcome. Mel, you mentioned that you had trouble at that salvage yard in the past. Any reason to believe this 'accident' wasn't an accident?"

"I have no idea."

"Assuming it wasn't," he said in a very quiet voice, "I don't expect it was the first attempt on your life."

"No."

Our gaze met and held.

I had finished bandaging his leg but was still kneeling on the floor in front of him. I started to stand up but didn't realize my leg had fallen asleep and fell over on my side.

Smooth, Mel. Real smooth.

"Mel, are you all right?" Landon, despite his injuries, leapt up to give me a hand. "Come, sit down."

I sat on the edge of the bed and he stood before me. Now his bare chest was right at eye level.

"Are you sure *you* weren't hurt earlier?" he asked.

"Not at all," I said, looking anywhere but at him. "I think you twisted midair so that I would land on you, ensuring your injuries, and my safety. Pretty smooth move."

"Nothing James Bond wouldn't have done. Say, would you like to see the letter from Chantelle?"

"I would love to."

He crossed over to a small writing desk and pulled the letter out of the top drawer, then passed the envelope to me.

"A real letter," I said. "On paper, with a stamp. I'm impressed."

"My sister was old-fashioned in some ways. It had to do with the 'vibrations' of computers—she preferred pen and paper. She still had an old-school answering machine because she didn't trust voice mail. Yet another way in which we saw the world differently."

It was written in dark purple ink on light green paper. The script was upright and easy to read:

Dearest Landon,
You and I haven't been terribly close over the years, and the last time we spoke you warned me

of this very thing. But please believe that I know what I'm doing. I am putting things into place, and will soon be able to pay you back every penny. I know you would say that what I'm doing is wrong, but you and I have never seen eye to eye on such things. Dad always said you were a good little soldier, while I was a free spirit and in this, if nothing else, he was correct.

I have a line on someone now, someone with more dollars than sense, and he'll pay through the nose. With luck, I'll have everything settled by the time you arrive!

Love, Chantelle (your Cheryl)

Below her name was a little drawing that looked like a ship with sails and a flag, with a pole through it.

"That drawing . . . ," I said. "It looks like the weather-vane from Crosswinds."

"Does it?" he peered over my shoulder at the note. "I assumed it was a doodle of some sort."

"No. . . . I'm pretty sure that's the weathervane. Karla showed me a photograph of it this morning."

Our eyes met for a long time.

"So maybe your sister's death really does have some-thing to do with Crosswinds."

He nodded.

I reread the note. "She says you warned her about something?"

"I can't remember what, but I'm sure it was some-thing general, such as don't play with people's hearts."

"And she owed you money?"

He nodded. "Chantelle did well, relatively speaking. But she always lived beyond her means. I—I feel as though I shouldn't be speaking ill of the dead."

"You're really not. All of us have some good and some bad in us; it's how humans are. Right now we're just trying to figure out what happened to your sister."

He went to gaze out the window. "Chantelle had gotten herself into financial trouble, and not for the first time. You saw where she lived. Do you have any idea how much that apartment cost? Though I suppose her business required her to convey the right image."

"Nothing succeeds like success?"

"Just so. But Chantelle was also a spender. She didn't drink, she didn't take drugs, but she did like to shop. You should have seen the number of shoes the woman had."

"Oh, sure, me too," I lied. "Can never have enough shoes. I wonder: Do you think this note suggests she was . . . well, blackmailing someone?"

"I hope not. It does sound that way, though it could mean she had found a wealthy client whom she was able to string along. Unfortunately it doesn't give the slightest hint as to whom the poor mark was—unless you're right, that this drawing is of the Crosswinds symbol. And truthfully, she'd been rather . . . obsessed with the Flynt family since she met them."

"She mentioned them to you?"

He nodded. "When I received the offer from Berkeley I phoned her to say I was coming to town. She was very excited about her association with the Flynts, even suggested I meet them, and perhaps invest in their latest venture, which was some sort of antiaging enterprise, I believe. I take it they're quite wealthy."

"Very," I said with a nod, thinking back on the information the Internet search had turned up about the Flynts. Grandfather George, son, Andrew, and his wife, Stephanie, were all involved in numerous public ventures and charities, and all, apparently, had more dollars than sense.

"Okay.... So where does this leave us?" I wondered aloud. "How do we find out who Chantelle was black-mailing—assuming she was actually doing such a thing?"

"I'm going to guess that Inspector Crawford would say it doesn't leave us anywhere," Landon said. "And that we should stay out of it."

"True. But I have work to do at Crosswinds, anyway. I planned to go over tomorrow afternoon. I'll look through the place more thoroughly, and see if the ghosts can tell me anything."

"The ghosts."

It wasn't a question, exactly, or an acknowledgment, but a statement.

Landon sighed and collapsed back onto the side of the bed. He hunched over and with his bared torso, his chin resting on steepled fingers, he looked like he could be a modern day *Thinker*. He was gorgeous. Really gorgeous, like his sister.

"Cheryl—I guess I'll go ahead and think of her that way, now that she's not here to object—she and I were so close as kids," he said. "Our parents died early, and we didn't have much, so we clung to each other. But when I went into the military, and she went off to 'find herself,' things changed."

"You were in the service?"

"Started out enlisted, but I wound up getting some training, going back to school. I'm good with computers."

"I hear you're *great* with computers."

"You looked me up?"

"Of course I did. You looked me up too, remember? You discovered the Diogenes Theorem. Very impres-sive."

The corner of his mouth kicked up, just barely. "Do you even know what the Diogenes Theorem is?"

"Not a clue. But I hear it's pretty good."

Now he smiled for real, a brilliant smile that made him even more attractive. I wouldn't have thought it possible.

"Yes, I guess it is pretty good. It certainly made me a lot of money. But then I got tired of the cutthroat world of business, and secured a lectureship at Cambridge thanks to the cachet associated with the Diogenes Theorem."

"I hear academia's pretty cutthroat too. You should meet my best friend Luz. She teaches at San Francisco State. Have you ever thought you may have gone from the frying pan into the fire?"

A humorless laugh. "I may well have. The funny thing is I really enjoy teaching. Calculus is my favorite, hands down. There's something so gratifying about watching students have that 'aha' moment."

"I only know enough to cut the right angle, I'm sorry to say."

He fixed me with a keen look. "Methinks there might be a little bit more to it. Not to mention, a little more to you than meets the eye."

Once again, our gaze held just a beat too long. I turned around too quickly and stepped on the first-aid kit, which flipped up and knocked over the bottle of hydrogen peroxide.

We hurriedly cleaned things up, then I packed the first-aid kit, shoved it under my arm, and fled.

Chapter Fifteen

I *had to stay away from Landon.* I wasn't sure what to make of my reaction to him, but I knew one thing for sure: It wasn't fair to Graham.

I checked my phone but Olivier still hadn't answered my increasingly frantic texts and didn't pick up when I called. Then I tried Brittany Humm, and asked if she trusted Karla, and what she made of the situation.

Brittany said that while Karla worked out of the same office, she couldn't really vouch for her since she hadn't known her that long. It was unusual, but not unheard-of, for a San Francisco property to be represented by an agent from Walnut Creek. Brittany had never met Skip. She did, however, agree that with an asking price as high as Crosswinds, there could be a lot of fishy stuff going on.

Frustrated, I decided to get back to the kind of work I knew I was good at. I dropped by the job we were finishing up in Bernal Heights and worked with the foreman for a while on developing the final punch list. Afterward, I headed over to Olivier Galopin's Ghost Supply Shoppe, located in an old brick building—Olivier claimed it was a former bordello—in Jackson Square, one of the oldest neighborhoods of San Francisco.

The store was large, with sections for books, maps, jewelry, art, all sorts of charms and amulets, electronic equipment, release forms, and other paperwork necessary for the ambitious ghost chaser. Upstairs was a classroom where Olivier held surprisingly popular classes about spirits and hauntings.

Inside, Dingo was standing behind the display counter. He was a short man with gray hair sticking out at all angles, à la Albert Einstein. He wore a black AC/DC T-shirt covered with a leather vest. Appearances to the contrary, Dingo was a sweet man with a love of bad puns.

"Mel! Welcome!" he said as I passed through the front door.

"Hi, Dingo, how are you?"

"In high spirits. Thank you so much."

"Is Olivier around?"

"Not a ghost of a chance," he said. "Sorry."

"When do you expect him back?"

"Not for a while. He's in Hungary."

"Hungary?"

"No, thanks," said Dingo. "Just had lunch."

I smiled. "Seriously, though, how long will he be out of town?"

"It's sort of hard to say. Pesky critters, demons."

I blanched. "He's gone up against a *demon*?"

I had only recently managed to wrap my mind around the idea that the spirits of humans sometimes lingered on this plane after their bodies had died. Demons were a whole other bag. Not only was I not sure if I believed they existed, I wasn't sure I even wanted to think about it.

Dingo did not seem particularly put off by the idea. His countenance didn't change in the least: grizzled chin sticking out, placid smile.

"He has help. So, somethin' I can do for you? May not seem like it, but I'm pretty good at spirits and the like." He tapped his temple with his finger. "Mind like a steel trap, is what."

Why not? I would take all the advice I could get.

"I've got a situation with a kitchen ghost," I said. "Cleans things up, slams cupboard doors, that sort of thing."

"Cleans things up? Usually it's the other way around—makes a mess."

"Not this one. Though she did throw the silverware drawer on the floor to scare me. But she probably picked it up once I'd left."

"Hmmm. Well, now, kitchen ghosts are usually female—there's a lot of reversion to old-fashioned gender stereotypes, on account of ghosts are usually from another era."

"Yes. Thanks. I was thinking that as well. That's probably why I refer to her as 'her.' "

"You sure you wanna get rid of her? Housekeeping services aren't easy to come by these days."

"It's not that I don't see your point," I said, "but some students have rented the place, put down first and last and security and now they can't afford to move. And she scares them."

"Students are slobs. No offense."

"As a general rule, I'd have to agree with you. Anyway, any thoughts on how I might get rid of her?"

"Same as usual, probably. Try to figure out why she's stayed, what she needs. Usually once things are resolved, they feel free to leave. Unless they're very stubborn, in which case they stick around no matter what you do."

I nodded. That had been my experience.

"What's the address?" He pulled a giant ledger out

from under the cash register and set it on the counter with a grunt.

"Address?"

"This here's a register of all known hauntings in San Francisco." He patted it like a pet. "Lots going on in this city. Real active, spirit-wise."

"Why isn't it on the computer?"

"Olivier maintains a database of hauntings, but I'm an old-fashioned kind of guy. This way I can keep notes, newspaper clippings, that sort of thing all in one place. And nothing gets erased—you might cross something out, but you can still see it. Nothing'll get this baby but a fire, and we got sprinklers. You got an address?"

I gave it to him, then perused the wide selection of spirit catchers and good-luck amulets while Dingo flipped through pages, searching. It took a while. The ledger didn't appear to be organized in any fashion, and there was no table of contents. Even though I'm not that much of a computer person myself, I did appreciate the advantages of a searchable database.

I checked out some of the high-tech electronics and wondered if I should invest in a new EMF detector or infrared camera. They were nifty little gadgets but the last ones I had didn't last very long, and truth to tell ghosts usually found me, rather than the other way around.

All this fancy equipment was more suited to someone like Olivier, who was trying to collect scientific proof of otherworldly specters. I didn't care about that; I was usually just trying to work my construction jobs, and help the ghosts resolve whatever they needed to so they would get out of my way. When you've been chased by a ghost with a broadsword, or seen a ghost throw silverware on the kitchen floor, or had a ghost yell at you to get off his roof, you don't need further proof of their existence.

Several minutes, one customer, and two phone calls later—during all of which he continued thumbing through the big pages of the ledger—Dingo had a hit.

"Aha! *Thought* it rang a bell. Overly active housewife, circa mid-1940s. Rental."

"Yes, that's it!" I said, surprised. I really hadn't expected him to find anything in that disorganized tome. "What can you tell me?"

He shook his head. "Nothing much here. Lessee. . . . See, this is why I like my handwritten book, 'cause of my notes. Sometimes the chicken scratch doesn't make it into the fancy-pants computer, but I still take 'em."

"What *does* it say?"

"Just conjecture, looks like," he said with a shake of his head. "That's why Olivier won't enter it into his database—the man believes in proof, hard-and-fast evidence. There was at least one death in that apartment, while it was rented to a Mr. and Mrs. White, no first names here."

"Anything about the death?"

"Nope."

"That's it?" I deflated.

"Nothing factual."

I perked up. "Anything not factual?"

"Apple pie mean anything to you?"

"Apple pie?"

He squinted at something written in pencil. "Says here 'apple pie.' I could swear that's my handwriting, but for the life of me can't figure out what that means. *Huh.*"

"While I was there I thought I smelled apple pie," I said. "But what would that mean? Is it a symbol, or something?"

"Maybe she's waiting for her husband to come home from the war," Dingo said. "But he never will."

"Well, that would be sad."

"Maybe she committed suicide, or like that?" he suggested. "Not sure, but I think maybe she was waiting and then got the news that he'd been killed."

"What makes you think that?"

He shrugged. "Suits the era. But I dunno anything, not really. Olivier says I got a mind for fiction. That's why he keeps me out of the computer. That, and on account of I don't like computers."

"I'm with you on that. So then I need to convince her that she doesn't have to wait for her husband anymore?"

"Exactly. I mean, that's if I'm right. Coulda been something else."

"Like what, do you think?"

He shrugged, scratched his stubbly cheek. "If her husband really was a soldier, well . . . violence isn't good for people. You know, back in the day when someone came back from the war troubled, they didn't call it PTSD. They called it shell shock."

I nodded.

"They didn't know much about it back then, and maybe it wasn't as big of an issue then as it is now, but I think it probably was, but just wasn't talked about. Like a lot of things back then—child abuse, sex abuse—that sort of thing *happened*, but it wasn't out in the open."

"So you think maybe her husband came back from the war with shell shock?"

"It's possible. Maybe while he was away at war, she had a life, you know, like Rosie the Riveter over at the Kaiser shipyards? And that didn't sit well with him, and he just snapped. It happened."

I took a moment to let that sink in. Dingo did the same, studying the scrawled comments in his book. A few customers roamed the shop, inspecting intricate woven dream catchers and sparkling crystals, perusing books on exorcisms and how to brew magical beer.

"Well, now, this is interesting," Dingo said.

"What?"

"Ya know, I mark down when people ask me about something," said Dingo. "See, right there? And I've had three different parties asking about this address. So that seems strange."

"So my students aren't the first group of renters to notice something amiss?"

"Can't say for sure if the other people asking were renters. But there were definitely other people asking."

"Do you have names or phone numbers? Maybe I could ask them about what they experienced?"

"No, I keep a tally, that's all, unless someone volunteers their name. But most don't—you know how it is."

"Okay, thanks for your help. I should let you get back to your customers. Oh wait, before you put that away—do you have a mansion called Crosswinds in that big book?"

"Crosswinds?"

I nodded. "I couldn't find anything much online."

He hesitated.

"What?" I asked. "You've heard of it?"

"Oh, sure."

"How come there wasn't anything online about it?"

"This is what I'm saying. You can't trust the online stuff—either it's made up, or people like Olivier insist it not be put up unless it's documented. Or people take stuff down because they don't want folks to know things about their house. But as far as Crosswinds, haven't you heard of the flower girl?"

"Let's assume I haven't heard of anything. What happened?"

"No one knows. She ran away. Maybe killed herself, who knows? Flora."

"A little flower girl named Flora? How old was she?"

"A young woman, I guess is more politically correct. And she wasn't a flower girl, I just call her that on account of her name was Flora. They say she disappeared from home on the evening of her eighteenth birthday."

"But her ghost is there, in Crosswinds?"

"Nope. According to legend her ghost roams California Street, between Jones and Powell, asking for rides to Crosswinds. It's one of those really sad cases. A lot of people have seen her, but don't know she's a ghost. If they give her a lift she disappears before they arrive."

"Have you seen her?"

He shook his head vehemently. "I don't got the eye. But Olivier's seen her, tried to help her get home, but she disappeared from him, too. Made him pretty mad, I tell ya."

"Do you know why she's trying to get home? Could this have anything to do with a weathervane, somehow?"

He shook his head. "No idea. But if you could help her get all the way home, maybe you could put her to rest."

Chapter Sixteen

One of the most frustrating things about being a clueless ghost hunter was that I frequently found myself at this juncture: All my investigations were opening up new avenues of inquiry instead of answering my original questions.

So now I knew more, yet understood how to address it even less.

I called Luz and told her what I learned about the students' apartment.

"Maybe poor Mrs. White was killed by her soldier husband, and ever since feels compelled to keep the kitchen spotless, a pie in the oven. If we knew the full story I could try to make her understand what had happened, so she could move on once and for all."

"I sent a letter to the landlady," said Luz. "An actual pen-and-paper letter that I dropped in the mailbox, can you believe it? But even if she gets right back to me, it'll take a couple of days. Don't know if I can hold out that long. Can't you just do an exorcism or something?"

"Doesn't work that way. Besides, I'd really like to know the whole story. Tell you what . . . ," I said, glancing at my schedule. "Why don't we meet at the Historical Society tomorrow? I need to look up Crosswinds anyway. We'll read through some microfiche together—it'll be fun."

"Looking up dead people in libraries is not my idea of fun, as I think you know. But whatever you say, *chica*. Just let me know when to meet you."

Next I headed to Marin to meet with the electrician and make sure everything was proceeding on track for the Wakefield Retreat Center's Grand Opening, scheduled a mere two months from now.

As I crossed the Golden Gate Bridge, taking in the incredible vista of the Pacific Ocean on one side and the San Francisco Bay on the other, I pondered. While in Marin I could check out a couple of other salvage yards and junk shops I knew up there. Which made me wonder ... Had the incident at Uncle Joe's been an accident?

Could Nancy have sent me there on purpose, somehow?

But why would Nancy do such a thing? I'd known her for years, and she'd never tried to have me killed before. If she didn't want me to find anything from Crosswinds, why not just deny she knew anything about it? Or could someone have followed us from Griega Salvage to Uncle Joe's? I hadn't been paying attention to a possible tail, and besides, big black trucks weren't exactly unknown in these parts. It looked exactly like half the trucks on any construction jobsite.

Could it have been Skip Buhner, or one of his men? Skip had struck me as squirrely, and not above violence if the odds were in his favor. But why would he bother attacking me? What would he have to gain?

Or maybe it really had been a random accident.

Then I thought about what Dingo had told me about

the Crosswinds ghost, Flora. Was the funny little guy reliable? He seemed so odd, but he worked for Olivier and as Dingo himself had pointed out, Olivier was pretty darned serious when it came to the business of ghosts and ghost hunting.

Still, the tale he told about Flora sounded like a story from childhood, the kind of tale told around the campfire, of hitchhiking ghosts who could never go home again. Perhaps it was because of that association that Flora's tale seemed spookier to me than encountering spirits in houses.

When I arrived at my destination, I riffled through my papers until I found the photo I had picked up in Crosswinds, and the ones in the file Karla had given me.

I studied the somber young woman for a few minutes. Could this be Flora Summerton, the girl who had fled her home on her eighteenth birthday? What might she have to say for herself? I surely would like to know.

One way to find out. I called Dad and told him I wouldn't be home for supper.

"I have to meet up with someone in San Francisco tonight."

"Have fun."

"Thanks," I said. "It's more business than fun, but it's sure to be interesting."

"Just stay away from dead people."

Good advice. Which I had no intention of following.

It wasn't really fun. Or interesting. It was dead boring.

Stakeouts imply action and secret adventures. In reality, they meant struggling just to stay awake. Also, for the past half hour or so I had been trying to convince myself I didn't need to pee, which I knew from experience was a losing battle.

I was sitting in my car on California Street, between

Powell and Mason, where Dingo swore Flora's ghost hung out. It wasn't far from Chantelle's Nob Hill apartment, and the competition for parking spots was fierce. I kept having to wave people off, even while trying to focus on spotting a ghost.

So far the best part of the evening, hands down, was the dumplings I had bought at one of my favorite Chinatown bakeries. But they were long since finished, and now I sipped cold coffee—even though it would make me have to pee even more—and tried to ignore the fact that the Scion now smelled like dumpling dipping sauce.

California Street had two sets of tracks in the middle of it, and occasionally a cable car would go clanging past. I remembered learning on a school field trip that the rich "nobs" who originally lived on the hill paid to have the tracks installed so they wouldn't have to climb the steep hill on their way home. But I had never heard about the ghost of Flora Summerton, walking these streets alone and trying to find her way back to Crosswinds. . . .

Someone banged on the window, rousing me from a semislumber.

I jumped, my heart thudding heavily in my chest. It was a cop, standing at my driver's-side window.

I rolled down the window. "Hi," I said.

"You got a problem?" he asked.

"Only that I need to pee."

He looked nonplussed.

"Sorry," I said. "No problem. Just waiting for . . . a friend."

"Someone reported suspicious activity."

Then I realized: He wasn't a police officer. He was a security guard, the kind that wore a neat uniform that made him look, at first glance, like a real cop.

"What kind of suspicious activity . . . ?" My words trailed off as I saw a woman walking in the middle of the street, between the cable car tracks. She wore a long flowing yellow dress, and her long hair half tumbled down her back, falling from an elaborate, old-fashioned coif.

I sat up, trying to see around the wannabe cop.

"I think . . . I think I see her now. My friend."

The man turned around. "Where?"

"There, in the middle of the street."

She was stumbling a little, as though confused or lost.

A couple of cars swerved to avoid her, while others passed right by. I thought of what Dingo said: "I don't got the eye." Funny how some could see and some couldn't, and how those who could often didn't realize that what they were seeing was a ghost. It was a little crazy making.

I climbed out of my car and pushed past the security guard.

"Flora?" I called as cars whizzed by.

She turned toward me. It was her, the woman in the photographs. I felt transfixed by her mournful gaze.

A cable car came between us at that moment, blocking the view. When it clambered past, she was gone.

"I don't see anybody," said the security guard.

"I don't either, anymore. She was just here."

Dammit. Part of me had known it couldn't possibly be that easy. It wasn't like me to set out to see a ghost and then simply see a ghost.

"Listen, lady, time to move along. You've got no business here," said the rent-a-cop.

"Am I breaking any laws by sitting here?" I asked, exasperated. "If so, by all means call the police. You might ask for Inspector Annette Crawford. She's a good friend of mine. Tell her you'd like to use up precious SFPD resources ousting people from legal parking spaces."

"I might just do that," he sneered.

"Use my phone. I've got the Inspector on speed dial."

He gave me a nasty look.

I got back into my car, annoyed by Deputy Doofus, but mostly wondering where Flora had gone, and what my next move should be. Would she reappear if I waited? Or was she now wandering somewhere else? Maybe she'd hitched a ride on the cable car, or with another passing motorist. I wasn't clear on how hitchhiking ghosts operated.

I reached up to adjust the rearview mirror to keep the end of the block in view.

Flora Summerton gazed straight back at me.

Chapter Seventeen

I froze at the sight of the ghost.

"Would you please take me home?" she asked.

Her voice was sweet and melodic, yet slightly echoey, as though she was speaking through an old-fashioned speaking tube.

Meanwhile, I was having trouble finding my own voice.

"I must get home," she continued. "Do you know it?"

"I think I know the way," I finally said. The security guard was watching me from the sidewalk, arms crossed. Sitting here talking to a ghost would no doubt reinforce his assumption that I posed a danger to the neighborhood. "It's on Broadway, isn't it? Crosswinds?"

Her eyes widened slightly. "You know it?"

"I do," I said, pulling out and heading up the hill. I kept the rearview mirror angled so I could watch her while I drove.

She looked so sad. I wanted to ask her what her story was, but it was hard to find the right words.

I have a ghost in my backseat.

"Flora, my name's Mel. Mel Turner. I'd like to help you get home. All the way home."

"Thank you. I must get home. Do you know it?"

"Yes. Crosswinds, on Broadway," I repeated. "I know right where that is."

"I must get home."

Her voice was so odd, almost disembodied. I'd interacted with ghosts before, held conversations with them even, but not like this. Once again I was reminded that every ghost was different. I felt shivers run down my spine at the thought of Flora sitting behind me, talking to me from beyond the grave.

"I think ... Is your father waiting for you at Crosswinds?" I asked.

"Father," she repeated.

We were about a block from Crosswinds now, and I was so preoccupied watching Flora in my rearview mirror that I nearly missed a stop sign. Talk about distracted driving. I could just imagine trying to explain that one to the cops. "You see, Officer, there was this ghost in my car ..."

A shiny Jaguar laid on the horn and I slammed on the brakes.

"Sorry about that," I said to my spectral passenger. "We're nearly there."

No answer.

I glanced in the mirror, then turned around to look in the backseat.

Flora was gone.

It was past ten by the time I got home. After Flora disappeared I retraced my steps to California Street but of course my parking spot had been taken, and though I drove up and down the avenue and circled the block for the next half an hour, I caught no glimpse of her.

Back home in Oakland, I hung out with Dog and poked my head into Caleb's room to say hi. A lot of people found it unusual that my ex-stepson would be living with me and my dad rather than with either of his biological parents, who both loved him and were active in his life. But it worked for us. Caleb's mother, Angelica, had a high-powered career in finance and wasn't home a lot, while his father and new stepmother, Valerie, were expecting a baby. Even before she launched into her high-maintenance pregnancy bliss, Valerie hadn't been overly fond of having her teenage stepson underfoot. Several months ago, when Caleb got into trouble, teenage-boy style, the adults had held a summit meeting. We all agreed he would benefit from my father's constant attention and old-fashioned parenting, which mostly consisted of keeping Caleb busy with chores when he acted up. It was a child-rearing style I was very familiar with, and it seemed to have worked wonders with Caleb, probably because he really liked my dad and wanted his respect. The feeling was mutual.

Other than Caleb and Dog, the house was quiet. I slipped into the Turner Construction home office to look up the legend of Flora, but found nothing more informative than Dingo's story. There were plenty of sightings of her, but she never found her way home. The haunted look in her wide eyes made me feel sad. She seemed caught in one of those dreams where no matter how fast you ran you never got anywhere.

On the other hand, if old cranky-pants from Crosswinds really was her father, why would she *want* to go home?

Next I flipped through the stack of today's phone messages atop my desk, including one from George Flynt, asking me to stop by the offices of Tempus, Ltd. in the morning. According to what I'd looked up yesterday, Tempus was grandfather Flynt's most recent pet project. He'd made billions in some Internet start-up years ago, but now that he was pushing eighty he was funding enterprises "just for fun."

I had intended to swing by the permit office tomorrow anyway, so it would be easy enough to stop in at Tempus. It was in the Hobart Building, right downtown, not too far from the havoc being wrought by Skip Buhner and his crew.

I thought back on my discussion with Skip: He had been lying, I was sure of it. I just couldn't figure out why he'd have any reason to lie to me. Then again, I was at that state in this mystery where I was pretty sure everyone was lying. Even Nancy at Griega Salvage. I looked at Dog, whose big brown head lolled over toward me.

"*You're* not lying to me, are you, Dog?"

He gave a couple of lazy thumps of his tail and I stroked his soft fur for a while. Then I shut down the computer and went to bed, Flora Summerton's sorrowful expression haunting my dreams.

The Hobart was a gorgeous old office building designed by Willis Polk in 1914, with a sculptured terra-cotta Baroque neoclassical exterior that was asymmetrical and idiosyncratic. The lobby's brass details and Italian marble walls retained its early twentieth century elegance. The walls on either side of the elevator were sheathed in solid stone slabs, and the stairs—which no one used— were a matching gray-and-white marble, bordered by elaborate wrought iron and brass rails.

And if all that sumptuousness wasn't enough: Between the two elevators was a mail slot—the kind lined with glass so you could see your letters fall. That was the sort of thing that had fascinated me as a kid, and I had to admit I still got a kick out of it.

The grace and beauty of buildings like this just tickled me. No doubt about it: I was in the right profession.

I took the elevator to the seventeenth floor.

Unfortunately, like so many older buildings, while the lobby and stairwell retained their original charm the offices had been gutted and updated with the trappings of the modern office suite: drop acoustic tiles, temporary walls and cubicles, and windows that couldn't be opened. I had the sense Skip Buhner, et al, would approve.

The offices of Tempus, Ltd. were down the hall to the left. A burly security guard at the door checked my name against a list on a clipboard.

Even though I had been summoned here to do the Flynts a favor, I was allowed to cool my heels for five minutes in the plush waiting room, where sage-green walls were covered in artistic black-and-white photos of attractive old people. I used the time to answer phone calls and some text messages, which the receptionist—a blonde, with her hair done up in a do as if she'd stepped off the set of *Mad Men*—seemed to find annoying. But if I was going to be made to wait, I was going to get some work done.

Finally, I was met not by George, but by Lacey Flynt.

She approached with a fake smile, and gave me the once-over, conveying the kind of dismissive disdain she had apparently learned from her father and grandfather.

"Thanks for coming, Mel. My grandfather will be right out. But in the meantime, I have a question of my own for you: This house has already cost us a fortune, and the carrying costs are eating into our profits every month. Whatever you're planning on doing will add to those costs. Can you guarantee that after you're done the ghosts will be taken care of?"

"I don't know that I can guarantee it, no. But I'll do my best, and I haven't failed yet."

I didn't always rid a haunted house of its ghosts— whether a ghost stays or moves on is really not up to me.

But so far, at least, I had been able to reach satisfying arrangements with all of the spirits I'd encountered on the job. In some cases I had been able to put the ghosts to rest, while others I had negotiated a settlement that allowed the ghosts to coexist peacefully with the living. But I wasn't going to go into such details with Lacey Flynt.

"I mean, shouldn't that be sort of assumed in a contract?" Lacey pressed her point. "That construction work would also get rid of any resident ghosts?"

If there was one thing worse than dealing with an overprivileged client, it was dealing with a *group* of overprivileged clients. I didn't mind dealing with Andrew, or Andrew and Stephanie as a couple. But I was not going to deal with the entire Flynt clan.

"Your father came to me for help, Lacey, not the other way around. If your family decides to work with someone else, that's your prerogative. But for simplicity's sake I would prefer to deal directly with your father and mother, as the owners of Crosswinds."

"Oh, hey, Mel," Mason said as he walked into the lobby. His gaze shifted to Lacey then back to me. "Oops, Lacey, are you screwing things up again?"

"Don't be ridiculous," Lacey said. "I'm just trying to get some assurance that she's going to take care of things so we can off-load that damned house."

"I thought you didn't believe in ghosts," Mason said. "But now you want a ghost-free guarantee?"

Lacey glared at her brother. "I just want this whole thing to be done with, once and for all."

"Don't we all," said George as he joined us. He had a blue blazer draped over one arm, and a manila envelope in his hand. "Your father's been obsessed with redoing that place, and with that ridiculous psychic." He seemed to realize he was being rude, and flashed an apologetic look at me. "May she rest in peace, of course. But it's high time to move on and get some damned work done. Mel, thank you for stopping by. Andrew was on his way out of town and asked me to give you the contract in person." He handed the manila envelope to me. "All signed, plus a check for your retainer. I had my lawyers look it over and they made a few small alterations. I trust there will be no problem."

I slipped the papers out of the envelope and skimmed them. The changes the lawyers had made were minor, so I nodded.

"Looks fine. Thank you. Will Andrew be out of town for long?"

George snorted.

"A few days, a week at most," said Mason, with an ingratiating smile. "Dad asked me to answer any questions you might have in the interim, but I'm going to assume you know what you're doing much better than I."

I had the sense that Mason, as family peacekeeper, had cultivated that smile and his negotiating tactics. It could not be easy to navigate the stormy seas of the Flynt Family, what with all that money at stake. Not for the first time I felt grateful for my far more modest upbringing. The members of the Turner Clan got on one another's nerves from time to time, but money, at least, was never an issue.

"And your mother, Stephanie?" I asked. "I assume she and your father are the legal owners of the property?"

George snorted again. I was beginning to feel sorry for Andrew, growing up with that sort of attitude from Daddy.

"Mom's busy," said Lacey. "She has her own work to do."

"I see." Given that Stephanie had turned over her re-

sponsibilities in the original renovation to Egypt, I supposed it wasn't surprising she would opt out now that
ghosts were involved. Still, I disliked getting handed off
from one family member to another. This job was almost
certain to be a headache, and if I weren't already so em-
broiled, I may well have torn that contract up and walked
away.

"Well, I have a business to run," said George. "Thanks
again for stopping by, Mel, and I hope you can whip that
place into shape quickly so we can all move on." He
turned to the receptionist. "I'm off to Sausalito, and then
I have lunch with the mayor at Garibaldi's. Should be
back early afternoon to meet the auditors."

"They're coming today?" Lacey asked.

George nodded. "Part of the IPO prep. Nothing for
you to worry about; it's an independent agency and your
brother put everything in order."

Another nod to our trio, and he left.

All of us—Lacey, Mason, the receptionist, and I—fell
silent for a moment, watching the door swing shut behind the elderly magnate. Whatever else one might say
about George Flynt, he commanded attention.

"Well," I said, as my phone beeped. More texts—I
was hoping one was from the sheetrock guy I was waiting on. "Nice to see you both again. I'd best be getting
back to work."

"You're not going to give her the tour?" asked the
receptionist, holding up a special visitor's badge.

"Good point," said Mason, passing the badge to me.
"Would you like a tour?"

Lacey rolled her eyes and crossed her arms over her
chest. "Why would she want a tour? She, like, builds
houses and chases *ghosts*. I'm pretty sure she's not interested in our business."

"Of course I'm interested," I said, feeling contrary. "Why wouldn't I be interested? I mean, it's Tempus, Ltd., am I right?"

"You don't have any idea what we do here, do you?" Lacey demanded. She might be rude, but she was also shrewd.

"I've heard of it, of course, but I'm fuzzy on the details."

Lacey snorted in an exact imitation of her grandfather. "Besides, I don't know if it's a good idea to give her a tour. We need to think about industrial espionage."

"Good point," I said. "There's always a chance I orchestrated everything having to do with the ghosts at Crosswinds in order to perpetrate industrial espionage at a company I've never even heard of."

Mason laughed out loud.

"Calm down, Lacey," he said. "Mel's not an industrial spy, and even if she were, just going on the tour wouldn't do her any good. It's not that exciting."

Lacey threw up her hands and disappeared down the hall, presumably to her office.

"Allow me to show you around," said Mason, still chuckling, and I followed him to a closed door, where he put his thumb on a screen. A buzzer sounded and the door clicked open. We passed a conference room featuring a gleaming twelve-foot acrylic table and a huge TV screen.

"Are you really concerned about industrial espionage?" I asked.

"It probably sounds paranoid, but there's nothing more powerful than an idea whose time has come. Who said that? Victor Hugo, I think?"

"Not sure," I said with a shrug, peeking into what looked like standard offices as we walked past.

"Here at Tempus we're devoted to halting the aging

process and allowing individuals to look and feel their very best at all times. To accomplish this, we have a multi-pronged approach: vitamins and supplements, an individualized exercise program, a series of hormone injections . . ."

As Mason rattled off his well-rehearsed promo speech, we walked past giant photographs of what I assumed were cutting-edge scientific procedures decorating the walls of the long hallway. Mason paused outside a room outfitted like a high-tech lab. Inside were a variety of monitors, vaguely scientific-looking equipment, and three people in white lab coats.

"The actual medical interventions are done off-site, of course. These are our offices for the clean work, but we also have research labs in Sausalito and several consulting physicians who work with us out of their offices."

"I see. But to go back to the first thing you said: You're dedicated to *halting* the aging process?"

He smiled, eyebrows lifting like a little boy opening a present. "Amazing, right? Think about it: New technologies are leading to the kind of cellular regeneration only dreamed of in the past. It's like the fountain of youth. It's incredible."

"Yes, it, uh, certainly is," I agreed. The fountain of youth was a work of fiction, of course, and I couldn't help but wonder if Tempus here might not be selling a fiction, as well. Eternal youth would no doubt command a very high price.

What I had originally thought was a lovely tribute to older people, I realized now was advertisement for the company's product. *Look how much younger you can look and feel!* proclaimed a series of before-and-after shots adorning the walls. But then what did I know? Perhaps science really had advanced to the point where we could at least slow the aging process, if not halt it.

On the other hand, I thought, watching a pampered

older woman being led out of one of the rooms marked "aesthetician," the place seemed a lot like a plastic surgeon's office. Nothing like a nip and a tuck to shave off a few years.

"I know what you're thinking," Mason said.

"Do you?"

"You think we're catering to the vanity and unrealistic expectations of the very wealthy."

"I . . . uh . . . I really don't know anything about this sort of thing, Mason. The only aging I'm familiar with is with buildings. Even there, there are ways to shore things up and make buildings last, but age always tells eventually, doesn't it? But that's part of their beauty. I mean, isn't that one of the nice parts of life?"

He chuckled. "I felt the same as you do when my grandfather first brought me into the business. But, think of it like ghosts: Once you see, you become a believer."

"I suppose—" I stopped short in front of a large photo of Chantelle, her ethereal good looks beckoning. Then I turned questioning eyes to Mason.

"Yeah, um . . ." He blushed. "I guess we should probably take that down, given what's . . . happened."

"Was Chantelle involved in Tempus?"

"She was interested in the project, of course. Who wouldn't be?"

Me, for one. Maybe I read *Frankenstein* at an impressionable age, but I was wary of anyone messing around with nature.

"Was Chantelle a client?"

He tilted his head a little to one side in what looked like a cross between a shake of the head and a nod.

"Or maybe a shareholder?" I suggested.

"The company hasn't gone public yet. We're preparing for an IPO this spring." He waved me into a beautifully outfitted office with a view of downtown San Francisco and the Bay Bridge in the distance. "And this is my office. What do you think?"

"Lovely," I said with a nod. "So, what was Chantelle's involvement in Tempus?"

"She was supportive of the idea, and wanted to get involved. Dad was negotiating with her to provide an endorsement. Her celebrity would have been a boon for the business, no doubt. But that's all a moot point now, of course."

"And Lacey's involved in the business as well?"

He paused.

"Yes," Mason said finally. "Yes, she is. Same as me."

Chapter Eighteen

I sat in the car in the garage, pondering what I had learned during my visit to the Tempus, Ltd. headquarters.

After Mason's rather cryptic response, I had tried to pursue the topic of Lacey, but he clammed up.

Probably it was nothing. Clearly there was no love lost between Mason and Lacey. And given what I'd seen of Grandpop George, he seemed to me the type to pit brother against sister in the boardroom as well as on the golf course.

And what was it George had said, that Andrew had been "obsessed" by Chantelle? That wasn't the impression Andrew had given me. Hadn't he said Stephanie had called Chantelle in? Then again, he had seemed quite shaken up by the news of her death. Chantelle was a beautiful woman, and I imagined she had been fascinating.

So why wouldn't Andrew have mentioned that she was a client—possibly an investor—in Tempus?

Was it possible Andrew had been closer to Chantelle than he'd let on? Maybe even having an affair? And if so, could that be the news Chantelle was planning to use to blackmail him?

I wondered if I should mention this admittedly vague suspicion to Annette Crawford. The inspector had told me, time and again, that people are most often killed by those who were supposed to love them: by parents and siblings, spouses and lovers. It was enough to feed the natural cynicism of a person like me.

But unless Andrew really had been having an affair with Chantelle, and was so desperately afraid of being blackmailed that he killed her in a fit of rage, there was still no tie that I could see among Tempus, Ltd., the Flynt clan, and Chantelle's death. No matter how off-putting the Flynts were.

Unless there was something else in play that I hadn't discovered yet. What might the other Flynts—George, Mason, Stephanie, or Lacey—have been trying to keep secret that would inspire blackmail?

There was the sale of Crosswinds. Had Chantelle somehow managed to keep people from buying it? There were twenty-nine million reasons to want her dead right there. But that made no sense. The ghosts were chasing people out of the house long before Chantelle arrived—it was why the Flynts had hired her.

Of course, there were no doubt a whole lot of corporate secrets hidden behind the heavy doors of Tempus, Ltd. Could Andrew have let something slip to Chantelle, and she used the information to blackmail him, or members of his family? Was that what Mason meant when he said Chantelle was interested in getting involved with Tempus, Ltd.—could it have been more than a mere endorsement deal?

Then again . . . Chantelle had been stabbed to death. Such an up close and personal attack suggested passion,

didn't it? Or had I watched one too many episodes of
Dad's favorite crime show?

As I sat there, thinking, George Flynt walked by, deep
in discussion with a woman.

That was odd; he said he was headed to Sausalito, and
then to lunch with the mayor.

Odder still was the woman he was talking to—make
that, *arguing* with. Or so it seemed, from this distance.
She wore a bright batik scarf and a pure white dress.

Egypt Davis.

I scooted down in my seat so they wouldn't see me,
and tried to listen in on what they were saying, but I
couldn't make out anything but a single word: *audit*.

I called Annette and left a voice mail saying that maybe
Andrew was having an affair with Chantelle but I had no
proof, and maybe Egypt Davis was somehow enmeshed
with George Flynt but I had no idea what significance it
might have. And then I tried to crack some joke about
not actually knowing anything, but it fell flat and it occurred to me that there should be a way to erase voice
mail messages from afar. Maybe I should ask Landon if
there was some sort of app for that.

Time to get back to work. I returned a few phone
calls, and then headed out to Glen Park to go over a few
backsplash tile choices with the clients at a residential
remodel—an *unhaunted* remodel that was noticeably
corpse-free.

Late in the afternoon, when I would normally be
heading home, I drove instead to Crosswinds to acquaint
my lead carpenter, Jeremy, with the house and the unusual job we had been hired to do. I had also arranged to
meet Nico, who had collected my salvage yard purchases
which we would stage in the home's three-car garage
that was serving as our interim workshop. I felt bad

evicting Egypt's little Ford from its spot, but Andrew had assured me she was happy to oblige.

When I arrived I went upstairs to speak with Egypt in person, but there was no answer to my knock on her door. Perhaps she was still convening with George.

I was beginning to feel a little like Andrew, wondering what was behind her bedroom door and fighting the impulse to break in.

Jeremy and I did a quick walk-through of the house and came up with a preliminary scope of work. It wasn't easy describing the situation to him. Normally Turner Construction did jobs right: completing every step of the process from A to Z. Contractors were famous for walking off jobs before they were done—in this business, a general was always looking for the next gig, so it was tempting to start up a new job before the old one was finished. We didn't do that at Turner Construction. So explaining to Jeremy that we were going to restore Crosswinds only to the extent necessary to appease a ghost . . . well, it was tricky.

Especially since I was not exactly "out" to my work crew as a ghost buster. The more perceptive among them had put two and two together, but it was a little complicated explaining this sort of thing.

We stood outside on the sidewalk, looking up at the roofline as I explained about the widow's walk and the weathervane.

"Nico's arriving with a truckload of stuff at five," I was saying. "I—"

Once again my words were cut off by the arrival of Landon Demetrius.

He was limping ever so slightly, but as he always held himself stiffly I couldn't tell if his ribs were hurting him. Once again I felt guilty that he had taken the brunt of the fall to protect me; my landing on top of him had no doubt made things worse for him.

"You're like a bad penny," I said after introducing him to Jeremy, who went to clear the driveway for the delivery truck. "Turning up in the oddest places."

"I hope you don't mind," Landon said. "Andrew Flynt said I was welcome to look around."

"Of course. But, why?"

"I thought it might help me find peace with my ... situation."

"Oh."

Again our gaze met and held just a tad too long. *Damn.* I'd been hoping to see Graham before meeting with Landon again, if only for the much-needed reality check. Graham and I had spoken last night, right before I went to bed; he was excited about today's meeting in New York, but I thought I detected a slight edge in his voice. I knew he was annoyed with me for not going with him. For *never* going with him. Last night in my in-box was an article he had forwarded about the importance of taking vacations.

I realized Landon and I were staring at each other, and I suddenly felt horribly self-conscious. My dust-and-grime-encrusted coveralls hung on me like a baggy, dirty jumpsuit and I didn't even want to think about what my hair looked like.

"Well ... ," I said. "I'm just waiting for some of those salvage yard items to be delivered, so I'll be in the garage. Feel free to look around; it's a huge house."

"Yo, General, the truck's here," Jeremy called.

"General?" Landon asked.

"My crew call me that sometimes, because I'm the general contractor." And because I'm bossy. "Like I always say, the G-word beats the B-word any day." I blushed. "Um ... would you like to meet Nico?"

Half Italian and half Samoan, Nico was a giant of a man with a large truck and a seemingly endless supply of muscled nephews. Whenever I needed something moved or demolished, I gave Nico a call. His huge smile and boisterous good humor were always welcome, despite his fondness for cheap cologne.

"General!" Nico enveloped me in a bear hug and lifted me clear off the ground. I am a substantial woman, but Nico was the kind of man who lifted pianos as an afterthought.

"How come you not married yet?" Nico, asked, standing back and looking me over. "A strong, strapping, gorgeous woman like you?"

I smiled. This was our usual greeting.

"Because *you're* not available," I said. "What other man can compare?"

"This is true," Nico said, puffing out his chest.

"Nico, this is Landon Demetrius, a friend. Be nice to him."

"Of course! How do you do?" Nico shook Landon's hand with the verve normally reserved for a professional wrestling match. To his credit, Landon appeared to give as well as he got. "You get to work with Mel, here? Lucky man! Hey, listen, my friend, you should marry her!"

"I will take that under consideration," Landon said.

Nico guffawed, clapped him on the back, then signaled to his nephews who started to unload the truck. They arranged the salvaged items in the garage: assorted fireplace surrounds, three old stained glass windows, lengths of decorative metal and various cabinets, carved moldings, and corbels. There were also half a dozen gold-gilt mirrors, andirons, fireplace backs, and one lovely old crystal chandelier missing a few glass drops.

None of it was original to Crosswinds, unfortunately, but I could make it look as though it were. I just wished I knew if any of this renovation effort would appease the ghost, or ghosts. Would they appreciate the replicas? Because at this point if they were insisting on the originals we were all up a creek. Besides, Karla Buhner had made a good point; it was going to look like a hodgepodge of styles unless we did it right.

Stan had put out the equivalent of a contractor's APB on the weathervane—calling around to antiques stores and collectors—but hadn't gotten a lead yet. If nothing shook out in the next few days, I would try Skip and Karla Buhner again. They had both seemed embarrassed when I asked them about the historic items from the house.

On the other hand, the salvage yards wouldn't have paid enough to make it worth Buhner's while. He was doing remodels—albeit ugly ones—for the likes of Andrew Flynt, and now was heading up a new office building construction in the financial district. The most he could have gotten from the likes of Griega Salvage was a few hundred dollars, maybe a thousand in store credit. Hardly enough to make petty larceny worth it.

Unless Skip was smarter than I thought, and had recognized that he had some valuable items. And held an auction for the Crosswinds Collection? I made a mental note to go back and talk with Nancy at Griega.

Jeremy, Nico and his boys, and I took a few moments checking out the new items, standing around, pointing and throwing out ideas and making bad jokes.

A lot of people who aren't in the industry might witness us at a moment like this and think construction workers don't actually *do* anything. But these informal sessions often set the stage for the best, most professional work. Builders need to be able to visualize the end result, to understand the final goal of a project, before diving in. Otherwise they might as well be working anywhere for an hourly wage, tending to what was immediately in front of them and not caring how the pieces fit together into a whole. Because of wealthy clients like the Flynts, Turner Construction was able to take a little more time and be sure that even the guy whose job it was to sweep up the jobsite understood—and respected—the final goal.

The metal worker arrived shortly after we'd finished unloading everything to examine the decorative metal railing I had purchased and see if it could be converted into a widow's walk for the turret. I had made some quick sketches last night, and gave him the approximate measurements. Then we went up on the roof to take the exact dimensions of the railing. I was wary as we clanged our way up the spiral stair and crawled through the sky-light, and kept my eyes, ears, and sense open to the grumpy old ghost.

Nothing.

Up on the old widow's walk I couldn't help but think of my encounter with Flora last night, how it had felt when I first saw her sad eyes looking back at me in the rearview mirror. The strange echoey sound of her voice, which even in retrospect made me shiver.

Why had she disappeared as we neared Crosswinds? What had driven her from her home in the first place, and what was keeping her from getting home now?

Once the metalworker left, I went back to the foyer, where I had heard the music yesterday. According to the discrepancies between my measurements and the blue-prints, I was sure there was space behind this wall. But . . . could it be something more? Something that would ac-count for the music and the other noises—whispering, a man yelling—I'd heard? The easiest way to find out was to peek behind one of the sconces—modern, of course, with sleek stainless steel details—mounted to the wall. I unscrewed one, pulled it from the wall, removed the plastic electrical box, and stood on my tiptoes, trying to shine my flashlight beam in the small hole left in the sheetrock.

"Lose something?" a voice from behind me said.

I squeaked and flailed as I whirled around.

"Sorry," Landon said with a smile. "Absorbed in thought?"

"Yes, actually," I stood back and handed him the flashlight. "You're taller than I am. Look in there and tell me what you see."

He peeked in.

"There's something behind here," he said, rearing back from the wall a little and looking surprised. "It looks like . . . a bookshelf?"

"That's what I thought, too."

"Who in their right mind would wall over a book-shelf?"

"Good question," I said, peeking back in the hole. "And get this: It's still full of books."

"Well, now, that's just a travesty. There's not a book in sight in this house."

"True."

"But then, I suppose if a person has his e-reader there's really no need for actual books anymore."

I bit my tongue to keep from jumping down his throat. I might feel just a little attached to paper books. And from what I could tell, the books on the shelf looked very old: They were bound in leather, with titles in gold gilt.

"Want to check it out?"

"How do you propose to do that?" Landon asked.

"Watch and learn, grasshopper," I said as I grabbed a heavy mallet, swung, and hit the wall as hard as I could. A sizable gash opened up, sending dust into the air.

"You can just *do* that?" Landon looked stunned. "Take a wall down, just like that?"

"Didn't win the handyman badge in Boy Scouts, huh?"

"I wasn't so much a Boy Scout as a member of Special Forces."

I smiled. "I'll leave the terrorists to you, then. But walls I can handle. As long as you make sure there are no hidden pipes or wires, you can just bash on through. Modern wallboard is made of pressed gypsum, lined with very thin cardboard. This stuff will disintegrate and go back to the earth if you leave it outside in the rain. Very easy to break through."

I grabbed a hunk of the ragged edge and pulled, peeling off a good foot of wallboard.

"Yes, I can see that," said Landon. He grabbed a chunk and pulled, a pleased look coming to his face.

"Pretty fun once you get into it, isn't it? Old-style lath and plaster is tough, but this sheetrock is for sissies."

In fact, I thought, this might be one reason why Skip Buhner had simply gone up over old walls: It was simpler by far than completing the demo on tough old plaster. Simpler, and sloppier, and most likely not what Andrew Flynt thought he was paying for.

Once we had opened a big enough hole in the drywall, I squeezed through. The original wall was set a few feet back. Overhead were original acanthus-leaf and dentil moldings, and at my feet a thick baseboard with an ogee trim met the floorboards. I took note: I could have a knife cut to re-mill these moldings and reinstall them all over the house—though back in the day, different moldings were often applied to different rooms, with the public areas by far the most elaborate.

Then I turned my attention to the bookshelf. It stood about seven feet tall and five wide, and it was set back so the front of the shelves were flush with the wall. Made of what looked like solid mahogany, its ample shelves were fronted with old brass trim. There were sconces on either side, graceful bronze arms holding handblown glass globes made of amber glass—though one was cracked.

Who puts a false wall up over a bookshelf?

The books themselves were caked with spider webs and the grime of age and neglect, in addition to the fine coating of white dust from our impromptu demo project. Many of the leather bindings were so old they were crumbling, leaving a chalky yellow residue on my fingers. A quick perusal revealed there were histories of the Americas, a social register of San Francisco, a few slim volumes of poetry. Mark Twain and Emily Dickinson. And old novels: *Ivanhoe*, and *The Hunchback of Notre Dame*. And Mary Shelley's *Frankenstein; or, The Modern Prometheus*, which seemed somehow extremely appropriate.

Frankenstein made me think of my visit to Tempus, Ltd. I wasn't wild about some of the side effects of aging I had witnessed in my own body, but trying to stop the hands of time just seemed wrong, somehow.

Behind me, I could hear Landon pulling off more of the wallboard, making a hole big enough for him to crawl through and join me.

I ran my hand along the spine of the ancient tomes. Sticking out from in between several of the books were more photos. I pulled one out. This time Flora was dressed as a peasant girl holding a water urn, her feet bare, her hair long and loose.

Her haunting gaze, though, was unmistakable.

Landon peered over my shoulder at the photograph. "She's captivating, isn't she?"

I nodded. When I continued to stare at the photo, Landon said, "Is she significant to the house, in some way?"

"I'm not positive, but I think so. Her name is Flora. Flora Summerton."

"She once lived here?"

I nodded. "But the ghost I've seen in this house was an older man, probably in his sixties. I haven't seen ... her here. Flora."

I was debating if to confide in Landon about last night's interaction with Flora's hitchhiking ghost, when I realized I heard the strains of an orchestra.

"Do you hear that?" I asked.

He nodded. "Lovely. I do adore a waltz."

"Of course you do. But where's it coming from? It sounds like it's coming from ... back here, doesn't it? Behind the bookshelf? Is that possible? There can't be another hidden wall behind this one, can there?" Skip Buhner was a lousy contractor, but even he wouldn't be that lazy, would he?

Landon was examining the bookshelf, his broad hands searching the edges and joints of the wood.

"What are you looking for?" I asked.

"At Cambridge there's a bookshelf set back into the wall like this, and it hides ..."

"What?"

"The entrance to a secret passage."

Chapter Nineteen

"A secret passage? Seriously?"

"The students are fascinated by it. As are a few of the faculty, I must admit. I may have gone through it once or twice myself."

I ran my flashlight beam along all the seams, looking for a trigger. "How do you get it to open?"

"With the one in Cambridge, if you remove the right book, there's a mechanism behind it that allows the shelf to slide open."

Our eyes met for a long moment. Then, as though of one mind, Landon and I started pulling out books. I went straight for *Frankenstein*, thinking it would be the most likely, but found nothing behind it.

"I suppose it's unlikely, isn't it?" Landon said when our search proved fruitless. "I mentioned it, of course, but it's not as though I know anything about such things."

"Of course it's unlikely," I said. "Just like chasing a ghost is unlikely, and the idea that your sister's death was somehow connected to this house is unlikely."

"Excellent point."

The music continued, growing louder. *Ta da da dan, dan, daaaan.* . . .

Landon started humming along, and I feared he might soon ask me to join him in a waltz.

"Shame about the broken lamp shade," he said, reaching up to look at the cracked glass on the sconce. When he rotated the glass to inspect the crack, we both heard a loud *click*.

Our eyes met.

"What just happened?" I asked.

"To paraphrase the immortal Professor Higgins, *'By jove, I think we've got it.'* Try pushing the bookshelf. Gently, gently."

I pushed the bookshelf gently, and it moved, just a smidgen.

"Now what?" I asked.

"Now let's try pushing it not so gently."

Landon and I lined up and put our shoulders against the bookshelf. "Ready on three? Ready, steady, go."

The bookshelf resisted, and rusty hinges screeched.

"This thing needs a little WD-40," I grunted.

"It probably hasn't been opened for decades. Let's try again."

A few more moments of pressure and the bookshelf had budged enough to create an opening we could squeeze through.

The strains of the orchestra were louder now, clearly emanating from deeper in the dark passage.

"You wait here," I said. "I'm going to check it out."

"As if I would allow you to go in there by yourself," Landon scoffed. "Pass me the torch so you can have your hands free to 'check things out.' I'll be your backup."

"I seem to recall you weren't a Boy Scout. Sure you're up for this?"

"You seem to forget I was in Special Forces. I'm up for this."

I carry a head-mounted flashlight in my toolbox, so I handed Landon the "torch" and strapped the headlight on.

We went in.

The passage was narrow, only a couple of feet wide. Thick cobwebs, furry with dust, festooned every corner. The air was musty, sepulchral, as though the space hadn't been opened for many years. The walls were unfinished and made of rough lumber—some of it, I imagined, old-growth redwood brought down from the Mendocino coast, in the decades following the Gold Rush when San Francisco was a boomtown.

Photographs were tacked to the wood here and there, the only decoration. They were all of the same young woman: Flora as a Grecian goddess, Flora as nymph . . . Flora as muse.

We made our way along the tiny passageway, following the sound of the orchestra. Despite my earlier bluster, I was grateful to have Landon at my back. I remained hypervigilant to ghosts or spirits of any kind, but apart from the music there was nothing otherworldly. Only the odd sensation of being in a secret passage that might well have been sealed up a century ago.

The passage ended in a T. Landon shone his flashlight down the passage to the right, then to the left. He shrugged.

"Eenie, meenie, miney, moe," I chanted and went to the left.

We descended a narrow flight of stairs to a small landing, where the passage came to an abrupt end.

Landon cast his light around the walls and ceiling, but there didn't seem to be any way out. I recalled the Flynts discussing their visit to the Winchester Mystery House, in nearby San Jose. Sarah Winchester, in an effort to appease the spirits of those killed by her late husband's rifles, had built onto the mansion incessantly. Stairways led to nowhere, doorways opened onto brick walls, and secret passages led to dead ends, just like this one. They were intended to confuse the spirits.

Could that be the case here?

While I was pondering this, Landon continued searching every inch of the passageway. At last he reached up to an overhead beam, and pulled a small brass lever.

The music stopped abruptly.

"What did you do?" I whispered.

"I pulled a lever. Maybe I shouldn't have."

"Too late now."

"Try pushing on the wall."

I did as he suggested, pushing then pulling. Nothing. But I felt something give and tried sliding a section of wall to the left, and it finally budged, squeaking loudly.

It opened onto an empty storage closet. I tried the closet door.

We were in a huge room, the far wall covered in mirrors.

"Where are we?" Landon asked.

"The Pilates studio," I answered, a little disappointed. It seemed only right that a secret passage lead to some fascinating hidden room or mysterious discovery. "Dog and I were here the other day."

"Is Dog another of your helpers?"

"In a manner of speaking. He's my dog."

"You named your dog 'Dog'?"

"Don't ask."

"So anyway, if this is where the music comes from," said Landon, "might it have been a ballroom?"

"It's certainly big enough."

The line of arched windows along one wall were

echoed on the opposite wall by a series of double doors. I remembered what Egypt had said, that there used to be a stage in this house. The orchestra's waltz was still playing in my mind in a constant loop: *ta da dan, dan daaaan.* . . . I could just imagine the couples whirling around the floor, liveried attendants at the doors, the cream of San Francisco's society dressed in their finery. . . .

"I think you might be right."

"But why would a secret passage lead from the foyer to the ballroom?" Landon asked.

"This storage closet might have been a wine cellar, or a small antechamber of some sort. . . . Maybe it was in case the host wanted to escape his own parties. Also, I think the main floor plan was significantly altered during the remodel—that bookcase upstairs was probably part of a library or parlor until the foyer was expanded."

Landon and I walked around the Pilates studio/ballroom, but there wasn't much to see.

"Waltzing would be a challenge on flooring like this," Landon said, bouncing slightly on the balls of his feet.

The flooring had been replaced with a slightly spongy surface which, I supposed, was helpful to bones while exercising, but held little romance. There was no sign at all of the old stage.

I tried to imagine the angry man I'd seen when out on the roof escaping a party through the cobweb-strewn passageway. Of course, back in his day it might have been neat as a pin, if he'd allowed the servants to take care of it—of course, that would necessitate them knowing about it, in which case it wouldn't have remained a secret for long.

And then Karla's story came back to me, about the poor woman from Dubai hearing a man's voice telling her to hit the floor. I remembered thinking I heard a man's faraway voice calling *"Oooooooor!"*

Could he have been crying out for Flora?

"According to my source, Flora Summerton has been seen wandering California Street, trying to get home." For some reason I didn't feel ready to share what had happened last night with me and the hitchhiking ghost. It felt private, somehow. "She wears a long gown; I suppose it could be a ball gown."

"Who is your source?"

"A little old man named Dingo."

"Ah."

"I take it where I can get it."

"Why do you suppose the ghost wanted us to see this, and led us here?"

"No idea. Although . . . it's possible that the ghost isn't orchestrating things, pardon the pun." I thought, again, of Dingo. He had urged me to help Flora get home, but he didn't say how. And frankly, I wasn't convinced she *should* go home if Papa Peregrine was so out of sorts. Imagine living with that scowling, yelling man for all eternity. "What I mean is that the music might be independent. There are different kinds of hauntings: some are residual, just the energy of that time caught in the walls and replaying over time. Only some ghosts are independent actors."

"I'm sorry, Mel, but it's going to take me a while to get used to speaking of such things like this."

"I understand. It took me a while, too, but I didn't really have much choice. It was get with the program or go insane."

He gave me an odd look, tinged with something like sympathy.

"I mean, it's not all bad. It can be a privilege, and it certainly makes life interesting."

"Of that, I have no doubt."

We retraced our steps, closing the secret door behind

us and mounting the steps. Behind us, the ghostly orchestra started up again. We arrived back at the T.

"Are you up for a little more exploring?" I asked Landon. I was hyperaware that not everyone loved the grime and funk that necessarily went along with secret spaces in historic buildings.

"I am at your command, my General."

I smiled, and turned down the passage leading off to the right.

The music swelled. I heard giggles, and whispers. The atmosphere shifted. The weathervane squeaked overhead, as though the wind had turned.

Anger pulsed through the air to confront us.

A sensation of rage and panic.

The smell of something strong and acrid.

And out of the corner of my eye I spotted the man I had seen through the skylight, dressed in a formal waistcoat, running through the passage behind us, yelling.

"Flora! Floooooraaaaaa!"

I staggered and slammed back against the wall, a few splinters from the rough wood poking through my coveralls and embedding themselves in my skin.

Before I could catch my breath, the apparition was gone.

"*Mel.* Mel, are you quite all right?" Landon asked.

"Um . . . yes," I said, trying to calm my wildly thudding heart. "Did you see that?"

"See what?"

I looked up and down the passage. All was still: cobwebs and old lumber, dust and grime. "Did you hear anything? Anything at all?"

He shook his head, looking concerned.

"Sorry. I just . . ." I looked around, simultaneously wanting to see him again, and yet not. "You might not believe this, but I just saw a ghost. And he wasn't happy."

Landon frowned, then shone his light around the passage. "Where?"

"He was running from the Pilates room. The ballroom, I mean. Calling for Flora."

"The young woman in the photographs?"

I nodded.

"Do you wish to get out of here? Or shall we carry on?"

His phrasing made me smile despite my fright. A few more deep breaths and my heart rate slowed to something approximating normal, and I reminded myself that as angry as this ghost was, he had yet to do anything to harm me. Other than nearly scaring me off the roof, but that was my fault more than his.

"Let's carry on, by all means," I said. "I want to know where this passage leads."

A few yards down the hallway there was an open door.

Landon and I stood in the doorway and surveyed the small room, equipped with two large sinks, wide trays, and shelves full of very old jars and bottles and canisters, made of glass and clay and metal. Many of the containers sported handwritten labels. There were papers hanging from lengths of rope, and the walls were peppered with tacked-up photos. The air was rank with something noxious.

"Wasn't there an old Frankenstein movie with a secret passage leading to the mad doctor's laboratory?" I whispered. I couldn't get my mind off Mary Shelley's story. This whole thing—the secret passages and now a hidden laboratory—seemed almost manufactured. A theater student's idea of a haunted house. Could someone—Egypt maybe?—really be screwing with us, as Skip had suggested?

"Yes, but this room is too small for a laboratory. . . ." Landon said. "Let's check it out."

Just then I saw an old man—the same man who had just appeared running through the passage—hunched over one of the trays, poking at something with long pincers.

He looked over his shoulder at us, and yelled.

"*Get out of here!* Leave me my photographs!"

I jumped back. Landon caught me and twirled around, as though to put himself between me and danger. In one smooth move he grabbed a metal rod leaning against the wall and held it up, as though to ward off an attacker.

But there was nothing to see.

"What was it?" he demanded.

"I—it was a ghost."

"Another one?"

"Same one, actually."

"It's gone then? Do you see anything now?" He was still holding me, protectively, eyes still scanning the perimeter, then looking down and searching my face.

"No," I croaked, then cleared my throat when I realized how husky my voice sounded. I pulled away from his arms, wondering whether my fluttering heart was due to the ghost or Landon's closeness. I blew out a long breath.

"You seem upset," Landon said. "What happened?"

"I was startled, that's all. He yelled at me."

"What did he say?"

"'Get out of here.'"

"Did he really?" And with that, Landon walked into the room.

Impressed by his bravery—or was it stupidity?—I crept in behind him. I searched my peripheral vision for old grumpy-pants, but saw nothing.

"This is no laboratory," Landon said, pointing to the rope from which hung a series of sepia-toned photographs, two ancient-looking cameras, and a tripod. "This is an old darkroom."

He picked up a couple of bottles from the shelf and read off the labels, which meant nothing to me.

"A former owner must have been a photographer—an early photographer," said Landon. "Some of this stuff is very old indeed. Fascinating."

"Maybe that's what I smelled."

"Smelled?"

"The first time I saw the ghost, I thought I smelled something . . . acrid."

"Like photographic development chemicals?"

"Maybe; I'm not sure what those smell like. But that doesn't make any sense, does it? Would he still smell of chemicals after all these years?"

Landon raised his eyebrows. "I didn't realize ghosts adhered to the laws of physics. If you can see him when he's clearly not here, it doesn't seem a stretch that you could smell him as well."

"Excellent point. But he lived so long ago . . . I guess photography goes back into the 1800s, right?" I asked, thinking of Civil War photos. "Before the turn of the twentieth century?"

"The earliest was in the 1820s, I believe."

"You know maths *and* history?"

Landon seemed absorbed in what he was finding, as he picked up one jar after another and poked through the cupboards.

"That's the fixative you're smelling. People were playing with the technology to take photographs quite early on, but it was the *fixatives* that proved to be the real challenge."

"What does the fixative do?"

"It fixes the image so that it doesn't fade away or turn dark."

"You know a lot about photography."

"My dad had a little darkroom made out of a base-

ment bathroom when I was lad," he said, looking back
with a small smile hovering over his lips. "Brings back
some nice memories. I even like the smell. I remember
one time—"

He stopped short.

"Landon? What is it?" As I said it, I realized that the
chemical smell had become stronger, almost overwhelming in the stuffy, claustrophobic room. Had we knocked
something over?

"Look." Landon stood in front of the rope, onto which
was clipped several photographs. He gestured toward
them. On the end, I recognized one of them: it was yet
another a photo of Flora—this time dressed like a maha-
rani, or an Indian queen. As Landon and I stood together
and examined the photograph, a second figure slowly
began to emerge.

"I think it's a woman," I said.

"Definitely a woman," Landon agreed. "In fact—"

It was Chantelle.

Chapter Twenty

Landon yanked the photo from the rope line, sending clips flying through the air. He gazed at it, then dropped it on the floor and stepped back, as though the image would burn him.

"This is not funny." He glared at me. "How dare you."

"It's not *me*! Landon, seriously. Not only would I never do such a thing, I would have no idea how."

"It wouldn't be difficult," he said, spitting out the words. "Computers and technology can do wonders. Piping in music to lead us through mysterious passages, setting up vintage darkrooms, using special filters to make photographs appear old . . ."

"I'm going to take your word that would all be possible," I said, slowly. "But not only do I not have any of the skills required to do what you suggest, I wouldn't do such a thing in the first place. Why would I? What could I possibly have to gain?"

"How on earth should I know? Maybe you're bored. Maybe this place is studded with cameras taking film footage that you'll upload to YouTube and become the next viral video."

"Okay, I realize we don't know each other very well, but has there been anything—anything at all—in our interaction over the last few days that would suggest I have the time, the ability, or the interest to set up some elaborate prank for a YouTube video?"

I bent down and picked up the photo. There was no mistake: It was Chantelle, dressed in Indian finery like Flora, looking very much of the time period.

"Of course not," Landon said, shaking himself and blowing out a long breath. "I'm sorry. I'm not at my best. I arrived from England two days ago, found my sister murdered"—his voice wavered—"and have realized that perhaps she did, indeed, have some relationship with the beyond that I simply can't fathom. Also, the Internet connection at my hotel is terrible. I am . . . off my game. I do apologize."

I smiled. "Apology accepted. You have been through the wringer, haven't you? I hope you can believe me when I say I'm trying to help. And while my route to figuring out these things is usually pretty circuitous, I tend to figure things out eventually. My boyfriend says I'm like a dog with a bone, once I'm onto something like this I won't quit until I figure it out."

He gazed at me for a long moment. "Boyfriend?"

I nodded.

"I would think he'd accompany you when you are dealing with certain . . . situations. Such as this one."

This made me laugh. "If the man tried to accompany me to every haunting, I suppose we'd be attached at the hip. This sort of thing happens to me fairly frequently."

"Hmmm."

"What does hmmmm mean?" I was beginning to ask, when another wave of noxious fumes enveloped us. A jar fell over into the sink, then another. Photos flew in the air.

Landon wielded his metal rod again, crouching just slightly, as though ready to throw himself on something.

"I think we should go," I said.

"Get out!"

"We're leaving!" I yelled in response to the ghostly command, then said more quietly but with urgency, "Landon, let's go."

"Right after you," he said.

We backed out of the room, me still clutching the photo of two women of mystery: Flora and Chantelle, together for eternity?

"Does this mean my *sister* is now haunting Crosswinds?" Landon asked after we stumbled out into the foyer, brushing off cobwebs and dirt.

It was the next logical question.

"I don't think so," I said. "In fact, though I've seen a lot of photographs of Flora, I've never seen or felt Flora in the house either. But I can't figure out why Chantelle would have shown herself like this . . ."

Landon took the photo from my hand and gazed at the image of his sister. She was wearing that same beatific expression, the same Mona Lisa smile she had when I had seen her spirit in the hallway outside her apartment.

I was trying to maintain my Experienced Ghost Communicator mien, but in truth my mind was reeling. What did this mean? Had Chantelle somehow existed at the time of Flora? Were we talking about reincarnation now?

More likely was that Chantelle was making herself known to us for some reason. I would have thought she'd be able to communicate with me, especially since she was able to go beyond the veil in her living days. Olivier had told me sometimes it happened like that. But then, since Olivier was nowhere to be found I guessed I shouldn't

base too much on his interpretation. With a lot of this
ghost stuff I was beginning to think I was treading on new
territory, seeing things Olivier had never experienced.

Setting aside the possibility of reincarnation for the
moment, what might Chantelle be trying to tell me? Why
would she want to be seen in a photograph with Flora?
Unless perhaps they appeared in that photo because of
Flora's father's ghost? Was *he* the one trying to communicate? Or had he shut things down? Could he be trying
to keep them from communicating—and if so, why?

Or were these ghosts just confused? Maybe killing a
few of the endless hours of the afterlife by having fun
with a gullible ghost buster?

I wouldn't put it past them. I was beginning to think
some of these spirits had very twisted senses of humor.

Landon's demeanor was always so rigid that I couldn't
tell whether he believed me or thought I was insane.
Which is a sensation I'm familiar with, since I sometimes
experience it when dealing with myself.

On the other hand, the poor man had found his murdered sister the other day, and was still dealing with jet
lag and, apparently, a wonky Internet connection. So he
might well be slightly more open to possibilities than he
might otherwise be.

We walked through the rest of the house, but other
than hearing the squeaking of the weathervane I didn't
hear or see anything else untoward. I called out to the
ghost, hoping he could hear me and might be willing to
communicate, but nothing.

"Karla mentioned her client threw herself on the
floor," I said, "but I suspect the ghost had been yelling
'Flora,' not 'floor.'"

"What does that prove?"

"Only that I'm not the only one to hear this particular

ghost. Which is strangely comforting. Not for the woman from Dubai, of course, but for me, there's some comfort to be had in company. Also, Dog saw him."

As we descended the stairs to the main floor, I remembered one book I had seen on the hidden bookshelf: a San Francisco social register. I went back, crawled through the opening, and took the old book off the shelf. I opened it to the "S's," found Summerton, and read: father Peregrine, mother Clara, two brothers Peregrine Jr. and Thomas Allen, one daughter, Flora. There were marriage dates for the boys, but nothing for Flora.

"Anything useful?" Landon asked.

"Not really. I—"

Without any warning, Egypt rushed into the foyer. She had her hair wrapped up in another brightly colored batik scarf, and a snowy white dress that I knew I'd be able to keep clean for about five minutes, tops.

She looked upset. "What are you doing here . . . ? What's going on?"

"I'm sorry to surprise you, Egypt. Andrew said he let you know we might be here. We're going to be using the garage as our staging area for the interim."

"Where am I supposed to park?"

"Well . . ." This really wasn't my problem. And yet it was, because I was the one who had to deal with it. "How about we make sure there's room in the driveway for you to park?"

She looked displeased, but nodded. "Okay. Thanks. You will respect my privacy, won't you?"

"We haven't gone in your room, if that's what you mean," I said.

"You don't seriously believe in this haunting thing, do you?" Egypt demanded, seeming suddenly angry. "I mean, I assumed that was just some gig you used to jack up your rates."

"'Fraid not," I said, glancing surreptitiously at Landon. "I'm really not that clever. Egypt, could I just take a quick peek in your room? I'd really like to cross it off the list."

"What list?"

"I just mean that I'd feel better if I'd seen the whole house, top to bottom. To rule things out."

"Another time, if that's all right? I just got home, found all of this going on.... I'd really like to just go relax."

It's true that it could be exhausting to live with construction projects. Still, we'd hardly made a dent, so if Egypt was already this disturbed by the little we'd done so far, she wasn't going to make it for the duration.

Her refusal to let me in could mean she was hiding something, or that she had left undies lying around on the floor, or simply was a private person. I supposed I could pull rank, call Andrew Flynt and force the issue, but I wasn't sure I wanted to use up my chips this way. And if Egypt was going to remain on-site, I needed her to be on my side.

Also, I was curious about her heated conversation with George Flynt, but couldn't think how to ask her about it.

"I understand," I said. "And I know you're tired. I hear you're good with computers. Is that your day job?"

"Sort of."

"I was wondering.... Could I ask you a question about the Flynts?"

"What about them?"

"You mentioned the other day that they argued about money. Was it about anything in particular?"

"From what I overheard ... Okay, now this is just plain gossip. But from what I've come to understand, it's George's thing, and it pisses Stephanie off big-time."

"What is 'George's thing'?"

"Apparently he was so disappointed in how his son Andrew turned out that he decided the grandkids shouldn't have access to the estate. They have to 'work for a living,' is how he put it. So he employs them at Tempus and they get paid, of course, but it's not like they're rolling in it."

"George disinherited them?"

"I don't think it's that extreme. It's just that he wants them to learn work habits, or something. Whenever I'm around he points at me like I'm some sort of symbol of working-class nobility. Creeps me out."

"I guess they would be pretty angry about that," I said.

"To tell you the truth, I think Stephanie is the one truly upset about it. She—Well, she's got a temper, underneath it all."

"I thought I saw you today, near the Tempus offices?"

She went very still. "Tempus, the Flynt company? No, I don't do any work for them. Too bad, right? Just imagine how juicy that IT position would be. But anyway, if you repeat any of this to the Flynts, I guess I'm out on my ear. I'm looking for a place to move anyway, though. Happen to know of an apartment with a reasonable rent?"

Yes, one that comes with housekeeping services, I thought to myself. But I just shook my head. "Sorry. I'll be sure to let you know if anything comes up."

"Thanks. And sorry about being so cranky before."

When she left, I expected Landon to ask me about Egypt, or the haunting. Instead, he said, without meeting my eyes:

"Would it be too much to ask to get a drink? I find myself somewhat at my wit's end."

"I . . ." I glanced at my watch. Dad usually expected

me for dinner, but I could call and let him know I wouldn't be there. Since he always cooked too much he was usually flexible, and we were big leftover folks. "Sure, why not?"

"Do you know of a good place around here?"

"Yes, as a matter of fact. Let's go sit down with the Big Four."

Chapter Twenty-one

"The Big Four were Central Pacific's C. P. Huntington, Charles Crocker, Mark Hopkins, and Leland Stanford," I explained as we walked into the clubby bar off the lobby of the Scarlet Huntington Hotel. "Four of the richest men in San Francisco, they had their homes here on Nob Hill."

The Big Four bar was very old-school, full of dark wood paneling and oil paintings—mostly of the four railroad tycoons. It was the sort of place I always half expected would throw me out on my keister, so, perversely, I enjoyed coming here in dusty sequins.

It also happened to be located on Nob Hill, just a block up from where I had been last night when I saw Flora. It wasn't dark yet as we arrived, but it should be full night by the time we left. Maybe I could try again to give her a lift.

"I thought the Big Four were the prime ministers of England, Italy, France, and the United States who met in Paris in 1919 to sign the World War I peace treaty," said Landon as we sat at a small table in the corner.

I gave him a blank look, then asked, "You sure you weren't a history major?"

He smiled and shook his head. The waitress came and took our orders: a Manhattan for me, straight whiskey for him.

"And," I continued, "when you put it like that, I suppose the four who put an end to the first World War were slightly more laudable than four guys who made bundles of money off the railroads."

"Depends on your point of view," Landon said diplomatically.

A group of rowdy tourists came in soon after us, jostling tables. The bar was clearly too intimate to accommodate their large party, and the hostess helped direct them to a sports bar down the street. By the time that got worked out, the waitress arrived at the table with our drinks. She was young and pretty, and clearly intrigued by Landon, who was paying no attention to her or to anything else in his immediate vicinity.

Instead he sat brooding, staring into the glass of amber liquid in front of him.

"I made arrangements for a memorial service, at the Chapel of the Chimes," he said finally. "Thank you for suggesting it. The service will be on Saturday, at eleven. I hope you'll come."

"Of course."

He gave a humorless chuckle. "I don't know a soul here, other than you and Inspector Crawford."

"Well, to be fair, we're two of the more interesting women in San Francisco."

"Now *that* I believe."

"Anyway, I'm glad you liked the Chapel of the Chimes. It's a pretty amazing place."

He continued to gaze into his glass. "I'm sorry. I probably shouldn't have asked you here. I fear I'm not good company."

"You don't have to try to be good company, Landon. Your sister was just killed. And, you know, your Internet's been wonky. You've had a tough couple of days."

Another barely-there chuckle.

"What was she like, your sister? You mentioned you used to be close."

He fixed me with a look. "You think this might tell you something pertinent to the crime?"

"It's possible. I don't understand why she would show up in that photograph. Maybe it's significant, somehow. Could she have felt some sort of special connection with Flora Summerton, do you think?"

He remained still, but his eyebrows lifted as though to say: *In what way?*

"It's a long shot, but this is sort of my process when trying to figure out murders. I ask a lot of seemingly random questions, most of which are completely off target, and then eventually I stumble across something, or someone, significant. It's worked three or four times now."

He took a deep draw on his whiskey, and tilted his head. "Do go on."

"I'm not going to get into the specifics, but as I said I've known Inspector Crawford for a few murders. And there was one even before I knew her. I'm sorry if this all seems strange, or out of your comfort zone."

"I think we can safely assume we're so far out of my comfort zone that we should just keep going." He signaled to the waiter for another round of drinks—even though my drink was still half full—and ordered *carne asada* fries. At my questioning look, he said, "I have never heard of such a thing in my life, and am intrigued beyond reason. Also, it's Happy Hour."

"And yet we're not very happy."

"Cheryl was my older sister by two years, yet I always felt protective of her. When our parents were killed, that feeling intensified. We went to live with my father's brother for a while, but he was rather ... inappropriate."

"Inappropriate?"

"With Cheryl. It didn't get too far, because I threatened to go to the cops. By then we were fifteen and seventeen. My threats were enough to keep him at bay, and we left on Cheryl's eighteenth birthday. That was when she was able to take control of the money our parents left to us—mostly a life insurance policy—and we left for England. Our mother was British, and we were both actually born there though we grew up in the States."

The waitress came by with the *carne asada* fries, which were a pile of shoestring French fries topped with chopped-up grilled meat, guacamole, *cotija* cheese, and sour cream.

"How astonishing," he said quietly, studying the plate. "I rather thought the actual meat would be made into fries, somehow."

"The wonders of American food," I said, stealing a fry.

Landon nodded and sort of prodded the food tower, but didn't dig in.

"Unfortunately," he continued with his story, "we had no close relations in England; no one who would take us in for more than a few days. But we had enough money for a while, got a small flat. Cheryl really fell in love with London. That's where she met Gobi. He was a guru."

"Gobi the guru?"

"Just so. It ... I don't want to say it changed her, as I imagine we were both changing by that time. But it intruded on our relationship, I'll just say that. Cher—*Chantelle*—I know she preferred that name—had been searching spiritually for some time, even before our parents passed away. After she began her study with Gobi, she came to believe there was a purpose to all of it: to our parents' deaths, to our orphanhood, even to our uncle's lecherous behavior and our move to London. It was fate, she said."

He tried a French fry dipped in guacamole, with a little chunk of *carne asada* on top. He looked confused.

"Please," he said, pushing the plate toward me. "Help yourself."

"Thank you."

"Anyway, I managed to finish high school in London. Then, since I was born there and my mother was British—I had dual citizenship—I was admitted into the military."

"So you served with the *British* military?"

He nodded. "I never saw combat, anything like that."

"You seemed pretty good with that iron bar in the secret passage."

He gave me a crooked smile and an insouciant shrug, and the waitress came by and asked him if there was anything, anything at all, she could get for him. She didn't ask me. In fact, she had eyes only for Landon, who didn't seem to notice.

"Would you like anything else, Mel? Something different to drink?" He gestured to the full glass sitting next to my half-finished one.

"No, thank you. I think I'm set for the evening."

The waitress slipped him an extra napkin.

"Oh, thank you," he said. She gave him a smile full of promise, then left.

"Anyway, while in the military ..." He trailed off as I reached over and turned his new napkin over.

Sure enough, the waitress had written down her name—Mia—and number.

"Aw, how cute: She dotted the *i* with a little heart," I said, then laughed at the surprised and discomfited look on Landon's face. I handed it back to him. "Go on. While in the military . . . ?"

"Chantelle was disappointed that I had chosen to go into the military, just as I was not happy with her following her guru. That was when we grew apart; our lives were just too different. I trained in Special Forces for a while, but what I truly excelled at was computer systems."

"Can you hack into things?"

"Why is that the first thing noncomputer people always ask?"

"It's the most interesting aspect," I said with a shrug. "Otherwise, what would I ask? 'How are the zeros and ones treating you?'"

"How about: Can you stop cyberterrorism? Can you save the world?"

My eyes widened. "*Can* you?"

He smiled.

"I'm just saying," I said. "If you can, you should probably get on that. All *I* can do is fix a sump pump. If you have a toilet backed up, I'm your gal. And I used to be an anthropologist so I know some fascinating factoids about the native peoples of Papua, New Guinea. But saving the world with a keystroke? *That's* impressive."

Landon laughed. It was the first time I had heard a genuine laugh from him, and it was a wonderful sound: deep and resonant and full of reluctant mirth.

It must have been the strain of the past few days, amplified by the whiskey, because I hadn't said anything that funny. Still, I couldn't help but smile in response.

He shook his head, still chuckling, and stared at me for a long moment. "You are really something, Mel Turner."

"I guess I would have them rolling in the aisles at Cambridge," I said. "Maybe I should book a gig."

"Maybe you should, at that."

Once again our eyes met, and held. *This was getting ridiculous.*

"Tell me about your boyfriend."

"Uh, Graham? He's a great guy. A green technologies consultant."

"I would assume there might be some conflict there, between historic restoration and green technologies."

"There are some issues, yes, but ultimately the carbon footprint of renovation is much less than new construction. Anyway, he's in New York right now."

"He's living there?"

"Oh, no, he'll be back soon." I snuck a couple more fries, more out of nervousness and something to do than hunger.

"And are you two serious?"

I stopped chewing. Something went down the wrong way and I started hacking and choking.

"I'm okay," I managed between coughs so no one assumed I had a chunk of *carne* stuck in my throat. I could only imagine some hero trying to apply the Heimlich maneuver to me. How much more glamorous could one woman get?

Once I downed some water and got hold of myself, Landon said, "I apologize if I was speaking too personally. Feel free to tell me to mind my own business. It's just that ... to tell you the truth, I think my coming to teach at Berkeley and reaching out to Chantelle was all part of my seeking something *more* in my life. I've been very successful by some standards, but I suppose I'm tired of feeling so ... temporary. I'm ready to set down some roots."

"Well, the Bay Area is a great place to set down roots if you have scads of money."

"So I hear."

"Hey! I happen to know a nice place for sale, great neighborhood, a mere twenty-nine million dollars."

He smiled.

"And it's a 'smart house'—you have to like that."

"Yes, but does it have any secret passages hidden behind bookcases?"

"You just might be in luck."

He smiled and pushed the now-soggy fries to the side.

"You're not blown over by this culinary sensation?" I asked. "I ate more than you."

"I think I've lost my appetite."

"Want to go look for a ghost?"

"Another one?"

"This would be Flora, the young woman in the photo with Chantelle." As I said it, it dawned on me: We weren't far from Chantelle's apartment. Had she seen Flora wandering up and down California Street over the years?

And their stories did share at least one parallel: They had both fled their homes on their eighteenth birthdays. Could they have shared more? Perhaps Flora had come into some money in her majority, as well, which she used to flee? And could the grumpy photographer—who I was going to assume was Peregrine Summerton, Flora's father—have been "inappropriate" with her? Was that what the dozens of pictures of her were about? Wasn't it odd to have fixated so on one's daughter?

But if that were the case, why would Flora be trying to find her way back to Crosswinds?

I told Landon about seeing Flora last night, and my trying to give her a ride home. He couldn't keep the expression of shock and discomfiture from his face. We walked up and down California a few times, then sat on the steps of Grace Cathedral for a while, on the lookout together. No Flora.

"Probably she's not that consistent," I said after a half

hour. "Since she was here last night, I doubt she'll show up tonight. Want me to give you a ride back to your hotel?"

"If it's not terribly inconvenient, I would appreciate it."

The trip across the bridge was largely silent, with both of us lost to our thoughts. We chatted a little about Landon's upcoming schedule at Berkeley—calculus but also a graduate seminar on business ethics—and he asked me again if I thought I would be able to make it to the memorial service on Saturday.

"I'll be there," I said as I pulled into the Claremont parking lot and explained to the guard at the kiosk that I was just dropping someone off. "I should have asked before: Is there anything I can do to help?"

"No, thank you. The staff at the Chapel has been very helpful. They've organized everything."

I pulled up to the hotel doors.

"Thank you for the ride home, and for a most interesting day," he said.

"Thank *you* for being my ghost backup. Not just anyone has the *cojones* for something like that."

He nodded, then hesitated with his hand on the door handle.

I was afraid he was going to ask me something, but then he smiled, climbed out of the car, and entered the Claremont through the double doors.

Chapter Twenty-two

The next morning I spent in a meeting with some new clients in the Sunset, their architect, their interior designer and landscape designer and someone who had been appointed as "project manager," whatever that meant. I supposed this was essentially the role Egypt had played with the Flynts. Perhaps this was a new trend among the wealthy: They were already too busy to tend to their own decorating and gardening and childrearing and cleaning, so now even the "coordination" of redoing a house was being handed off to a third party.

It was another example of the group process applied to construction work. After about twenty minutes I was about to chew my arm off to escape, but the meeting went on for an excruciating three hours.

Next, I spent nearly two hours at the bed-and-breakfast in the Castro, which was a job that should have been done until Kim Propak, the owner, decided she wanted to change the layout of the living and sitting rooms.

Ghosts were looking better all the time.

Afterward, I grabbed a late lunch from the falafel cart and then called Luz.

"I need a dose of sanity," I said. "See you at the Historical Society?"

"Believe it or not, I'm already here. I have to go to a faculty meeting this afternoon so I thought I'd come early."

Half an hour later I pushed open the heavy door to the archive and was immediately greeted by the unique aroma of the past, a scent I had come to love. I had spent many happy hours here searching for information to help with the renovation of one historical home or another: photographs and floor plans and the occasional ghost story or disturbing legend.

I breathed in deeply and savored the atmosphere. The hushed calm of the archive was oddly rejuvenating.

I didn't see my friend Trish, head librarian at the archive. But Luz was already at a desk in the back, scrolling through microfiche, so I went to join her.

She was so absorbed in her reading that she barely looked up.

"Look at this," she said. "A woman *died* in that apartment. Her name was Suzanne White. Apparently she had been dead for a while by the time they found her."

"Was she killed by her husband?"

She shook her head. "It says here she was a widow. Her husband died a couple of years earlier. How sad."

"How did she die?"

"No one knows. She was found in the kitchen, no signs of violence, but with a rolling pin beside her. She was only thirty-three. Plus, there was a pie in the oven, burnt to a crisp. The neighbors called her the Pie Lady, said she used to bake all the time."

"So why is she hanging around the apartment?" I wondered aloud.

"She's waiting to take the pie out of the oven?"

I shrugged. "It could be just that simple, though probably not. Often hauntings are the result of a spirit that gets stuck in time and space, usually due to a traumatic event, like a sudden death, murder, or suicide." Just call me Mel Turner, ghost lecturer. "But occasionally, if they're strong enough or stubborn enough, spirits will stick around because they've got some unfinished business."

"Trying to put things right, maybe? Can't shuffle off this mortal coil unless the dishes are done?"

"Being murdered tends to interrupt plans," I nodded.

"That would explain why she's so upset, anyway." Luz said, yawning and rubbing her eyes. "So, now that we know a little about her ... where do we go from here?"

"When's the last time you slept?" I asked.

"What day is it?"

"That bad?"

"Worse. You know how small my apartment is. I got rid of some throw pillows because they made the place feel too crowded. The students are all lovely people, but having them underfoot is getting on my nerves. If the situation isn't resolved soon, I may break out a rolling pin and resort to self-help."

"Tell you what: How about I ask my dad if they can stay at our house for a few days? They'd have to sleep in the living room, but there's plenty of space to spread out, not to mention three bathrooms."

"Seriously?" Luz breathed.

"For you, *chica*? Anything."

"That would be wonderful, but ... isn't that a lot to ask of your dad? I mean, I know he likes having Caleb over, but Caleb's his grandson. He doesn't even know the students."

"So we'll introduce them. You know how my dad is: He loves cooking big meals when we have company, and is happiest when he has something to grouse about. A bunch of hungry college students fits the bill perfectly.

I'm surprised he didn't suggest it himself the other night at dinner."

"He was probably distracted by the thought of your finding another body."

"Could be. Though, not to nitpick or anything, but *I* didn't find the body, Landon found her."

"Ah yes, Landon. You've mentioned him a few times."

"He's Chantelle's brother."

"I know who he is."

"We've spent a little time together."

She raised an eyebrow. Luz and Annette Crawford both had this particular gesture down. It was so effective that I had spent some time in front of my bedroom mirror trying to master the technique, but gave up. No matter what I did both eyebrows always waggled, and I looked like an idiot.

"It wasn't like that."

"Uh-huh."

"Really. He went with me to a few salvage yards, that's all."

"That's all my Aunt Fanny. Continue."

How did Luz always know when I was holding back? "Okay, there was . . . an incident."

"Spill."

"A car hit the fence, and we were almost crushed under lumber and metal."

"And that happened how?"

"Not sure. It could have been an accident."

"Or it could have been on purpose?"

"Maybe."

"And then . . . ?"

"And then yesterday he came to Crosswinds and we found a secret passage, and saw some ghosts, and then we got a drink. It was completely innocent."

"Was it, now?"

I knew before I said anything that this conversation would turn out this way, and yet I kept talking. Luz was the only person in my life who had this effect on me.

"It was indeed. Completely innocent."

"And yet you feel the need to keep insisting it was innocent."

"Don't pull that psychoanalysis on me, Dr. Cabrera. Do you think I shouldn't have gotten a drink with Landon?"

"What do *you* think?"

"Luz!"

She laughed, then fixed me with a pointed stare. "Let me ask you this: Did you tell Graham about having drinks with Landon?"

"Not in so many words. Do you think that means anything?"

"I think if having drinks with Landon was as innocent as you keep insisting, then you either would have mentioned it to Graham, or you wouldn't be wondering if you should have mentioned it to Graham because it wouldn't be an issue for you. The fact that it *is* an issue for you tells me that something more is going on, and that you probably haven't even admitted it to yourself yet."

Damn. "Graham's a great guy."

"He *is* a great guy," Luz confirmed.

"Handsome, smart, kind."

"Loyal and true."

"He's perfect for me."

"Maybe that's the problem. He's too perfect."

"What do you mean by that?" I demanded.

Luz shrugged. "Just that you two became awfully comfortable with each other, awfully fast. Sometimes . . . I don't know, Mel, I'm not a relationship guru—I live alone, remember? But sometimes it's the guy who isn't so obviously perfect who sparks the passion."

"Graham and I have passion," I mumbled.

"Which is wonderful. Don't misunderstand me; I'm not trying to talk you out of being with Graham," Luz said. "Graham's a great guy, and if he's what you want then go for it, with my blessing."

"Thank you."

"But you're not a kid, Mel, you're a grown woman who has been married, has raised a child—who's now on the brink of leaving for college—and runs her own business. I think there's a reason you haven't settled down and started the family Graham has made it clear he wants. Maybe you don't just 'need a little time.' Maybe you need someone else."

I gave a little sound between a gasp and a moan.

"On the other hand," she said, shutting down the microfiche machine and rewinding the film. "What do I know? And who is this Landon person? Maybe *he's* the psycho killer you're looking for, and that's why he's spending so much time with you. Then you will have much bigger problems on your hands."

"Landon is *not* a psycho killer," I said. "He doesn't have any friends here, and he's trying to deal with the sudden death of his sister; that's why he's been hanging around."

"I'm just saying. He lost his parents early, had very little familial support, apparently has no current friends, and his sister was killed right after he arrived. Also he's rich but not married, which I find suspicious. All I'm saying is that with your track record, you might want to be cautious."

"Luz ..."

"Anyhow, as fun as it is to scroll through microfiche, I have to get going. Faculty meeting. Sorry I can't hang out," she looked around the library, where three patrons were quietly absorbed in reading. "You think you're safe here?"

"Very funny. Even *I* can't get in trouble at the California Historical Society."

She raised one eyebrow again. "Don't tempt fate, *chica*."

I went up to the counter and asked for help finding any information on the Summerton family, of Crosswinds. After ten minutes the young man handed me a slim file.

"Doesn't look like much. Sorry," he said. "Mostly about the house."

Well, that was something. And in fact I did find something useful: a photograph of Peregrine Summerton. Beetled brow, muttonchops, broad, florid face. Looking supremely unhappy. That seemed to be his status quo.

So at least I was sure that it was, indeed, Peregrine Summerton's ghost haunting Crosswinds. Calling out for his daughter.

I couldn't find out anything more about the Summerton family, or Crosswinds, beyond some original drawings and blueprints of the home, which I photocopied. The older son went to school back east to become a lawyer, the younger went into the lumber business. Flora seemed to have disappeared entirely.

I approached the readers' services desk to hand the file back, and let out a sigh of relief. Trish, archivist extraordinaire, looked up from the papers she was working on and smiled. I was saved.

"Well, well, if it isn't Mel Turner," Trish said. "Of all the archives in all the world, you had to walk into mine. Long time no see."

"Good to be back. How's life in the archives?"

"Oh, you know, it's not all it's *stacked up* to be. Get it?"

I groaned. "What is it with puns, lately?"

She laughed softly. "What can I help you find this fine, fair day?"

"I need the lowdown on the Summerton family who used to own Crosswinds mansion in Pacific Heights. I don't suppose you have a Top Secret file with all their dirty laundry, do you?"

She frowned slightly. "Can't swear we don't have some dirty laundry hiding around here somewhere, but nothing leaps to mind. Did you do the usual searches?"

"Yes, but no luck finding anything juicy on the Summertons."

"Murder, suicide, scandal?"

"The usual."

She tilted her head back and stared at the ceiling, and I waited silently while she did a mental search. Trish had a near-encyclopedic knowledge of local history thanks to years spent curating the Historical Society's collections, though she claimed she was just nosy. "Nothing leaps to mind. . . ." She trailed off, then cocked her head at the file lying on the counter, upside down to her. "What street did they live on, upper Broadway?"

I nodded.

"The Rutherfords, of course!"

"Who, now?"

"The Rutherfords lived on that same block."

"Okay . . . and they're significant—why?"

"The Rutherfords were big boosters of the city and all things cultural, gave a lot of money to save and archive documents from San Francisco's early days. That happened a lot in the late nineteenth century: Families with money sought to celebrate their accomplishments, and ensure their legacy, by building monuments and founding historical societies. Hard to be forgotten when you've endowed an organization dedicated to remembering the past."

"I don't follow."

She waved a hand in the air and started to type something on the keyboard in front of her. "It doesn't really matter. I only mention it because the Rutherfords not only endowed the Historical Society but donated their extensive collection of family papers."

"Oh. You mean the Summertons might have done the same thing?"

"No such luck; what you have there in the file is all there is on the Summertons. That's not that unusual; a lot of people burned their private papers before they died...." She focused on her computer screen, jotted something on a pad of paper, tore off the top sheet, and said, "Let's go."

I followed Trish through a door into the archive's closed stacks. I'd seen this area once before when I'd taken the tour. Tightly packed metal shelving soared three stories high and held tens of thousands of bound volumes: some small, some large. The area was climate controlled to prevent mold and mildew, and the lights were kept low so as not to fade old ink. Trish strode briskly past the books, heading for a door marked MANUSCRIPTS. Inside the Manuscripts room were more shelves filled with archival boxes of various sizes, each meticulously labeled with the name of the collection.

"Let's see ..." Trish muttered as she scanned the boxes. "Randolph, Remington, Roscoe ... Here we are: Rutherford." Box after box contained what was clearly an extensive collection of the Rutherford Family Papers. She glanced at the paper in her hand, and selected a few boxes and set them down on a large wooden table in the center of the room. "Have a seat," she said, and I pulled up a chair.

"The Rutherfords were neighbors of the Summertons, not that that mattered. The families that made up San Francisco's high society in the late nineteenth century were a close-knit and interconnected group. A lot of them had nothing to do but spend money and gossip, and their favorite topic was one another: who was doing what to whom, who said what about whom. 'Twas ever so, I suppose."

As she spoke, Trish carefully opened an archival box, which was full of large labeled folders. She removed one folder from the box, and set it on a square of felt on top of the table. "Here's the deal: Manuscripts require special care and handling. The old paper is vulnerable to the oils on your hands, so do not touch the letters. To turn a letter over, lift it gently by one corner. Whatever you do, do not cough or sneeze on them. Take notes with a pencil and paper only; no ink of any kind is allowed. Deal?"

I nodded.

"It's very likely the Rutherford family correspondence will include some mention of the Summertons. The Rutherford daughters went to school in Boston, and when they were gone Mrs. Rutherford wrote numerous letters to them, relaying all the local news. Remember, these were the days before telephones and text messages; when the only way to stay in touch across distances was through letters. Reading the entire collection would take quite a bit of time—the Rutherford women had decent handwriting, all things considered, but it can be slow going—but if you can narrow the search down by suggesting some dates that would be helpful."

"1896."

"Okay, let's start with 1896."

Chapter Twenty-three

It took a while to get used to the slanted, stylized hand-writing, but once I got the hang of it and started to figure out the cast of characters, the correspondence of the Rutherford family made for fascinating reading.

A lot of it concerned the minutiae of everyday life, the sort of thing that might seem tedious and expected at the time—the weather, favorite recipes, complaints about the difficulties of finding reliable servants—but the letters were a fascinating window into another time and way of life. Much like the sort of stuff I typically found behind walls in houses; everyday objects like newspapers with the ads for current movies playing or worker's scrawl about where to splice wires.

The personalities of the letter writers shone through: Mrs. Rutherford was high-strung and a bit of a snob, but loved her daughters fiercely. The elder daughter, Beth, was quiet and devoted to her studies, and expressed a wish to pursue a career as a nurse that her mother quickly squelched as "unsuitable for a girl of your station." The younger daughter, Virginia, was a riot: high-spirited and outgoing, she must have been a handful.

Every letter from Mrs. Rutherford to her daughters began with anxious inquiries into their health and home remedies to treat a cough or an ache. Rumors that an epidemic of typhoid fever or scarlet fever had appeared in Boston would prompt Mrs. Rutherford to barrage her daughters with maternal warnings about avoiding unhealthy miasmas and pestilential immigrant neighborhoods. I marveled at how little control even the immensely wealthy Rutherfords had over their world; in the years before antibiotics even a minor scrape or illness could result in death.

And then, just as Trish was standing over me, car keys in hand, telling me it was closing time and everyone else had gone home, I found a reference to Crosswinds and the Summertons.

> *... apply the mustard plaster and leave it on until the skin starts to blister. It will draw out the bad humours.*
>
> *I have news of a delicate nature concerning the neighborhood. I cannot imagine how Mr. Summerton will be affected by it. I believe your dear father has spoken in the past of Mr. Summerton's political ambitions, but though Mr. Summerton has many friends in the state legislature your father believes his election to the Senate is no longer a viable proposition. I am sure you remember Mr. Summerton's daughter, Flora? She was two years behind you at Miss Smith's School for Young Ladies, and I believe you were reunited with her at the tea hosted by the Remington ladies last summer. I always thought she was a lovely girl, though a bit headstrong, with a quick wit and a sharp tongue, and in this regard I am sorry to say I am proven right. Flora chose the occasion of the announcement of her engagement to*

Mr. Caruthers (of the Caruthers copper fortune) to fly the coop—at exactly the stroke of midnight, which ushered in her 18th birthday!

It is said that in the weeks leading up to the ball, Flora was oft witnessed standing atop the widow's walk, looking out to sea. Our neighbor Mrs. Landingham declares the object of Flora's heart might well be a seaman! Just imagine, if you dare, how Mr. Summerton must regard such an association.

The betrothal ball was the event of the season, and I wore a beautiful velvet gown with garnet beads and Alençon lace made especially for the occasion. Mr. Summerton's home looked splendid: the ballroom was decorated in garlands of evergreen and hydrangea, with cascades of bougainvillea and huge urns with bouquets of pink roses. A full string orchestra serenaded us! We were waited upon most solicitously by servants in proper livery offering imported French champagne, steamed shrimp and crab, and oysters in a wonderfully rich sauce called "Oysters Rockefeller" that I understand is all the rage these days. We were breathless from waltzing when all of a sudden we heard Mr. Summerton cry out, a mixture of agony and ire that made my blood run cold. I have since been led to understand that Flora rebelled against the fiancé her father had chosen for her, and decamped from her own ball in quite a dramatic fashion. She was there one moment, and gone the next, and no one can countenance how she accomplished it.

Your Aunt Helen will be arriving by steamship next week from Los Angeles for a nice visit; I do hope she will bring a crate or two of oranges with her. How lovely it must be to live in a land of endless orchards. . . .

"This is amazing. Trish, you're a genius."

"I'm sorry, Mel. I don't mean to rush you but we officially closed twenty minutes ago, and I have plans with friends tonight."

"Of course," I said, though I was frustrated it had taken me so long to find the reference to Crosswinds, and now all I wanted to do was to read through the rest of the letters.

"We open tomorrow at ten, and I'll keep the file for you right behind the counter."

"Oh, great. I'll be back . . ." As I said it I realized that tomorrow at eleven was the memorial service for Chantelle, in the East Bay. "I'll be back tomorrow if I can, or the next day at the latest."

"We're closed on Sunday."

Dammit. "Of course. Okay, I'll be sure to come back tomorrow."

We walked out together, and I rescued my car from the garage and headed over the Bay Bridge in thick Friday evening traffic, pondering Flora fleeing her own engagement ball at the stroke of midnight, chased by a furious and politically ambitious amateur photographer father.

Where had she gone? What would an educated young woman have done on her own, back in the day? And the question that kept preying on my mind: Why was she trying to get back?

At home it was just the immediate family: Dog, Stan, Dad, Caleb. Stan was helping Caleb go over some college applications, and I washed greens for the salad. The kitchen was redolent with the aroma of roasted chicken, and Dog made sure he was underfoot at all times in case something good fell to the floor.

"So, Dad," I said. "What do you think about providing temporary housing for some young people in need?"

"What goes on in that mind of yours?" he growled, basting the chicken.

"There are five of them. They seem quite responsible, and very nice. And they got chased out of their apartment by a ghost."

"This is the ghost Luz was talking about the other evening?" Stan asked as he and Caleb joined us in the kitchen.

"Yeah, did you find another body there?" Caleb asked.

"No, I did *not* find a body, thank you very much," I said with some pride. The moment it came out of my mouth I realized how twisted my sense of reality had become. "But the ghost is"—I searched for the word—"*active*, and they really can't live there until I can get rid of her. I'm going to Chantelle's memorial service at the Chapel of the Chimes tomorrow so it might be another day or two until I can try to put her to rest, presuming I can figure out how to do that. The students are sleeping on Luz's floor but she only has one bathroom...."

My father muttered something under his breath while he checked on the potatoes.

"Ah, go on, old man," said Stan with a grin. "You know you can't refuse the combined forces of Mel and Luz. They're a formidable pair. You might as well give up gracefully."

I didn't think of myself as particularly formidable, but I appreciated the comment and gave him a wink.

"Huh," said my dad, taking the chicken out of the oven with a grunt and setting it on the stove to rest.

"Anyway, may I tell them they can stay here?" I persisted. "Just for a few days, max."

"I could move back to my dad's if you need the room," offered Caleb.

"No, Caleb," I assured him. "I wouldn't ask you to do

that. The guys can sleep in the living room, and the girls . . ."

"Or maybe I could sleep on the couch with the guys," Caleb suggested. "And the girls could have my room."

"That's awfully nice of you, Caleb."

"No problem," he said.

My dad gave him the very slightest smile and nod, the kind that had motivated me to bend over backward to make him proud of me when I was a kid. Then, as a teen-ager, I'd gone through a rebellious phase, but now Dad and I got along just fine, as long as we avoided talking politics.

"Table needs setting," Dad said, and Caleb hopped-to without having to be asked.

Then our unusual little family sat down to a dinner of roast chicken, tiny new potatoes in butter sauce with parsley, and asparagus.

"This looks great, Dad," I said. "And you call *Stan* Martha Stewart? I think you might be giving him a run for his money."

Dad grunted. "All the best chefs are men, you know."

"I'm not going to get roped into this discussion," I said, digging into the asparagus.

"So," Stan changed the subject. "How goes the ghost busting in the other place, what is it, Crosswinds?"

"I saw him yesterday," I said, and popped a tiny new potato in my mouth. The herbs and butter and salt were perfect.

"You *saw* him?" Caleb asked.

"Landon and I found a secret passage leading from the foyer to the Pilates studio." As I said it I realized what I had read at the archive earlier: Flora must have used the secret passage to disappear from the ball, then went through it and upstairs to the main floor, and ran away.

"You and 'Landon'? This the brother of the dead gal?" my dad asked.

"Chantelle," Caleb put in.

"That's right. Chantelle. So, Landon's her brother? And he's running through secret passages with you why, exactly?"

I shrugged and bit into the succulent chicken, which was juicy and perfect. "He wanted to look through the house. It seems . . ." I wasn't sure if I was supposed to be talking about this crime with civilians, but after all, this was family. "It seems Chantelle might have been blackmailing someone in relation to Crosswinds."

"Someone in the owner's family?"

"It's hard to tell. And it might not have been blackmail per se, but maybe she came upon a secret, or something? There are a lot of suspects. And then it's not even a given that the person being blackmailed was the one who killed her. But it's not out of left field to think there might be a connection between Crosswinds and her death."

Dad snorted. "Not if *you're* involved."

"Thanks, Dad."

"I still don't see why this Landon person is running around secret passages with you."

"First of all we weren't 'running around,' he simply happened to be with me when I realized there was a gap behind a wall. Frankly, I was glad to have the backup."

"A gap behind the wall?" Stan asked.

"There was a false wall, essentially."

"What," Dad said. "You mean the remodeler just went right up over the old one?"

"It gets better: He went right up over an entire bookcase, full of books."

Everyone at the table, even Caleb—who had been around Turner Construction enough to understand some of the basics of construction—gasped. Dog came to attention, hoping for food.

"We heard music that seemed to come from behind it," I continued. "And Landon knew of a bookcase in Cambridge that covers up a secret passage, so that was how we found it."

"I can't believe anyone would build a wall over a *bookcase*," said Stan. "That makes no sense at all."

Dad just shook his head and passed around the Parker House rolls. The table was quiet, all of us lost in thought.

When it came to the folks at Turner Construction, ghosts and murders were one thing, but shoddy construction techniques were downright inexcusable.

Chapter Twenty-four

Saturday morning Luz had invited me to a yoga class, but I begged off. Since I was going to Chantelle's memorial service at the Chapel of the Chimes at eleven, I decided to take a walk in Mountain View cemetery beforehand. The way you do.

I loved this cemetery. I hadn't been kidding when I'd told Landon: It offered some of the best views from Oakland, hands down. The graves marched up the hill, and on "millionaire's row" big names in Bay Area history, like Crocker and Merritt and Ghirardelli had commissioned elaborate crypts. Statuary included mournful angels and triumphant heralds and caryatids—female figures used as columns. The Crocker memorial featured a circular bench, which locals like me used for picnic lunches from time to time, looking out to the bay, Yerba Buena Island, San Francisco, and the Golden Gate Bridge.

I passed by one family plot and paused to read the names. Several of the gravestones held little ceramic cameos with a photo of the deceased. It seemed like an old-fashioned custom, but I noticed several modern-looking ones as well. It was sort of nice to be able to put a face to the names.

Old photographs put me in mind of what Landon and I had found in the secret passage at Crosswinds. So Peregrine Summerton was a photographer. Judging by the darkroom and the quantity of photographs, it seemed he was pretty serious about it.

Was Flora his one and only muse? I thought of what Landon had told me about their uncle's behavior toward Chantelle. Could Flora have run away from Crosswinds because her father had crossed the line? But how would I ever find out? Things like that weren't talked about back then, were they?

I closed my eyes for a moment and imagined the popping sound as the flash went off, the explosion of the little glass bulb, the violence of the moment. Flora jumping.

At ten thirty I returned to my car on Piedmont Avenue to change into my one decent pair of dress shoes. Unsure of what to wear to a memorial service but pretty sure it didn't include spangles, I had dressed in a simple blue dress but wore my athletic shoes for the cemetery walk. I refuse to walk in heels, even low ones.

Sitting in the open door of my car, I looked up to see Stephanie Flynt approaching.

"Isn't it just *awful?*" she said. She wore a gauzy black dress and a hat with a black veil. I wondered if black was still de rigueur at funerals. It had been a long time since I'd attended one.

"Yes, very sad," I said, wrenching my petty thoughts from my wardrobe to the reason we were here: a woman's tragic death.

"Have the police made any progress on the case, do you know?" Stephanie asked. "That rather ... *daunting* inspector came to speak with us. She wasn't very accommodating."

I presumed she was speaking about Annette, and the thought of Stephanie asking her to be "more accommodating" made me smile.

"I don't think they've figured it out yet," I said. "But I don't actually know."

"So sad that her *brother* found her. How very awful for him."

I nodded.

"And you arrived soon after, you said?" Stephanie said.

"Yes, I went by the apartment and found Landon with Chantelle," I said, trying to gauge just how invested she might be in my answer.

Mason and Lacey joined us. Both ran true to form: Lacey looked like she wished she were anywhere but here, and Mason looked just a tad too eager to please.

"Will Andrew be joining us?" I asked.

"He's still out of town, unfortunately," said Mason. "He sent flowers."

"Cost a fortune," said Lacey.

I stood, feeling awkward in my grown-up shoes—I really did prefer my boots for almost any occasion other than exercise and funerals—and locked the car.

The Flynts and I walked together into the building.

I loved Chapel of the Chimes even more than Mountain View cemetery. Famed local architect Julia Morgan had been commissioned to transform the old trolley station—at the end of the line of what used to be called Cemetery Avenue—into a columbarium, which is a mausoleum for cremated remains. She brought her special style to the place, creating a series of differently shaped arches leading down long hallways, mosaics and wall paintings and quatrefoil windows and concrete tracery. It was stunning.

Probably it's strange that I should so enjoy cemeteries and columbariums ... though now that I'm a ghost specialist, it seemed rather fitting.

It dawned on me, however, that I'd never seen a ghost at Chapel of the Chimes. I was much more likely to find them in private houses than in the places most people associated with spirits: cemeteries and mausoleums. Still, I wouldn't go sneaking around this place at midnight on Halloween. If an actual ghost didn't scare the daylights out of me, my imagination surely would.

Within the columbarium were several chapels. Landon had told me he had reserved the small, intimate chapel on the third level of interior courtyards; it was my favorite, located beside a courtyard rife with plantings, lit by peaked sunroofs, and studded with fountains. But when the Flynts and I arrived we discovered the service had been moved to the largest chapel to accommodate an overflow crowd.

We had arrived twenty minutes early, but it was already standing room only. I had hoped to say hello to Landon before things began, but it was too much of a crush. Many of the people attending appeared to be paparazzi rather than mourners, and the management had to make an announcement asking everyone to cease snapping photos.

As we found a spot to stand at the side of the chapel, Stephanie slipped her arm through mine as though we were long lost pals united in grief for a good friend. What had Karla said, that she and Stephanie were "instant sorority sisters"? Stephanie had the open, easy friendliness I had noticed with a lot of people who practiced the kind of spiritual work common to Marin Country retreats. It was appealing, but at the same time it was hard to know when they were being sincere.

Before I could give Stephanie much more thought, an older woman, short and round and wearing minister's robes, went up to the dais and began a nondenominational, slightly New-Agey homily about embracing life and happiness while we have it, and not asking why unfair things are visited upon us from time to time.

Then Landon stepped up to the dais. He paused a moment, looking out at the crowd, his hands gripping the sides of the podium so tightly his knuckles went white.

"Many of you knew my sister, Chantelle, better than I. I"—he choked up, ducked his head and cleared his throat—"I am Chantelle's brother, Landon Demetrius. And I, for one, am full of regret. Regret for the way in which Chantelle was taken from us. Regret for years of separation and time lost. Regret that I was not able to protect her. But I will make this vow: I will not rest until her killer is known. I owe her that much, at the very least. I will not rest."

Now he looked directly at me. Or was he looking at the assorted Flynts standing with me? I heard Stephanie gasp, and caught Mason and Lacey exchanging a significant look.

After Landon stepped down, several others took the podium in turn and spoke about Chantelle as a friend and colleague, but primarily as a talented psychic who had brought solace to many by helping them to connect to their deceased loved ones, or by giving advice about major life decisions.

While they spoke, my gaze fixed on the blown-up photo of a smiling Chantelle on an easel next to the low stage. She really had been beautiful, and those ethereal eyes seemed to promise otherworldly insight.

Why couldn't she communicate with me, if she had

been so talented with such things? Probably Olivier would tell me the supernatural lines of communication didn't work that way, but I found it bewildering and frustrating.

What had she been after? Had she really tried to blackmail one of the Flynt clan? If so, it would stand to reason that it had to have been Andrew or Stephanie, right? Had Chantelle even known any of the others enough to know their secrets and threaten them?

On the other hand, Karla had mentioned the entire family was present at Chantelle's reading of Crosswinds. Could she have discovered something on that night?

Egypt told me the kids didn't have access to any significant amounts of money, so there would be no point to blackmailing them. But would Chantelle have known that? She was a psychic, but did that mean she would *know* everything? Did her obvious popularity mean that she was truly gifted, or simply that she was so attractive and intuitive that she was able to convince people she had special sight?

I wish I could have met her—when she was alive—so I would have a clearer sense of what I was dealing with.

My thoughts were brought back to the memorial service with a jolt when the massive pipe organ started playing, and the chapel was filled with muted chatter and shuffling sounds as the audience stood and slid out of the pews.

"I'm going to try to say hello to Landon," I said, excusing myself from the Flynts.

"Please do give him our condolences," said Stephanie. "I don't feel up to braving the crowd, but I would like him to know we were here."

"Of course, I'll tell him."

I slipped off and tried to find a way around the milling throng by scooting around the head of the chapel, but no luck. Short of actually shoving my way through, I was stuck.

I scanned the crowd for Landon and found him on the opposite side of the chapel, surrounded by a flock of well-wishers.

When our gaze met, I read deep sadness in those extraordinary eyes of his, but there was something else, as well. A tingle of connection, even among such a crowd.

I held up a hand, and he gave me a sad smile and a nod.

I imagined Landon would be swamped for a while, so I would have plenty of time to use the restroom before finding him and giving him a big hug. Or ... maybe a hearty handshake.

What *was* it about Landon? Was Luz right?

Please oh please don't let him be the killer. That would be just like me, wouldn't it? To develop a crush on the bad guy. Talk about inappropriate.

The women's room on the main floor—the relatively modern one with several stalls—already had a line out the door. But familiar as I was with the columbarium I knew there was another bathroom upstairs, tucked into a corner of one of the building's endless interconnected chambers.

I went up to the third tier of the courtyards, then down the endless corridors lined with glass-fronted cabinets holding urns or bronze "books" of cremated remains, each fronted with a brass plaque.

The bathroom was two small adjoining rooms, one with a sink and mirror and a second with the single toilet. It was empty so I slipped into the toilet room and locked the door behind me.

Moments later I heard someone come into the outer room and rattle the knob on the toilet door—which went all the way to the floor—without knocking.

"It's locked," I heard Lacey's distinctive sneer. "Told you I don't think we're supposed to use it. Besides, it's so old and creepy it probably doesn't even work. Let's go back downstairs."

"Oh! My hair," came Stephanie's voice. "I look a fright."

"Told you not to wear that ridiculous hat. What are you, Jackie Kennedy? Now you have hat head."

"May I borrow your lip balm?" Stephanie asked in a small voice. I heard a loud sniff, and the sound of the towel dispenser.

"Honestly, Mother, you're *crying*? I don't know why you even dragged me to this thing," said Lacey. "I say she got what she deserved."

"Don't say that," said Stephanie. She blew her nose and sniffed again. "It sounds terrible when you say that."

"I notice Dad didn't feel the need to come. And he's the one who *should* be here. Or would that be Grand-pop? What, did they take turns? It's disgusting."

No reply.

I remained frozen, afraid to breathe.

"Seriously, Mother, how can you stay so calm?"

"She's *dead*," came Stephanie's voice in a surprisingly harsh tone. Gone was the breathy, dreamy quality. "It's *over*, do you hear? *Over*. We will never speak of this again. We are Flynts, and Flynts stick together. No matter what. Understood?"

"Um . . . yeah. Understood. Sorry, Mom."

"Now, may I *please* borrow your lip balm?"

Chapter Twenty-five

I remained where I was for another couple of minutes after I heard them leave, before leaving the stall and washing my hands.

I was having a hard time believing they had spoken so openly. Number one rule of espionage: Check to see if anyone else was in the restroom before spilling the beans. Any child playing Spy vs. Spy knows that.

On the other hand . . . what had I actually learned? It wasn't as though either of them was admitting to being the killer, or even knowing the killer. Their conversation did imply, though, that perhaps Andrew—and even George?—had been much closer to Chantelle than either had admitted.

What bothered me more than anything, though, was the abrupt shift in Stephanie's tone. I often wondered if people who appear outwardly placid and virtually impervious to emotion might blow up from time to time. Could it all be an act?

I slipped out of the lavatory, looking to the left and the right for any sign of a Flynt, but saw no one. Just in case, I took a circuitous route back to the chapel, descending the set of stone stairs that were said to have been leftovers from Julia Morgan's work on Hearst Castle. But by the time I returned to the chapel the crowd had thinned dramatically. I didn't see Stephanie or Lacey . . . or Landon Demetrius for that matter.

"Have you seen Chantelle's brother anywhere?" I asked a young man who looked the part of a cub reporter. He had been snapping photos with an actual camera, not his cell phone, and taking notes on a pad of paper.

"I think he took off. Didn't want to answer questions. You know him?"

"Just barely."

"Something's troubling me," he said, a thoughtful look on his face. "How come such a badass psychic didn't know she was going to be killed?"

An excellent question, I thought. And one for which I had no answer beyond the frustrating: "I don't think it works that way."

"What's the point of having a sixth sense if it doesn't work when you need it most?" he asked, then shrugged. "Well, have a nice day."

"You too."

I sat in my car and dialed Annette Crawford, then told her about the conversation I overheard.

"That's it? The whole thing?" she asked.

"Yeah, pretty much."

"So it doesn't actually tell us anything, except that they're a clannish group."

"I guess you're right."

"That's okay, it's not like you were going to trip on a spontaneous confession. And even if you had, that's not the sort of thing we can use in court so it's of limited use, except to point us in a direction. I'll see if any of this plays out, maybe apply some more pressure to the lovely Mrs. Flynt."

"Okay. Also, I saw Egypt talking with George Flynt the other day."

"And?"

"It just seemed strange, because George said he was going to Sausalito, and then I saw him with Egypt, and she denied seeing him, as well."

"You think they're having an affair too? And if so, why do I care?"

"I really don't know. It just struck me as odd. Egypt did say that the family fights a lot about money—"

"Like every other family in the world . . ."

" —and that George essentially disinherited his grand-kids, which made Stephanie mad."

"Lacey and Mason? They don't seem to be hurting for money. And wouldn't that be motive to kill George instead of Chantelle?"

"I'm just reporting what I heard."

"You hear anything about financial impropriety at Tempus?"

"I . . . overheard that they were expecting an audit as part of the preparation for the IPO. And I think maybe Egypt and George were talking about the audit."

"But no specifics?"

"No, sorry. Oh! I forgot to tell you: Someone might have been trying to kill me the other day."

"Go on."

"Or it might have been nothing."

"Why don't you let me decide?"

"Yeah, so Landon and I went to a salvage yard in Richmond—"

"Oh, this is the thing where a truck went into the fence? He already told me. So, how come you're taking Landon to salvage yards?"

"Um . . . he asked me to. He's trying to figure out what happened. You know, with his sister."

"Yes, I'm aware of that. But I'm not clear on why you took him to Uncle Joe's."

"It's sort of a long story . . ."

"Save it. I gotta go."

"Okay, so you don't think anyone was trying to kill me?"

There was a slight pause. "There's always that possibility. But I'll leave you with this thought: What makes you think they were trying to kill *you*?"

And with that she hung up.

I stared at the phone for a moment. Why would someone want to kill Landon? If Chantelle really was killed because she was blackmailing someone, did he or she know Chantelle had written to her brother, and fear exposure? Someone cold-blooded enough to knife Chantelle to death wouldn't hesitate to ram a fence at a salvage yard.

Which again raised the question: Why did Nancy send us to Uncle Joe's?

Determined to try to figure out the connection, I drove to Griega Salvage in Berkeley.

"Oh, I totally screwed that up, didn't I?" Nancy said when I asked her about it. "That's why it seemed so weird, even as I said it. It wasn't Uncle *Joe's*, it was Uncle J's, in Walnut Creek. What can I say? Menopause; I forget my own name these days."

"Uncle J's?"

"Yeah. In Walnut Creek, do you know it? I mean, it's weird enough Uncle J's is having an auction—can you imagine Uncle *Joe's*? Ha! Sorry if I sent you on a wild-goose chase," she repeated. "I've got to get more help in here."

The phone rang again, as though to make her point.

I went back out to my car. So if someone really had

been trying to kill—or intimidate?—me or Landon, or
both of us, they must have been following us. But why?
Skip himself told me to check Griega Salvage. So he
might have known I would go there, but he still wouldn't
have known when, exactly, unless he was watching the
place. On the other hand, he would have known I was
meeting Karla that morning, so could he have tailed me
from Mama's Royal Café?

I checked my phone for the time. If I went out to Walnut Creek first I still might be able to get to the Historical Society before it closed, but with barely enough time
to get much reading done.

The phone rang. It was my dad, and there was lots of
noise in the background.

"What's up?" I asked.

"We're having a tamale festival with Luz and the students tonight," said Dad, sounding buoyant.

"That was fast work. When did they move in?"

"Came over an hour ago. We've already started cooking. Seems making tamales is a group event."

"That's great, Dad," I said, wondering if he'd kill me
if I arrived a little—or a lot—late.

"We need a few more things at the store. We don't
have nearly enough corn husks and *masa*," he said, and
immediately started reading off a list.

"I'm a little busy, Dad."

"You invited a bunch of kids into my house and now
you're too busy to do a little grocery shopping?"

I sighed. "No, of course not. You're right. I've got to
run an errand first, but I'll swing by Mi Pueblo on the
way home."

"Don't be late."

"I won't."

"And be careful, babe. You're not running after a
killer, are you?"

"Nope. Just stopping by a salvage yard."

What could possibly go wrong?

The only problem was that Walnut Creek was in the opposite direction of San Francisco; there was no way I could get both places and get home on time for the tamale festival.

I called Trish at the Historical Society.

"Actually," Trish said, "I was so intrigued by your questions that I've been doing some digging. I came up with some really good stuff."

"Are you serious? Trish, is there an award for best librarian or research guru or something? Because I'll nominate you."

She chuckled. "No worries, this is the sort of thing I live for."

"So what did you find?"

"Lots of interesting stuff. I made some copies for you. Unfortunately we close at three on Saturdays, so you're already cutting it close."

"Darn, I was afraid of that."

"But if you want, I'll come to you. No big deal, I could hop on the bridge. I like Oakland. Want to meet somewhere for a drink and I'll show you what I came up with?"

"I'd love to, but I foisted a bunch of college kids on my dad and they are, even as we speak, in the process of making tamales. He just gave me a shopping list."

"I love tamales."

"Really? I don't suppose you'd like to join us? I have to warn you, it's a crowded house with students and a dog and my dad. . . ."

"Sounds like a blast," she said, adding something in Spanish that I didn't follow.

I gave her the address and she said she'd be over in a couple of hours.

So I headed east through the tunnel, toward Walnut Creek, to Uncle J's. I had been there only once, many years ago. It wasn't the kind of salvage yard I frequented, because it was much more antiques shop than junk store. I didn't often shop at places where the owners knew exactly what they had.

Also, I never shopped on the other side of the tunnel if I could help it. It was an East Bay thing.

Uncle J's was located in a darling little house with a darling little garden, chock-full of darling little accessories, antiques, and—I was pretty sure—at least a few darling reproductions. There was no dust or grime anywhere, not even on the outdoor garden statuary.

I passed through the garden and into the main house, where a handsome twentysomething man sat on a high stool behind the counter. Unlike the fellow at Uncle Joe's, this man looked in charge of things.

"Hello," I said as I stepped inside.

"Hello, there! Welcome. Lovely day, isn't it?"

"Yes, it is. Could I ask you a few questions?"

"Of course," he said, slipping off the stool and standing, giving me his full attention. "Could I help you find something special?"

"I'm looking for items from the Crosswinds estate, in San Francisco. Skip Buhner was selling some things. . . ."

He was nodding. "Sure. But that was a while ago. I think all we have left . . ." He started typing into his computer, then scrolling through something, nodding. "Yeah, let's see. . . . There might be a fireplace surround, and there's one ceiling medallion over here. . . ." He left the computer and led the way to a smaller room. He gestured to a creamy limestone fireplace surround featuring carved cherubs. Then he started moving aside a few other items to reveal a plaster medallion in a scallop shape, with acanthus leaves and ivy swag.

"These came from Crosswinds?" I asked, feeling almost reverential as I ran my hands over the hand-carved decorations, original to the haunted manse.

"Yep. There was a whole bunch of stuff, but most of it sold at auction."

"I don't suppose you know who bought the weather-vane, or the widow's walk?"

He frowned. "I don't remember either of those items, actually. Are you sure they were in the Crosswinds Collection?"

"Very sure. I heard there was a picture of the weathervane on the brochure."

"Oh, that's right." He went back to the computer and started typing again. "Yes, I do remember that, now that you mention it.... Like I say, it was a while ago. Uh-huh ... unh-huh ... looks like they decided to keep that piece."

"'They' who?"

"Well, according to the records, Mr. Buhner and Mr. Flynt, it looks like. They were the ones who asked us to curate the auction. We don't do a lot of that sort of thing, and suggested they go through Clars or Butterfields, but they preferred to do it here."

"Mr. Flynt? Andrew Flynt?"

"You know ..." He gave a little laugh and his voice dropped. "I wasn't actually in charge back then. To tell you the absolute truth, I was mostly driving the delivery truck until a few weeks ago. Mrs. Jennings, the owner, is in Europe right now. She's going to be sending over an entire container full of European antiques, can you believe that?"

"So, you don't know which Mr. Flynt it was? Did you ever meet them?"

"I wasn't working that weekend. I just know Mrs. Jennings was very excited to have the collection. She said it was very exclusive, and only allowed our private mailing list in the audience."

"Okay," I said, nodding and trying to think of what else to ask. "Hey, my office manager Stan Tomassi has been calling around, asking some of these questions. Did he call here?"

"We don't take phone calls anymore," he said with a laugh. "It's something Mrs. Jennings came up with: Everything's done in person or by e-mail. She doesn't want anyone to walk in and see us on the phone, or have to leave a customer in order to answer the phone. She's quirky."

I thought about Nancy constantly on the phone and thought, quirky or not, maybe Mrs. Jennings had a point.

"Okay, thanks. I'll take that fireplace surround and medallion—are those the only items you have left?"

"According to the computer, yes." He was typing something in, then looked up with me and smiled. "That'll be five six."

"I'm sorry?"

"Five thousand, six hundred."

"Five thousand, six hundred *dollars*? For a fireplace surround and a ceiling medallion?"

He nodded.

This was why I didn't shop in places like Uncle J's. Good thing Andrew Flynt had more dollars than sense; this was going on his bill. Interior designers usually charged clients a full one hundred percent markup, but I was nicer than most designers. I would only inflate the bill by a small percentage to cover my time. All in all, it was a good day's work, and I was thrilled to have found at least a few items original to Crosswinds.

While the young man rang up my bill, I wondered which Mr. Flynt had coordinated this Crosswinds Collection with Skip Buhner. Was Andrew somehow playing both sides of this? But that made no sense—he was eager to lay these ghosts to rest so he could sell Crosswinds. Still, George or Mason seemed just as unlikely. The money involved—while big bucks to mere humans—wouldn't have meant much to the wealthy Flynts.

"Do you think the Flynt name might have been attached to the Crosswinds Collection just as a courtesy?" I asked.

"Could very well be," he said, not looking up from the computer screen. "Mr. Buhner does a good deal of business with the store, so he might have simply attached his client's name to keep things straight."

"Mr. Buhner does a lot of business here?"

"Oh, sure. Mostly in trade. His wife simply can't get enough of our Americana collection," he gestured toward a corner that featured eagles and wooden items painted in red, white, and blue. Most were rather primitive wooden carvings, but there were also some fine examples of framed cross-stitch samplers and the like.

"This would be his wife, Karla, the Realtor?"

"That's her! You know her?"

"Sure, we go way back."

"Well as you know, she lives right around the corner. Darling place, and just about the cutest garden you'd ever like to see, isn't it?"

"*So* cute. It's right around the corner, you say?"

He nodded. "I just sold her a new whirligig: half the fins are red-and-white stripes, half are blue with white stars! As the kids would say, it's adorbs!"

I drove around one corner, but all I saw were standard suburban houses with standard suburban lawns. So I made a U-turn and went back the other way, and there it was: a midcentury ranch-style split-level with an American flag waving by the front door. The mailbox was carved to look like Uncle Sam, and the picket fence–enclosed garden featured mini-lighthouses and figurines of frolicking children and several whirligigs, one of which was painted in the stars and stripes.

None of this captured my attention, however. I was too distracted by the weathervane on the roof. It was shaped like a ship, and had a lovely copper patina.

Oh no they did *not*.

I stopped the car with a jolt and jumped out, passing through the cute little picket gate with nary a glance at the oh so Americana decorations. On the door was a brass knocker shaped like an eagle with its wings spread. I banged loudly.

I could hear voices, and then Karla swung the door wide. Her welcoming smile faded to a guilty, hangdog expression when she saw me.

"Mel," she said, breathless. "What are you—?"

"We need to have a conversation," I began, barging into the house. "Is Skip here?"

The contractor was lurking near the kitchen, looking just as chagrined as his wife. A hand-painted wooden sign over the doorway read KARLA'S KOUNTRY KITCHEN.

"Nice place you've got here," I said. "I would have figured you for a modern, Eichler-type home."

"There's a place for tradition," said Skip, puffing out his chest a little. "And in this, our great nation, we can all do with a little home-grown patriotism."

"I get the flags, but are you saying a purloined weathervane is somehow patriotic?"

Skip and Karla exchanged glances, and I lost my temper.

"I am *done*, do you hear me? Done with subterfuge and skulking and guilty looks. One woman has been brutally murdered, and someone made an attempt on my life, and I want somebody to start talking."

"We had nothing to do with any of that!" Karla gasped. "It's all a silly misunderstanding, really. Honestly. Now, let's all sit and have a cup of tea and talk."

"I'll skip the tea, but thanks." At this point I wouldn't put it past her to slip a little hemlock into my teacup.

"Please," she said, gesturing to a sofa upholstered in blue denim, adorned with a red-and-white-striped afghan. "Sit."

I sat. Karla and Skip perched in wing chairs on the other side of a low coffee table.

"All right, all right. It's true," Skip began. "I kept the weathervane for myself. It's just . . . They didn't want it, and I thought it would be perfect for Karla."

"I'll admit it," Karla said. "I'm an absolute *nut* for Americana!"

Skip winked at her, and she beamed.

"But . . . why didn't you *say* anything?" I asked. "I thought you wanted to speed up the sale of Crosswinds."

"I figured you'd find another one from the same era," Skip said. "How hard could it be? And then I wouldn't have to go into the whole story."

"You knew perfectly well I was trying to track down the original items from the house. Chantelle said—"

"Why does everyone believe that kook was right?" demanded Skip. "What I saw—" He cut himself off with a shake of the head.

"What did you see?"

He shook his head some more, and looked down at his hands, folded together almost primly on his knees.

"Please tell me, Skip. It might be important," I said.

"The ghost, or whatever it is." When he looked up at me, his eyes were shadowed. "I *heard* it. Yelling at us to get out, to leave. That's why . . . I put up those walls, hoping to close it in. I thought . . . I thought if I could just shut it all away, it wouldn't be able to get to anyone. And then Chantelle comes in and suddenly the Flynts are wanting to tear everything up. I knew it would be trouble. I *knew* it."

Chapter Twenty-six

"We tried our best to talk Chantelle into changing her mind, taking back what she said. It was all so absurd," said Karla, patting Skip's hands reassuringly.

"And yet you stole the weathervane," I pointed out.

"It really wasn't like that. That junk sat in the garage for months, and Andrew didn't want to deal with any part of it."

"So you set up the Crosswinds Collection auction at Uncle J's."

Skip shrugged. "I figured if we kept it exclusive to their mailing list, word wouldn't get out. No one comes over here from the other side of the tunnel."

"You invited Nancy, from Griega Salvage."

"We did?" He shrugged again. "Well, she didn't come. Proves my point."

"And did any of the Flynts work with you? The man at the shop mentioned a Mr. Flynt."

Skip shook his head. "That was just a formality. The only Flynt really interested in anything was Lacey, but even she didn't want to be saddled with getting rid of it all, though she did demand a cut of the profit."

I studied him for a moment, trying to discern whether or not he was telling me the truth.

"Okay, how about you skedaddle on up to the roof and bring that weathervane down."

"Couldn't you just put up a reproduction?" asked Karla. "All this emphasis on originals, it's absurd, really."

"It's probably for the best, sweetheart," said Skip as he rose and left the room to do my bidding. "I'm beginning to feel strange about having anything from that place in—or *on*—our home, anyway. It's . . . That Crosswinds is a bad place."

Skip left Karla and me staring at each other for an awkward moment.

"Do you have any more photos from Crosswinds?"

She looked guilty again, and hesitated.

"Karla, please just give me all that you have. I'll take them back to Crosswinds. I think this might be part of what stirred up the ghost of Peregrine Summerton—people have been removing his photographs."

She pressed her lips together. "If he didn't want people to take them, he shouldn't be sprinkling them about the house."

I saw her logic, but I wasn't sure Peregrine—or any ghost—was totally in charge of what he managed to manipulate in the material world, much less how the effects might be experienced by the living. But at this point I wasn't willing to discuss the intricacies of crossing the veil with Karla Buhner.

"In any case," I said, "I'd like to bring back all the photos I can."

She crossed over to a rolltop desk and extracted a large manila envelope. As she handed it to me, she asked, "Do *you* think Crosswinds is a bad place?"

"No." I was rather fond of the huge old mansion. "Old

buildings are like people. Crosswinds has a lot of unre-
solved issues, but then so do a lot of us."

She tittered nervously.

"What do *you* think about all of this, Karla? Who
might have killed Chantelle?"

"Oh, oh I couldn't! My, my," she blushed and wouldn't
meet my eyes.

"It seems like it's somehow embarrassing to you?" I
was fishing; I couldn't quite figure out her reaction.

"Why would *I* know anything about the embezzling?"

"I'm sorry? Embezzling?"

"I thought you were talking about . . . the embezzling." She blushed some more.

"What embezzling?"

"At Tempus, Ltd. Oh dear, did I say something
wrong?"

Skip Buhner's boots tread heavily on the roof above
our heads. I could hear the wood shingles cracking.

"What embezzling would that be?"

She waved a hand in the air, then stroked a pillow
embroidered with a train and yet another eagle. "It's all
just silly gossip. Stephanie was very upset, because apparently there were allegations of someone skimming
off the books at Tempus. And somehow it had to do with
Chantelle."

"How? How would Chantelle have any access to
Tempus finances?"

"I simply have no idea. Really, I've told you all I know,
and so much more than I should have."

There was a great deal of thumping and the sound of
splitting wood overhead. I looked at the ceiling, wondering if I should offer to help.

Karla smiled brightly.

"Well, now," she said. "He'll just box that weathervane right up for you, and you can be on your way. The sooner you finish up at Crosswinds, the sooner we can put the house back on the market!"

I stopped by Mi Pueblo for the provisions Dad had requested, and arrived home to find the air redolent with corn *masa* and spices, reminding me of the Mission District.

Stan, Dad, and Luz were in the kitchen with Sinsi and Venus and Eddie, filling corn husks with *masa* and meat in a red sauce, then wrapping them up. Dog wagged his tail, on high alert for any and all edible items—and "edible" was a loose term—that might hit the floor. He took a quick break to greet me with enthusiasm, and then returned to scrap patrol.

"Hey, Mel," said Dad. "Venus here tells me there are sweet tamales with raisins and pineapple and coconut in them. You believe that?"

"Yeah, I've heard that," I said, putting the bags on the counters.

"Oh, great," said Eddie, rooting through the bags. "We needed more corn husks."

"And some tamales are wrapped in banana leaves instead of corn husks," Dad continued. "Whaddaya make of that?"

"I guess you use what you have at hand, right? So how many tamales are we making?" I asked no one in particular, eyeing the already huge pile of yet-to-be-steamed tamales.

"These are chicken but we're also making pork," said Venus. "And I promised your dad if we had extra I'd show him a couple of sweet variations—he's got some raisins in the drawer."

"And I'm guessing that's why he requested a pineapple?" I asked as I drew the spiky fruit out of the paper bag.

"Ah, perfect!"

Stan and I shared a smile. There was nothing Dad liked better than complaining about having to cook, and then cooking for a big group. Especially if he could make it a group project.

A quick peek in the living room confirmed Dad had brought out our old family camping gear: sleeping bags and foam mats. A bed had been made up on the couch—I recognized Caleb's flannel comforter.

Diego and Carmen were sitting at the dining room table giving Caleb advice on his college applications. By the way Caleb was looking at Carmen I was pretty sure he already had developed a crush on the young woman. She was probably only a year or two older than he, now that I thought about it. I still hadn't gotten used to the fact that my ex-stepson was very nearly old enough to vote.

"Oh, Dad. I invited my friend Trish to come by."

"Don't know if we'll have enough to eat," he said.

Not only would there be far more than any of us could eat, he was probably going to wind up inviting the whole neighborhood soon.

"So, I was thinking," I said as I sat down next to Luz, grabbed a corn husk, and made a little boat out of the soft *masa*. "What if their landlady knows perfectly well that there's a ghost in that place? Dingo knew about it, after all."

"Who's Dingo?"

"Little old man who works at Olivier's Ghost Shoppe."

"Ah."

"Wait," said Sinsi. "So you think maybe she *knows* there's a ghost, and that's why it's cheap?"

"I wondered about that. That blows," said Venus.

"Maybe not just that," I continued. "Call me a cynic, but what if she knows the renters will go fleeing into the night, and she gets to keep first month, last, and security deposits?"

"That would be a pretty low-down thing to do," said Luz.

"Yep. It would," I agreed. "But she seems awfully hard to get ahold of. Keeping herself scarce for some reason, maybe?"

Luz nodded. "Okay, clearly we need to track her down and make her give the money back."

"Maybe," I said, wrapping up the tamale and starting on another. "Or . . . maybe we should have the students sign a four-year lease at that below market rate, and then get rid of the ghost so the students can live there in peace. Let the landlady feel a little of the pain."

"I like the way you think," she said with a grin.

"What's that rattling sound?" I asked.

"The penny at the bottom of the pot," Dad said. "You put a penny in the water for the tamales, and when it's nearly gone the penny starts to rattle. Let's you know the tamales are almost done."

"That's clever."

"Sure as heck is. Who needs the newfangled stuff when there's good old human ingenuity?"

Dad and Eddie launched into a discussion of simple ways of doing things versus "newfangled" ways. It was on the tip of my tongue to point out to Eddie the irony of such views coming from someone desperate to get his iPod back, but reconsidered. I was becoming as grumpy as my father could sometimes be.

Trish arrived, and said something in Spanish to the students, who burst into laughter and shouted in reply. Since my Spanish was limited to a little construction site vocabulary, the conversation left me behind pretty quickly. Still, it was fun to see Trish in a social setting. I knew she had traveled to Cuba and all over Latin America, and worked with Pastors for Peace and Doctors Without Borders. But I had never actually seen her outside the library.

"Where's my margarita?" Trish asked, turning to me. "We need to talk."

I couldn't wait to hear what she had found, so I fixed her a drink and we left the others to finish making the tamales while we went into my home office.

Trish had a big smile on her face.

"What is it?" I asked.

"I found her."

"Her? Her who?"

"Flora Summerton."

"Seriously?"

"I read the Rutherford letter you read, the one that describes how Flora ran away from her engagement ball when the clock struck midnight on her eighteenth birthday. And I got to wondering what she was running *to*. She might have gotten married, of course—"

"Wait—didn't the letter say Flora was in love with a sailor?"

"It did, but that seemed more like idle gossip to explain why Flora spent so much time on the widow's walk gazing out to sea. Think about it: Where would Flora have met a sailor? Young ladies of her social class did not hang out down at the docks. That got me wondering: If Flora wasn't up on the widow's walk looking for the ship bringing her lover home, what was she doing up there?"

"Getting a breath of fresh air?"

Trish laughed. "Maybe so. Or maybe she was imagining a different life for herself in a faraway land. People in the past weren't all that different from ourselves, Mel."

That was more true than Trish realized, I thought. "So what were her options?"

"How about missionary work?" Trish opened the file and handed me some photocopies. "I thought about her being a schoolteacher, or a nurse, then realized I might find a clue in the archives."

"I thought you said the Summerton family didn't leave many records?"

"They didn't—but family papers aren't the only kinds of records. So I looked up Peregrine Summerton's will. Turns out he was a big supporter of the American Board of Commissioners for Foreign Missions. For years he sent an annual donation and left the organization a substantial bequest. Then I checked the records of the church the Summertons attended, and what do you know: Flora was a member of the church's Missionary Sewing Circle, and helped to raise money for overseas missions. The ladies of the sewing circle were especially fond of supporting women missionaries. Nothing in the church records suggested Flora had gone on a mission, but there are large gaps in the records. So I dug a little deeper."

Trish paused and took a sip of her margarita, licking salt off the rim.

"You're amazing," I said.

"I'm a *librarian*."

"Well, then, librarians are amazing."

She smiled. "One of the databases the Historical Society subscribes to includes old newspapers devoted to covering overseas missions. I started reading the issues for the months after Flora's disappearance and finally found a reference to her in an article about missionaries in Hawaii."

"Flora went to Hawaii?"

"To Maui, to be precise."

"You're getting a kick out of this," I said, enjoying her enthusiasm.

"Flora Summerton must have been a gutsy young woman. Just imagine what it took for her to leave her home and everything she knew, and sail off into the sunset to a foreign land. I went back to the Rutherford Family Papers and read some of their earlier correspondence. Apparently the neighbors were buzzing about how disappointed Peregrine Summerton was in his sons. He was fond of saying that his daughter Flora was 'twice the man my boys should be.' "

"Yikes. Sounds like a fun family dynamic."

"Indeed."

"Did you find anything about Peregrine Summerton being a photographer?"

"Actually, yes!" She brought out a copy of a small handbill. "He had a show of photographs, right there in the ballroom. 'One hundred faces of Flora,' he called it. It was really much more about the wonders of photography than about Flora herself, but she was his favorite model. A young John Caruthers, heir to the copper-mining fortune, saw the show and fell in love with Flora. He asked for her hand in marriage right there and then, without even meeting her!"

"So Flora escaped her father's home and marriage to a man she didn't love, and made a life for herself in Hawaii?"

Trish nodded. "It turns out that she also became entitled to a small inheritance from her grandmother upon reaching her majority, which helps to explain why she waited until her birthday for her dramatic escape."

"Did Flora ever return home?"

"Good question. I wondered that myself." She handed me a photocopy of a pamphlet entitled *California*

Women of Distinction. "This little gem was published in 1910 to support the fight for women's suffrage in California. A library patron requested it, and I looked through it when she was done. It consists of a number of very short biographies, including several women missionaries. According to the pamphlet, Flora met a young American physician in Hawaii. They married, but she was widowed after only a year when he died of some sort of fever in the islands. Then she received a letter from Peregrine saying he was ill and wanted to see her, and take one more photo of her, before he died. He obviously knew where to find her, but had left her alone until he fell ill. Perhaps her dramatic exit led him to see the error of his ways."

"Or maybe he assumed a wife's first loyalty was to her husband."

"Quite possibly."

"Anyway, she sailed back to San Francisco, but never made it to Crosswinds. She was struck and killed running across California Street to catch the cable car."

"That's so sad. I mean, I know she's been dead a long time, but—what a waste."

Trish nodded. "Life was tough back then. Fevers, accidents, so-called 'childhood diseases' that killed tens of thousands of young people every year. And don't get me started on the dangers of childbirth."

"So Flora's been trying to get home, all this time," I mused.

"Pardon?"

"Nothing, never mind." I noticed she had also brought some newspaper clippings from the 1940s. "What are these?"

"Something else I thought you'd be interested in. That address your friend Luz was looking up? There was lots more to that story. As Luz discovered, a woman named

Suzanne White lived at that address and was known locally as the 'Pie Lady.'"

"That might explain why I smell pie there."

"Better than sulfur," grumbled Luz, who was now standing in the office doorway. "I heard my name. You found out more about Suzanne White?"

Trish nodded. "During WWII, while her husband was serving in the military overseas, Suzanne turned her love of baking into a part-time business, making pies, cupcakes, strudel, what have you. Kept her busy and supplemented the family income, I imagine. When her husband was badly wounded in battle, and came home in a wheelchair, the money the Pie Lady made was even more important."

"She must have been quite anxious about their future."

"Very likely. There weren't a lot of options for women who needed to support their families at this time; men were assumed to be the breadwinners and if a man was unwilling or unable to take on that role, then a family could be in serious trouble. Anyway, when Suzanne's husband passed away about a year after he came home, everyone assumed it was due to complications from his war injury."

"You think it may have been from something else?"

"I think it's possible. Not long after Suzanne's husband died, the neighbor across the street fell ill after eating one of the Pie Lady's pies. She died, too."

"You think Suzanne was poisoning people?"

Trish nodded. "Nothing was ever proved, but the neighbors were convinced of it. Check out these articles."

Luz came into the office and took a seat at Stan's desk, and Trish handed us photocopies of newspaper articles.

Mine looked like it came from a tabloid paper, the kind with large print and lots of exclamation points. Surrounding the story about Suzanne White were tales of out-of-wedlock celebrity sex and visitors from outer space.

"A tabloid? And you, a librarian ..."

"Hey, if you want idle gossip and conjecture, the *New York Times* won't help," Trish said with a shrug. "It's not enough to prove anything, of course, and in principle I can't support this kind of yellow journalism. But if you want to take the pulse of a community, read the tabloid newspapers."

According to the article, the neighbors suspected Suzanne White of having an affair with her across-the-courtyard neighbor while her husband was away fighting for his country. When he returned she continued with her pie business and quickly grew tired of taking care of her disabled husband. She fed him a poisoned pie—the article went on at length as to whether it was apple or strawberry-rhubarb—wore widow's weeds until his modest life insurance check cleared, then resumed her affair with the neighbor. A few months later the neighbor decided he wanted to break it off. Suzanne invited his wife over for coffee and pie. The wife became violently ill shortly thereafter, and died later than night.

She used to make the children cupcakes, but no one will take them now, the article quoted one neighbor as saying. *Still, she bakes. Every day.*

"But nothing was ever proved against her?" Luz asked.

Trish shook her head. "A couple of the neighbors contacted the police—including the husband of the woman who died—but they didn't find anything. Forensic techniques were pretty crude at the time. I couldn't find any notice of official charges."

"What happened to her in the end?"

She handed me another newspaper article.

Suzanne White, age 33, was found dead in her home at the Mermaid Cove Court apartment complex. Known to one and all in the neighborhood as the Pie Lady, she was widely believed to have been a murderess! Mrs. White's husband, a proud American G.I., survived terrible wounds sustained defending his country in the recent war only to be felled by the treachery of his wife, a greedy adulteress! Not content with burying her brave husband for the insurance money, Mrs. White is believed to have poisoned the wife of the man with whom she carried on the adulterous affair when he, realizing the depths of her wanton depravity, inevitably spurned her love. Soon even the neighborhood children refused to partake of her baked goods though she spent hours in her kitchen no doubt to distract herself from her evil deeds. The Pie Lady's dreadful corpse was discovered yesterday in her kitchen, a rolling pin by her side. This reporter was able to learn that she had died some days previous, and the natural course of decomposition rendered the identification more difficult. According to eyewitnesses, the police found an apple pie on the kitchen table, with but a single slice missing, and one dessert plate and fork in the dish drainer. Another pie still in the oven had burnt to a crisp! The neighbors at Mermaid Cove are breathing a sigh of relief that the deeds of a murderess most foul will no longer haunt their comfortable abodes.

"Quite a story, isn't it?" Trish asked.

"She killed herself, after killing her husband and her lover's wife?" Luz asked.

"Who knows? That's certainly what the neighbors thought. Gossip is often wrong—but a lot of the time it's right on the money."

"So you're saying the apartment is being haunted by the ghost of the Pie Lady, who used to *poison* people?" asked Eddie.

I looked up to see Eddie, Sinsi, and Carmen lurking in the doorway, listening in. Dog pushed his way past the bottleneck, but upon noting we weren't eating anything, he went back out to scout the kitchen.

"Um, yeah. It looks that way," I said.

"I'm sorry . . . ?" said Trish. "Did you say 'haunted'?"

I realized I wasn't fully out to Trish. Time to come clean.

"You know how I'm forever looking up the histories of the houses I'm working on? It's partly for the sake of architecture, and partly because I have a little side business wherein I put ghosts to rest."

Trish looked at me appraisingly, as though to assess whether or not I was kidding. Then her gaze flickered over to Luz, and the others.

"Cool," she said finally.

Dad, who was now looking over the students' shoulders to see what the commotion was all about, snorted.

Chapter Twenty-seven

After we had all eaten our fill of tamales—and rice and beans, of course, and guacamole and chips and margaritas and lemonade—we sat around the dining room table, digesting.

"I was thinking . . ." I began.

"Serious trouble," grumbled Dad.

"Maybe we should go and try to talk to the Pie Lady. Maybe kick some ghost butt. What do you think?"

"I think that's the margarita talking," said Luz.

The students exchanged glances. "We were kind of thinking of watching a movie."

"Hey, it's okay by me if you all want to sleep on Dad's floor forever, but *somebody* asked me to get rid of a ghost, so that's what I intend to do. Besides, if this ghost is the type to kill off her husband and neighbors with poisoned pie, I have very little sympathy for her. Time to send that nasty piece of work on, let her get started cleaning the big kitchen in the sky."

"Fine," said Dad. "Let's go."

"Let's?"

"We're not gonna let you run around chasing down

homicidal ghosts all by yourself. It's the middle of the night."

"But it's okay if I do it in the middle of the day?"

"There are limits."

"Wait," said Venus. "A friend of mine gave me a sage bundle. You should take it, just in case."

"What's that for?" asked Diego.

"You 'smudge' the room with it. Supposed to get all the bad juju out of the corners," Sinsi explained. "They do it on the ghost shows on TV."

"Well then," I said. "It's good enough for me. Hand it over."

In the end Dad, Stan, Caleb, the students, and Luz joined me. Only Trish bowed out, saying that while she could accept the idea of my ghost-hunting ways, she didn't particularly want any part of it. Which I understood.

Also, we left Dog at home; I didn't need his special sense to prove there was a ghost at the Mermaid apartments. At least this time I was pretty sure I knew whom—and what—I was dealing with.

On the way over, on a hunch, I stopped at Safeway and picked up an apple pie.

Our convoy arrived at the apartment complex. I had nine folks backing me up, like a ghost-hunting posse. Trouble was, I barely knew what I was doing; I certainly didn't know what to do with all my helpers.

"Okay, why don't you guys wait out here for the time being?" I suggested. "Let me see if I can talk to her. Now that I know her name and some of her story, maybe she'll be willing to have a chat."

"She's a murderess, don't forget," said Dad. His insistence on using the old-fashioned *-ess* on the end of the word cracked me up. But I appreciated his concern.

"*Alleged* murderess," I said. "And anyway, ghosts can't hurt people."

I was almost sure about that. They could certainly scare a person, and every once in a while there might be dangers posed, but the more I was around ghosts the more I realized: *We* are the ones who freak ourselves out. The ghosts are just being themselves, carrying on with their lives—or afterlives—the only way they know how. Often they aren't even aware of the effect they're having on the live people around them.

"Anyway," I said. "Hang out here and I'll shout if I need you."

I stroked the ring at my neck and took a few deep breaths to ground myself. Then I walked into the apartment, pie held high in one hand, my toolbox—including the sage bundle—in the other.

"*Helloooo?* Mrs. White? I brought pie."

The apartment was silent and seemed vaguely sinister in the dark shadows. I crossed through the living room and flicked on the lights in the kitchen.

As I had expected, the silverware drawer had been replaced, all the cutlery picked up. The kitchen was spotless.

I set the pink cardboard box on the little breakfast table, then rummaged through a few cupboards and found a pile of mismatched dishes, took out a chipped ceramic plate with a picture of a rooster, and placed the pie on it.

Then I found a knife and cut two slices of pie. I put them on small dessert plates.

"Anyone hungry?" I asked. "It's store-bought, which is a shame. Nothing like homemade, am I right?"

The aroma of a fresh apple pie began to waft through the kitchen. Now we were getting somewhere.

I was stuffed from the tamale feast, and truth to tell the grocery store pie didn't look all that appetizing. But I was here with a purpose. A ghost buster doesn't shirk her duty.

Sitting at the table, I took a bite of pie. No reaction.

I was hyperaware of the folks waiting for me right outside the front door, and of the fact that I really didn't know what to say to Suzanne White. If what the neighbors had said was true, then she was probably unhinged. Maybe she always had been; maybe the stress of taking care of an injured husband with very limited resources had simply become too much, and she had snapped. Or maybe the whole thing was a terrible misunderstanding.

I was halfway through the pie when I heard dishes clattering inside the cupboard above the refrigerator. It was too high to reach, so I looked around for a step stool. I checked the little gap by the refrigerator, and then a small utility closet right outside the kitchen.

As I reentered the kitchen, the remaining apple pie sailed through the air, landing with a splat against a cabinet.

"Hey!" I yelled. "I hope you know you're going to have to clean that up."

Lame, Mel. Of course she would. That's what she did with her time. Which, apparently, was all of eternity.

"Anyway, that was just rude. Mrs. White? I want to talk with you. Please, could you tell me why you're here?"

The refrigerator door banged open and a plate with some dubious-looking leftovers sailed past my right shoulder and shattered against the sink. At least she had a bad pitching arm. "Mel, are you all right in there?" Dad shouted from the doorway.

"Yes, Dad, I'm fine. Please shut the door and stay outside unless I call you."

Eggs started flying out of the carton, one after the other. I was so busy ducking that I slipped in some apple pie that had slid down a cabinet and onto the floor.

I fell on the linoleum with a thud. Now I was mad.

"Hey! *Knock it off!* You don't belong here anymore. Do you understand me? You are not alive. Your body has passed. You DO NOT BELONG HERE."

There was a pause. Maybe I was getting to her.

An egg smashed onto my head. "Ow!"

I was prostrate on the floor, flour raining down upon me, then milk, then whatever else the supernatural scamp could find in the refrigerator. It was a phantom food fight and I was on the losing end.

I still hadn't seen a vision of Mrs. White. For some reason it seemed important that she appear to me. Ignoring the deluge of food as best I could, I rubbed my grandmother's ring, centered myself, and reconfirmed my resolve.

"*Suzanne White.* You are accused of poisoning your husband and your neighbor! Is this true?"

The barrage of food abruptly ceased. I slowly got to my feet and looked around.

"Mrs. White? May I call you Suzanne? Please talk to me, Suzanne. I want to hear your side of the story."

And she appeared. The image was flickering, like a ghost one might see in a movie. As though she was having a hard time manifesting, possibly because she had used up a lot of her supernatural energy throwing food at me.

She was a pretty woman in a simple blue dress and a starched white apron. Her short brown hair was set and she wore bright red lipstick. She reminded me of photographs of my grandmother in her kitchen, back when proud housewives used to dress up to cook.

Mrs. White looked decidedly peeved.

"Look at this mess!" she exclaimed, reaching for a sponge.

"Don't blame me," I said. "Don't you remember? You did this."

No answer. She had her back to me, scrubbing the sink.

Now what?

"Mrs. White. Do you know that you died? You are no longer of this world. It is time for you to leave, to move on. Get out of here."

Her scrubbing became even more frenetic. When she spoke, it was as though she were talking to herself.

"I've got to get everything just so. The kitchen is the soul of the home. The kitchen must be spotless and *don't let the pie burn or I'll beat you to within an inch of your life!*"

The aroma of apple pie ceded to the stench of smoke, and Suzanne disappeared.

"Suzanne? Mrs. White? Please listen to me." I lit the sage bundle and started to walk around the kitchen, smudging the corners. I had no idea if this would have any effect, but it gave me something to do. "I think you've done some things you aren't proud of, but you don't have to be afraid anymore. Your life was difficult, but it is over now. Your body no longer exists, your life here has ended. Do you understand me?"

Something rattled in the cupboard over the refrigerator again. This was the cupboard Eddie told me he couldn't open. I took a hammer and chisel out of my toolbox.

My father always warned me against climbing on chairs, but I didn't have a lot of choice. I dragged one of the kitchen chairs over to the refrigerator, stood on it, and reached for the cupboard doors.

I was doused with a cold liquid from behind and tee-tered on the rickety chair, but I tried to ignore it.

The cupboard doors had been painted shut with several thick coats of paint, and clearly hadn't been opened in years. I jammed the tip of my chisel into the crack between the cabinet door and the frame, and hit the end with the hammer. The paint in the crack began to split, and I moved the tool over an inch. After several minutes of this—during which I tried my best to ignore the things Suzanne White was throwing around the kitchen—I was able to apply enough force to pop the cabinet door open.

Inside were several metal canisters, labeled SUGAR, FLOUR, COFFEE, TEA, and BAKING SODA. They were old, blackened with dirt and grime.

"Hey, Suzanne. Were these yours?"

The havoc in the kitchen ceased and Suzanne reappeared, wringing a dish towel in her hands. "Mustn't open those!"

"Is this what you're trying to hide?" I carefully stepped off the chair and placed the sugar canister on the counter. I used the chisel to pop the top off. Inside was a substance that, as far as I could tell, was regular old sugar. A little caked and lumpy, but otherwise white and crystalline.

Suzanne's eyes were huge, as though terrified. If she really had poisoned her husband and a neighbor, could one of these canisters hold the poison? It would take a little lab work to figure it out, and since Suzanne White was long gone, I wasn't sure I was willing to pay to find out the absolute truth.

"How about I get rid of these?" I offered, getting back up on the chair and bringing down the rest of the canisters. Behind them, in the far back, was an ancient package of rat poison. "And . . . the rat poison?"

"I—" Her eyes were huge, and she looked mortified. "I'm so sorry, I'm so so so sorry! Please, I'll clean the kitchen, I'll make it spotless, I won't burn the pie.... *Please!*"

"Mrs. White," I said in the firmest voice I could muster, while still trying to sound sympathetic. "Listen to me, Suzanne: You will no longer clean this kitchen. I know your secret now, so you don't have to worry about it anymore. No more pies, you understand? You are free. I will take care of it, I will clean it, I promise. I will clean up everything, even the cupboard over the refrigerator."

Slowly and deliberately, the ghost reached behind her waist and untied her apron. She hung it on a hook by the sink. She smoothed her hair and her skirt, and stalked out of the kitchen.

And disappeared.

Chapter Twenty-eight

"What the hell happened to you?" Dad asked as I emerged from the cottage. I had been doused with flour and milk and a variety of condiments, and I had egg in my hair. But I was smiling.

"Are you okay?" asked Venus.

"Yeah, you look pretty bad," said Caleb.

"Yes, well, what can I tell you? This ghost busting is a messy business."

Nonetheless, I was triumphant. I felt as though Suzanne White had moved on, which meant that I set out to rid the apartment of a ghost, and I had succeeded. And there weren't even any bodies associated with this place. Other than those long dead, that is.

"I think she's gone."

"You mean gone, gone?"

I nodded. "Put up a bit of a fight, but I think she had been hiding her supplies in that cupboard over the refrigerator. I brought the things down, told her I would take care of them, and then told her to leave. And she did."

"After covering you in foodstuffs?" asked Stan.

"She was trying to make herself known. Ghosts don't have much choice as to how they communicate with the living. They can't manipulate things the way we do, so sometimes it's . . . unexpected."

As I spoke, I thought about the Crosswinds ghosts. When Peregrine was yelling at me, was he trying to protect me? To get me off the roof for my own good? Could he be trying to keep me from discovering something dangerous in the darkroom?

"Looks to me like this particular ghost was pretty good at manipulating things," Dad snorted.

"So what do we do now?" asked Carmen.

"I'll meet you guys here tomorrow and we'll do some cleaning. Not just regular cleaning—and there's a big mess in the kitchen, I have to warn you—but also spiritual. We'll use the smudge bundle, and sweep everything outside and then burn the broom. And ring a bell in all the corners."

"What's with the bell?" asked Luz.

It struck me as funny that the gang went along with the crazy ghost who throws food but drew the line at ringing a bell.

"Some people say it breaks up old energy, making it easier to dispel. Not sure if I believe that, but it couldn't hurt."

"I don't know if I even want to go back in that place," murmured Carmen.

"Yeah," Caleb said, nodding sympathetically. "It's creepy."

"That's why we're doing the spiritual cleansing. It gets rid of all that weird juju, and then you can fill up the apartment with the joyful vibrations of youth."

They continued to look at me like I was suggesting they play with doggy-doo-doo.

"Tell you what, guys, you wanted my help. It's the

middle of the night, I look and feel like a baking experiment gone horribly wrong, and I'm suggesting we be sure this place is clean and ghost-free by taking a few extra steps. And besides, do you have any idea how hard egg is to clean up once it's dried on?"

"In that case, why don't we take care of it tonight?" suggested Luz. "Why wait until morning?"

Because some of us habitually get up at five a.m., I thought. But Luz was right: The students were clearly night owls, and there was no time like the present.

"Well, Stan, I think our work here is done," said Dad.

"You're not going to help with the cleanup?" I teased. "I thought you were my backup."

"We were," said Stan. "And we fulfilled our job description: You have emerged from the fracas battered but not dead. Get it? Battered? Flour, milk, and egg . . . ?"

I groaned. "What *is* it with the puns lately? Okay, fine, go home you two, and get some sleep. If I'm not mistaken there's a pretty messy kitchen to clean up at home, as well."

Luz and the students got started in the kitchen while I took a few minutes in the bathroom, trying to rid myself of the worst of the food residue. After that, it took us over an hour, but Diego hooked his iPod up to speakers and the kitchen cleanup was actually fun. Caleb and Carmen were whispering and giggling, Sinsi rocked a karaoke version of "Total Eclipse of the Heart," and Eddie turned out to be a scrubbing machine.

We ended the process by turning off the music and reclaiming the house, sweeping out every room as the students proclaimed in loud voices that this was their place, and ringing the bell in each corner. Finally, we burned the broom in an old barbecue pit in the tiny backyard.

By the time we had finished it was nearly two in the

morning, and as we gathered around the fire pit I wondered if the neighbors would see and wonder if a coven had moved in.

Gazing at the fire, Luz said, "Shouldn't we say something? You know, to her memory?"

"She killed two people!" said Sinsi.

"Allegedly," I felt compelled to say. "Not to excuse what she might have done, but I think she had a tough time of it. She was tortured by her fears—from what she said, her husband might have been abusive—and then maybe her guilt. Plus, she's been trying to make sure no one accidentally got into her poison stash," I said, thinking of the canisters sitting in a cardboard box in the back of my dad's truck. He had promised to take them to the hazardous waste dump on Monday.

I wasn't certain Suzanne White was sorry, or that she even fully comprehended what she had done—assuming she was guilty as charged. All I knew for sure was that it had happened a long time ago, and whatever judgment Suzanne White would be subject to was not an earthly one. At the very least, I thought, I had helped her move on to a place where she could face the consequences, or come back and try again, or whatever the next step was for us.

"Suzanne White," I intoned. "May you move on and find solace, peace, and serenity, and the opportunity to right whatever wrongs you may have committed."

"In a galaxy far, *far* away," added Diego.

"*Amen,*" we said in unison.

"So what do we do about the landlady?" Luz asked around a yawn. It was two thirty in the morning, and we were sitting in her car chatting. Claiming that stress made her hungry, Luz was eating one of the dozen tamales my father had wrapped up for her to take home.

At the moment I was certain I would never eat again; though I figured that sensation would wear off tomorrow right around lunchtime.

"Tell her if she doesn't sign an extended lease at the current low rate we'll sic the ghost on her. Tell her I'm a professional, and I say ghosts aren't put off by post office boxes."

"Hmm. All right, I'll send her a note tomorrow. And I will threaten her with ghosts." She took a swig of mineral water. "Now *that* is a phrase I never thought I'd utter."

"Luz, my friend, we've been through a lot together."

"Meaning?"

"You should tell me about your ghost experience. Because I *know* something happened to you. And if you don't tell me . . . I'm going to take home all the tamales."

"Your dad would kill you, and then bring them back anyway."

"True."

There was a long pause. I gazed out the window, but there was nothing to see at this hour, even on a Saturday night. The bars in San Francisco close at two, so the only folks on the streets were working the swing shift, or sneaking into after parties, or up to no good. But Mermaid Cove Court was quiet as a tomb.

Finally, Luz said, "When I was little, I was really close to my grandmother, my *abuelita*. She got sick, but no one told me."

"How old were you?"

"Five, maybe? Or six, I guess. . . . I was in the first grade. The thing is . . . I kept seeing her. She would come after school to meet me at the gate, and walk me home. I was so happy to see her, she used to have trouble walking but now she was able to go everywhere with me. One day we went to the park, and had long conversations about life, and her favorite flowers—lilies of the valley.

It was all in Spanish, which was why I thought other people couldn't understand her. And when these older kids tried to beat me up, she intervened and they ran away. She was my hero."

I smiled. "Grandmas are the best."

"I adored her," she said with a nod. "But when I came home, my mother and a bunch of my aunties and cousins and neighbors were there—they had been looking everywhere for me, they thought I'd gone missing. I told them *abuelita* had taken me to the park, that she was much better now. They started crossing themselves, and one of the neighbors called me a *bruja*, a witch."

She had tears in her eyes.

"Then, my cousin turns to me and says, '*Abuelita died*, dummy.' Apparently she had died the weekend before. They thought I was too young, so no one told me. When I insisted I had just been with her, they told me I had seen something *evil*, unnatural."

I wanted to reach out and comfort Luz, but knowing her as I did, a hug would be exactly the wrong thing to do right now. "That must have been pretty traumatic."

"My mother was shaken, I could see that. She didn't know what to think. But in the end I learned my lesson: When *abuelita* appeared to me again, I ran away, screaming and crying. I *learned* to be scared, I suppose."

"This is hard stuff to comprehend, Luz. Everybody has a different take on it, depending on their religion, their life philosophy, the way they're raised. . . ."

"I know, but—I'll never forget the look in her eye when I ran away from her. It was like I broke her heart. Now, seeing what you do with spirits, I wonder . . . Do you think she was looking for help?"

"It's hard to say. Probably she just wasn't ready to leave you."

"And I screamed and ran away."

"Don't be so hard on yourself, Luz. You were only a little girl. Don't you think your grandmother understood? And if you haven't seen anything since then, you probably don't have a particular sensitivity. It's likely she manifested because she hadn't had a chance to say good-bye to you."

She nodded and finished off the tamale, the emotional upset apparently having no effect on her appetite.

"Hey, I have an idea," I said.

"Like your father would say: That's serious trouble."

"Cute. You and he really are quite the pair. Anyway, want to join me on a stakeout one night soon?"

She groaned. "I just spent tonight going up against a kitchen ghost! Wasn't that enough to redeem myself?"

"Since *I* was the one getting egged, no, I don't think it was enough. Also, I got the students out of your house, so you owe me one."

She let out a big sigh. "I don't like stakeouts. I always wind up having to pee. Guys have a definite advantage in that regard."

"True. But nonetheless, I will pick you up Monday night, nine-ish? Just don't drink a lot beforehand."

When the phone rang the next morning, I let it go to voice mail. After all, it was Sunday. My crews had the day off, so theoretically so did I. Although, since I work for myself, and the office is in the house, I often wound up spending Sundays catching up on paperwork that didn't get done the previous week, and anticipating the schedule for the next.

But last night, when I crawled into bed well after three in the morning after ejecting a kitchen ghost from the Mermaid Cove apartment and standing in the shower for a half hour trying to get egg out of my hair, I had decided that I wouldn't work this Sunday. It had been an exhaust-

ing week. In addition to my construction work I'd con-
fronted two ghosts and almost been killed and felt
attracted to a man other than my boyfriend.

I needed a day off.

Too bad said boyfriend wasn't flying in from New
York until tomorrow night. I could only imagine how
pleased Graham would be if I suggested we take in a
matinee or pack a picnic. As I lolled in bed and tried to
convince myself to go back to sleep, I thought about going to the beach. I lived in California, after all. People did
things like that.

The phone rang again. *Don't look don't look don't. . . .*
I couldn't stand it. I opened one eye and checked the
screen: Annette Crawford.

Dammit.

"'Lo," I croaked.

"I thought you were an early riser."

"I am, normally, but last night was a little . . . active."

"Hold it right there. I really don't need to hear about
your sex life."

"Believe me—it wasn't *that* kind of active."

"Did somebody try to kill you again?" she asked, her
voice taking on a serious tone.

"I wouldn't have put it past her, had she been able.
She threw eggs and stuff at me. And a pie."

Annette chuckled. "Who was this? One of the Flynts?
Let me guess: Lacey?"

"No. It was a ghost at that apartment complex I told
you about."

"I thought you told me ghosts couldn't hurt you?"

"She didn't hurt me, exactly. . . ."

"But they can throw things?"

"As I think I've made clear, I don't really know what
the ghost rules are. But this one did, indeed, manage to
throw foodstuffs. But what I'd like to focus on is that

she's gone now, and I didn't find a single body. She probably killed a couple of people, but it was a long time ago."

"Okay, I'm going to let that one go for the moment, because I have my hands full. Could you meet me at Chantelle's apartment?"

I groaned.

"What, you have something better to do?" she demanded.

"I was going to the beach."

"Which one?"

"I hadn't gotten that far with my thinking. It just seemed like something people do on their day off."

Another chuckle. "When's the last time you went to the beach, here or any other place?"

There was a long pause while I thought. "High school, maybe? No, wait—college!"

"You are pathetic. You're a workaholic, like me. Might as well face it."

I checked the clock and blew out a breath. "Okay, I can meet you there in an hour. Should I bring any special ghost stuff?"

"Do you *have* any special ghost stuff?"

"Not really. I accidentally dropped the EMF reader in the toilet, and I've never really gotten the hang of the infrared camera. But I could go by the ghost supply shop if you think it would help."

"Nah, it's not that sort of thing. I just wanted your take on a few of the items we found at her place. If Chantelle decides to appear to you, great, but it's not about that."

We signed off.

Chapter Twenty-nine

There was no one in the lobby when I arrived.

"Gabe?" I called, then realized that the man probably didn't work here twenty-four/seven. Probably there were other people on staff—and most likely one of them had run to park another guest's car.

Just then I sensed something out of the corner of my eye, an arm going up . . .

I whirled around, dropping the bag I was carrying and crouching slightly the way I'd seen Landon do.

But it was just Gabe in the small side corridor, doing some sort of Tai-Chi thing, apparently so focused he didn't hear me come in or call for him.

I took a couple of deep breaths and tried to relax. My heart pounded, and my bones ached. I don't do well with too little sleep.

"You okay?" Gabe asked, picking up the bag I dropped.

"Sure," I croaked, exchanging my keys for the bag.

"S'okay," he said with a shrug. "Everybody's been on edge since the murder. Lot of blood."

Annette walked in. Her intelligent eyes flickered from

my face to Gabe's, then back to me. "Everything all right?"

"Sure," said Gabe.

I nodded.

"Let's go," she said to me, and Gabe watched as we got in the elevator.

"I'm going to assume you checked him out?" I asked as the car sped silently up nine floors.

"Gabe? Of course. We have a pretty good idea of when Chantelle was killed, because you called and talked with her, and her brother arrived at two fifty. Gabe was on the security cam the whole time, except when he ran for cars. I think he's just weird."

"Is that a professional assessment?"

"Yes, indeed."

"Oh, hey, these are for you," I said, handing her the bag.

"What is it?"

"Tamales. Be careful, a couple of them have pineapple in them. I tried to stop it from happening, but I was outmaneuvered."

She smiled. "Thank you. I love tamales."

"So tell me what you want me to look for in Chantelle's apartment."

"I'd rather not. I was hoping you could just see if you saw anything you found pertinent, first, so I don't color your expectations."

The elevator doors slid open and we headed down the hall to the right. Crime scene tape had once crisscrossed Chantelle's door, but it now hung down in limp strips.

"That doesn't bode well. . . ." Annette murmured, her hand hovering over the gun in her holster.

She gestured to me to stay where I was, out in the hall, then stood to the side of the door, her back to the wall. She leaned over to turn the knob and pushed open the door.

"SFPD," she called. "Police! Anybody here?"

Silence. Finally she peeked around the doorframe, then entered with caution, her gun drawn.

"Police!" I heard her call again. I could hear a door opening and some muted thumping from inside the apartment. And then, silence.

"Annette?"

I peeked my head around the corner. When I didn't see anything, I crept inside.

"I told you to wait outside," Annette said from behind me.

I jumped. "I was . . . just making sure you were okay."

Her mouth kicked up in a half smile. "I'm the one with the gun, remember?"

I nodded. "Did you find anything?"

"No, but it looks like the place has been gone through. I gotta say, I don't think this building has what you'd call a crack security team. There's a camera in the lobby, but the ones on the back door and the garage weren't working when Chantelle was killed."

The mess on the floor where Chantelle had lain had not yet been cleaned up. I had learned on my first murder scene that when a crime takes place on private property, it is up to the homeowners to bring in the crime scene cleanup folks. Sometimes they had to replace carpets and wallboard to get the bloodstains out. My early-morning coffee churned in my gut.

"What do you suppose they were looking for?" I asked.

"The same thing I was hoping you'd see," she said. "Which is: I don't know. I was hoping you might see something out of place, something that might serve as a clue."

We spent the next several minutes looking around, but saw nothing suspicious, nothing that might tell me anything.

Neither did I see Chantelle. I had really been hoping she might appear, send a sign, throw a pie, anything.

And then my eyes alighted on a silver frame hanging over Chantelle's desk. It held a sepia-toned photograph of a young woman holding an Italian half mask up to her face. A little Post-it note stuck to the frame had the name, Flora, along with a series of dates, written in purple ink.

"Every couple of weeks for the past few months," Annette said, reading the dates on the note. "Mean anything to you?"

"I think it's possible that Chantelle saw Flora Summerton's ghost walking on California Street."

"You wanna back up and explain that sentence to me?"

I gave Annette the rundown, as best I understood it, of Flora, the hitchhiking ghost. "I saw her myself the other day, and it occurred to me that her favorite stretch of California is awfully close to Chantelle's apartment. If Chantelle was as gifted a psychic as everyone seems to think, it's not hard to imagine she encountered Flora's ghost."

"So you think she finagled this job, somehow, to get into Crosswinds and figure out how to get Flora home? Seems rather convoluted, without a lot of payoff."

"When you say it like that, it does sound a little far-fetched. But . . . maybe it all just came together, like it was meant to be."

Annette looked worried. "I can handle the fact that we're discussing ghosts as though we're rational people, but you start throwing around phrases like 'meant to be' and I might have to strangle you."

"Got it. Annette, would it be all right to take the photo back to Crosswinds? I have a theory that one of the things that has stirred up the ghost there is that people have been removing these photographs."

She nodded. "Sure."

"Thanks. Anyway, I don't really see anything else—"

On a bureau was a bright batik scarf, full of Caribbean flowers. I picked it up, the silk soft in my hands.

"This looks familiar . . . ," I said.

Annette nodded. "Egypt's scarf, right? She has been high on the list of persons of interest."

"You think she was here, looking for something?"

"Could well be. Egypt and Chantelle, after meeting at Crosswinds, formed an interesting kind of partnership."

"Seriously? Chantelle certainly knew how to make friends and influence people. She must work fast; it wasn't that long ago she did the reading on the house, was it?"

"Almost a month. A lot can happen in a month."

"Do you think all this has something to do with allegations of embezzlement at Tempus?"

"What makes you think that?"

"Karla Buhner mentioned Stephanie was upset about it."

Annette nodded slowly. "And on top of that, someone hacked into the Tempus computer system."

"Was it Egypt?"

"Not sure. But apparently she's quite the computer whiz. She wouldn't give us access to her room, though, and because of her association with Chantelle and Chantelle's connection to the Flynts and Tempus, Ltd., I was hoping to get a warrant to take a look at her computers. But . . ."

"But?"

"She was found down by Fisherman's Wharf. Hit and run."

"*What?* When?"

"Last night. She's in serious condition, hasn't been able to talk to us yet. Witnesses saw a black truck, no markings. Only a partial license plate. Not much to go on."

I let that one sink in for a moment.

"Who brought the allegations of embezzlement at Tempus?"

"Official questions were raised during a routine audit, but there were whispers before that. It's quite a money-making place, lots of cash changing hands, so it's hard to pinpoint what's going on. The Flynts have not exactly been cooperative. You're right, by the way: that Stephanie is a piece of work."

"You talked to her again?"

She nodded. "She tried spouting a bunch of Buddhist crap, but lost it when I pushed her."

I had to smile. "Buddhist 'crap'?"

"I'm just saying, if you walk the walk I respect you. If you use it as a shield to hide behind, it's crap. Anyway, it turns out Andrew was having an affair with Chantelle. And get this: George and Chantelle appear to have had a brief encounter, as well. With what you overheard in the restroom, and what we found in her appointment book, they both fessed up."

"Hard to imagine of old man Flynt, isn't it? He always spoke of Chantelle so ... dismissively."

"She was a beautiful woman. And by all accounts, fascinating. I find those two factors go a long way when it comes to attraction."

"I see why *they* were attracted to *her*, but it's harder to understand from her vantage point."

"Never underestimate the power of money."

"She was blackmailing them?"

"No, actually. But she was using her influence—I'm gonna let you use your imagination as to what that entailed—to get in on the ground floor of Tempus, Ltd. Egypt was helping her to position herself as a spokesperson, and if everything went according to plan they stood to make some big bucks when the company went public." She tilted her head and looked at me. "You think Chantelle had any special knowledge about it doing well in the IPO?"

I smiled. "I think if her special sight worked that way, she wouldn't have had to ask her brother for a loan."

"Good point."

"Speaking of that ..." I had to ask. "What about Landon?"

"Chantelle's brother? His taxi from the airport arrived about four minutes before you did. Gabe verified that, and it was backed up by the security tape of the lobby. There's no way Landon could have let himself in here, killed Chantelle, and gotten cleaned up before you arrived. Not with this amount of blood splatter."

My stomach lurched again. Not enough sleep and too much coffee and talk of blood splatter didn't make for an easy morning. "Okay, good, if you're sure."

She tilted her head and gave me a questioning look. "You have some reason to suspect Landon Demetrius that you haven't shared with me?"

I shrugged. "Not really. I mean, not as such."

"That means nothing to me. Spill."

"No, I mean it's really nothing ... just that I sort of like him."

"Like him?"

"I mean"—I could feel my cheeks burn—"*like* him. I feel ... attracted to him."

"I thought you were with Graham?"

"I am. It's not like I've *done* anything about it."

She fixed me with one of her intense cop looks. "So you're saying that because you sort of like this guy ..."

"It made me wonder if he might be a murderer."

She gave me the lifted eyebrow treatment.

"I'm just saying," I tried to clarify. "It doesn't seem totally out of the realm of possibility that I'd fall for the main suspect. You know, given that it's me we're talking about."

She seemed to be trying to stifle a smile. "You do give yourself a hard time, don't you? Couldn't it just be as simple as the fact that you like him, and maybe you and Graham need to have a talk?"

"I suppose," I said, noticing a huge crystal ball sitting on an elaborate stand on the coffee table and wondering, if I stared long enough into its depths, would it hold any answers for me? "Though things are rarely simple when it comes to me and mine."

We headed back down to the lobby. Annette told Gabe the apartment seemed to have been broken into and she was going to need to see the security tapes for the past several days. Annette was one of those people who never had to yell to get her point across. He blanched and apologized obsequiously, then ran for her car.

"To be fair, if he's running in and out, parking and retrieving cars he can hardly watch over the desk all the time," I said.

"Well, I'll check the tapes and see if they tell us anything. Are you off to the beach, now?"

"Yeah, maybe," I said, though truth to tell I hadn't planned for it when I left the house, so I had no picnic or blanket or anything. Still. I could head out to Stinson Beach, talk a walk along the cliffs, soak up a little sun if it was warm enough....

Gabe pulled up in Annette's car, tires screeching.

"Have fun at the beach," Annette said. "And stay away from ghosts of shipwrecks past."

"You bet. Thanks, Annette."

Chapter Thirty

Who was I kidding? I wasn't going to the beach. I headed to Crosswinds.

I still had the weathervane in my car, and my toolbox. On the one hand, I knew darned well I shouldn't be traipsing around up on a roof by myself. It was against basic safety procedure.

But on the other hand, I wanted to put this weathervane back where it belonged. It was the first haunted thing I had ever heard at Crosswinds, and what Nancy had said made sense to me: The vane seemed, somehow, magical.

Maybe if I installed the antique and let it spin in the wind and squeak for real, Peregrine's ghost would warm up to me a little and tell me something useful. Or perhaps Chantelle, if she was connected to Flora somehow, could manage to make contact with me here.

Chantelle seemed like a force of nature; I wished I could have gotten to know her when she was alive. Not to mention that had I been closer to the psychic, I would have had a much better idea of who could have committed such a heinous crime.

Egypt mentioned Chantelle had met with each of the Flynts separately when she did her reading at the house. What if one of them was embezzling from Tempus, Ltd., and Chantelle had intuited enough to figure it out? In the run-up to the IPO such allegations might have been devastating, right?

I didn't really know enough about big business to understand how that would work. In Turner Construction the principals—Dad, Stan, and yours truly—drew our salaries from the company, and shared any profits on a quarterly basis. If one of us was embezzling funds it would reduce the others' share of the profits, but it wouldn't affect salaries unless the theft was extreme.

But surely the bookkeeping for a company like Tempus, Ltd. was not nearly as straightforward as Turner Construction. Probably someone could have been skimming off profits for a very long time without getting caught.

Just as I pulled up to Crosswinds, I realized I had forgotten to make contact with Landon after the memorial service yesterday.

I hesitated for a moment, then texted, *Sorry I wasn't able to say hello in person yesterday. Hope you're doing well. Guess what! Found the weathervane!*

Then I let myself in through the front door, mounted the stairs, passed by Egypt's still-locked door—saying a little prayer that she'd be okay—and climbed out onto the roof. I moved carefully, taking note of the varying slopes and treading carefully on the cantilevered eaves. Mounting the weathervane in its original position on the roof didn't take much: I attached the Phillips head screwdriver bit to my power drill and used it to screw the bracing onto the peak of the roof, then attached the weathervane. It was a temporary job—I would ask Jeremy to build a new metal brace to make sure the vane could withstand whatever storm might whip in off the bay.

But it would do for now. I watched happily as it spun around in the breeze. Looking out at the stunning view, I imagined Flora standing on the top of the turret, hearing the squeaking of the weathervane as she gazed out to the vast unknown of the world beyond the horizon.

And then I imagined her father, Peregrine, scowling at her and yelling at her to come back in. So he could take more pictures of her? I imagined him trailing around after her, like those really annoying people at parties so intent on having a photographic record of everything that they ruin the evening.

But this was back in the day, when taking a photo required a lot of equipment, and the subject had to keep absolutely still for the long exposure or the final result would be blurred.

Again I thought of old movies from the Wild West, the popping sound of the old-fashioned flashbulb, the burst of smoke and fire.

I imagined Flora standing stiffly in her costumes, trying not to move, acceding to her father's wishes even while plotting her own escape on her eighteenth birthday, when she would come into her inheritance. Fleeing during a celebratory ball marking the announcement of her engagement to another rich man.

Peregrine didn't materialize on the roof, nor was he scowling from the other side of the skylight when I went back down. But I thought of him throwing Landon and me out of his darkroom the other day.

Was there something he didn't want us to see?

I climbed down the spiral stairs, and descended to the huge foyer, where I had left my bag. Inside was the framed photo of Flora from Chantelle's apartment, along with the manila envelope Karla had given me. With these in hand,

I crawled through the hole in the wall, moved the lamp shade until I heard the click of the mechanism releasing the bookcase, and then pushed. It opened a little easier this time, loosened up from our last trip through.

I shone my flashlight as I made my way through the cobwebby passage. It dawned on me that I hadn't talked to Andrew about what to do about the false walls and secret staircases and darkroom. Should I try to incorporate them into the remodel? Maybe Karla was right, after all: Maybe it was absurd to try to reclaim Crosswinds. It was too far gone; unless Andrew was willing to spend another year and a *lot* more money there was no way to return it to its former glory.

That was a depressing thought.

When I got to the darkroom I lingered in the passageway for a moment. The rational part of my brain knew that the ghostly yelling couldn't actually harm me, but my gut didn't seem to be getting the message.

Peregrine Summerton frightened me when he yelled. His anger and despair felt immediate, and overwhelming.

But now the darkroom seemed quiet. The dusty old canisters and jars, the cobwebs, the photos hanging on the rope, the ancient camera on the tripod—all was still. The room looked just the same as it had the other day and, rather like in Suzanne White's kitchen, all the things that the ghost had knocked over and scattered had been put back in order.

I stepped into the room. "Mr. Summerton? I'd like to talk to you."

Turning around slowly, I searched my peripheral vision, looking for his apparition. I had been buoyed by my success with the ghost of Suzanne White and it occurred to me that maybe, just maybe, I was getting better at calling spirits.

Or not.

"Mr. Summerton? Please try.... I brought back some more of your photographs. I want to help you."

Another moment passed. Nothing.

I set the framed photo on the counter, and then took out the contents of the envelope, splaying the photos in an arc. They showed Flora as a proper Victorian lady, Flora as a tavern wench, Flora as a goatherd. I still had a few more photos of Flora in my jobsite file, so I made a mental note to bring those back next time I came.

I started searching through cabinets and stacks of old photographic plates and papers. The only problem was, I didn't know what I was looking for.

But finally I unearthed an old ledger that reminded me of Dingo's big book of hauntings. And just as with Dingo's book, this one was stuffed with yellowed newspaper clippings and random advertisements, mostly regarding photographic equipment.

The paper was so fragile it crumbled, so I took care to turn the pages with the gentlest touch of my fingertips along the edges.

Peregrine's handwriting was shaky and hard to read, and the ink was faded, but I could make out several of the entries: notations on experiments with different chemical baths for his photographs, and lists of costume ideas for Flora: Peasant Girl, Southern Belle, Dance Hall Girl.

And there were other, more telling notes.

She is too much like me. When she hears the wind shift, she clambers up to watch the sea. It is indecent for a girl. The things she says ... She is twice the man my boys should be.

And:

I feel almost as if this camera, these photographic renditions might capture her, hold her here. Otherwise, she will slip through my fingers. I fear for her. What will the world make of my girl's unseemly bravery and independence? She will be destroyed.

And finally:

She has gone. Fled. And I have only myself to blame. Along with her go my political aspirations, my best hopes for the Summerton family. And the very finest part of me. Her mother is distraught and treats me with silence. I am left with my photographs—that is all.

While I read, I realized I could hear the strains of a waltz. And a man's anguished voice.

It wasn't Peregrine. This was yet another old man. I closed the ancient journal and made my way along the passageway and down the stairs. I stood on my tiptoes and pressed the brass lever to open the door, and stepped into the exercise room storage closet.

Cautiously, I opened the door to the Pilates studio.

George Flynt was standing by the window, his head in his hands, moaning loudly.

"Mr. Flynt? Are you all right?" I asked as I approached him.

When he looked up at me, his eyes looked wild. His gray hair was askew, he appeared unshaven.

"Where did you come from?" he asked, twisting around to look around the room.

"I was upstairs, on the roof. Installing the weathervane. I found the original."

"Oh," he said, underwhelmed.

"I apologize. I think I'm intruding. I'll go."

He let out a sound of despair. "Do you have any idea how much the Flynt name means to me? Do you? I've spent my entire life building my fortune, my reputation. I came from nothing—you know that? Not like my son—I gave that boy everything, but it turned out it was too much. Silver spoon in his mouth did him no damned good. So I went the other way with the grandkids, and where did that get me?"

When I first saw him, head hanging low, I thought he was a distraught old man. But now I wasn't so sure.

"I think I've intruded on your privacy," I said. "I'll just go—"

"You damned psychics. First Chantelle, now you. And if you're so good at reading minds, I guess you know what I'm doing here," he said, walking toward me. He was between me and the doors. I could probably take him, but what if he had a weapon? I backed up slowly. "Mason tells me you and that computer genius from England hacked into my business accounts."

"I don't know anything, believe me," I said, my mind racing. He had nearly backed me into the corner. "And I'm no good at computers. Truly wretched. Hacking's wrong, isn't it? Illegal, even. I mean, it's hard to know the intricacies of such things, but really—"

As he loomed toward me, I shoved him, hard. He wasn't a large man, and he was elderly. He stumbled backward.

I ran into the closet and slammed the door, then rushed into the tunnel, closing the door behind me. Unless George was superstitious enough to believe I had somehow mastered the skills of disappearing, he would quickly figure out the secret passage. I had a few minutes, tops.

It was enough. It would have to be.

I could hear the weathervane, and the sound of the

waltz, which didn't surprise me—this sort of thing was probably stirring up old Peregrine's ghost. Violence had a way of doing that.

As I rushed through the dark hallway I pulled out my phone and tried to call 911 but I didn't get any reception. *Dammit.*

Cobwebs stroked my face, and I tripped over an errant bit of trim as I raced through the dark corridor. Finally I found the back of the bookcase at the foyer, and shoved as hard as I could.

It swung open and I lost my balance, falling flat on my face.

I had to hurry. Chances were good old man Flynt had either figured out the secret passage, or was even now racing up the stairs. The only thing I had in my favor was his advanced age.

I scrambled to my feet and climbed through the hole in the sheetrock, only to realize that Mason was standing in the foyer.

"Mason! Your grandfather—"

"He's a mean old coot, isn't he?" Mason said. "He fired me today, *and* disowned me. Can you believe that? His own grandson."

Realization was dawning, and it wasn't looking good.

"But unless I'm mistaken he hasn't had a chance to tell anyone. Nor will he." Mason looked around and casually pulled a gun out from under his jacket. "Speaking of Grandpop, have you seen him? He was supposed to meet me here. To 'talk.'"

"I have, yes," I said. "He's up on the fourth floor."

"Liar," he said quietly. "He has a hard time with the stairs. Arthritic knees. And he's claustrophobic, afraid of elevators. You believe that? A captain of industry, but he's scared of elevators. Hey, that's not a bad idea—thanks!"

Ugh. I hated to think what idea I might have given him. I had pegged George as a nasty piece of work, but it was friendly, peacekeeping Mason all along.

"You know, Mason," I began. It occurred to me to point out that he couldn't possibly track down everyone who might know about his crime in order to kill us all; that would have been quite the bloodbath. "I'm not the one who uncovered the embezzling of Tempus. I think Egypt—"

"Egypt?" Mason swore a long streak. "I took care of her."

So much for using logic when facing a murderer. When would I learn?

"You want to hear something funny?" Mason asked.

"Sure. You bet," I said, hoping to stall until something, anything, came to mind. I thought about making a grab for the gun but while I'm no waif, Mason was a healthy young man. He probably had me in the pure strength category. And it was just too easy for him to pull that trigger.

"I thought you could read my mind, like Chantelle did, so I followed you to that salvage yard. But I finally realized you didn't know anything, you were so clueless when you came to Tempus. Just a clueless idiot, like the rest of them."

"Well, now, that's true," I started to say when I realized I heard the sound of a waltz coming through the wall, and the squeaking of the weathervane spinning overhead. A faraway door slammed, and the lights blinked.

A worried look passed over Mason's pleasant features.

"What are you *doing*? Stop it."

"I'm calling out to Chantelle," I lied. As I said it I decided it wasn't half bad, as far as ideas for not getting killed went.

"Stop it!"

"She's already on the other side, Mason. As you know better than anyone, since you put her there. And I gotta say, she isn't very happy about it."

He started looking around him.

I rolled my eyes skyward and held my hands out to my sides palms up, thumb touching forefinger, as I'd learned in that infernal yoga class.

I don't know any actual spells or chants, so I took a chance that he wasn't bilingual, and started rattling off the names of tools in Spanish: *"Destornillador, herramienta,* Chantelle. *Llave inglesa, hilo de plomada!"*

"Stop that! What are you doing?"

"Calling on Chantelle, of course," I said, closing my eyes and continuing to chant: *"Martillo, piquet,* Chantelle. *Sierra circular!"*

"That's crap! You said you can't do stuff like that."

I opened one eye. "I said I could talk to the dead, and I can. Chantelle couldn't tell me who killed her, but she sure as shingles can show up right now and give me a hand."

Someone was coming down the staircase.

Mason whirled around and fired off a shot.

Chapter Thirty-one

The bullet had no effect on Peregrine Summerton, who stood looking as full of rage as ever—though now that I'd read his journal, I thought I saw deep sorrow in those ghostly eyes.

At that moment George Flynt emerged from the stairwell from the ground floor. He was pulling himself up with help from the rail, yelling, "Mason, stop!"

Mason fired at Peregrine again, but hit George, who went down like a sack of potatoes.

"Damned old man!" I wasn't sure at first whether Mason was referring to Peregrine or George, but then he clarified: "Everyone *else* at school had a trust fund, but I have to work every damned day of my life?"

"Listen to me, Mason," I said. "Hey! Only your grandfather knows about the embezzling, right?" That was a blatant falsehood, since Annette told me the police were already investigating this angle. But I was desperately trying to think of some way of distracting him, so he didn't shoot again and hit his target. "I can fix this!"

"Fix it, how?"

"Up in Egypt's room she has all that high-tech equipment, she knows about what was going on, right? Well, I happen to be a computer genius myself. Remember? You told your grandfather I hacked into the computers at Tempus."

"I was lying when I said that. I was hoping he'd go after you."

"Okay, but it happened to be true. Let's go up there, and I can wipe away all traces of the evidence. How hard could it be?"

He studied my face, as though trying to decide whether or not to believe me.

"You mean like Dad did, when he hired Egypt to wipe the Internet of all the references to Crosswinds being haunted?"

"Exactly. That's exactly what I mean. Look how successful she was, and we'll do the same."

I didn't have much of a plan. But old cranky-pants Peregrine had disappeared, darn the man, and I didn't know how badly George was hurt. If I could get Mason away from him, maybe George could call for help. And maybe I'd see Peregrine again and freak Mason out, or I could trip him as we climbed up the stairs, or I could send a computer message for help, or . . . something.

"Come on, Mason. I understand how you feel, you've been working so hard and it just doesn't seem fair. You know what? My dad's just like that: No matter how hard I work it's just not good enough." I was working on my lying skills. "But we'll go take care of things, and then you won't have to worry."

I wasn't kidding myself. Mason had been cold-blooded enough to knife Chantelle at close range because he thought she read his mind. He would dispatch me just as dispassionately as soon as I was no longer useful.

I had my own cell phone in my pocket, but I couldn't manage to dial 911 without looking. And it would be too risky to take it out.

"All right," said Mason. "But I have to do something with Grandpop."

Grandpop opened his mouth, no doubt to say something sneering and dismissive. Behind Mason, I held my finger to my mouth in the universal "shhh" sign and widened my eyes. *Now would be the time to shut the hell up, old man.*

"How about we tie him up?" I suggested. "He's so old and he can barely walk and you shot him. Let him bleed out right here."

"You think?"

"I don't think you should risk another gunshot. Not in this neighborhood. Somebody's bound to hear and call the cops."

"Good point. Okay. Use that drapery cord and tie him up. Tightly."

I took the cord over to where George sat on the floor. He was fully conscious, and I didn't think he was in any danger of bleeding out, as his white shirt showed only a small red stain.

"Sorry," I whispered as I crouched and started tying his hands. "Are you okay?"

"My golf game will be shot to hell," he muttered. "But I think it's a flesh wound."

"Oh, and sorry for knocking you down earlier."

He snorted.

"Stop talking!" Mason said.

But as I finished tying the knot, I leaned in and whispered, *"Fake a heart attack."*

George immediately started hyperventilating and as I was pretending to tie up his hands, moaned and keeled over.

"What happened? What did you *do*?" asked Mason, as though worried I had just hurt his beloved Grandpop.

"I don't know," I said. "It's . . . probably a heart attack. All this stress."

Mason nodded slowly. "It's hard to believe, someone like him, you think he'll go on forever but he's mortal like the rest of us."

"That's true. We should probably call nine-one-one, get the paramedics here."

"Are you crazy? If he dies now, I won't have to deal with him later."

It had been worth a shot. George lay on the floor, convincingly pale and inert. Part of me feared he'd had a real heart attack, but whether the family scion was alive or dead wasn't the biggest of my problems at the moment.

Mason moved in and checked to see that the cord was tied tightly enough. He nodded.

"Good job. Now, hand me his cell phone. And yours too, now that I think about it."

I set my hopes on tripping Mason as we mounted the stairs to the fourth floor. Or maybe Peregrine would be helpful for once and scare the crap out of the man with the gun, or throw a pie or something.

"Here, let's use the elevator," said Mason in that friendly tone I was used to. As though he just wanted to spare me the exertion of the stairs.

"I'd rather use the stairs."

"What, claustrophobic too? What is it with you people? Time to face your fears, young lady."

He gestured with the gun and I headed to the elevator, which was small, making for a very tight fit. Mason and I were basically chest-to-chest in there.

I was trying to avoid his eyes.

The doors opened at the fourth floor, and Mason scanned the scene before allowing me out.

"Okay, let's go."

Egypt's door was locked, as usual. Mason rattled the knob, in a way that reminded me of his father trying to get in, just a few days ago, the first time I set foot in this haunted mansion.

"*Dammit.* Why would she lock it?"

I had to laugh. Until he raised the gun in my direction.

"I'm sorry, Mason. It's just that your father said exactly the same thing, the first time I took a tour of the house with him. I think you're more like him than you know."

He looked uncomfortable, torn between being pleased and insulted.

"He seems like a good man," I said.

"He slept with Chantelle. She rejected me but went for him? It's like Grandpop always says: It's all about the money."

"Why did you kill her?"

"She read my mind, you believe that? When she came here to figure out what was going on with the ghosts. . . . I should have skipped that particular family night, but Mom insisted."

"So she threatened you with exposure?"

"At first she wanted money, but I pointed out that was why I had to steal it, because I didn't *have* any money. Not *real* money, because of Grandpop's insistence on treating us like salaried employees. So she said she would keep quiet if I worked with her, got her in on the ground floor at Tempus in time for her to make a killing in the IPO."

"And you were living up to your end of the deal, right?"

"I was! And I had to go up against Grandpop to do it. But then Egypt hacked in and figured things out and wanted part of the action, and now Grandpop . . ."

He shook his head, and I saw tears in his eyes. He swore and kicked the locked door, a frustrated little boy.

"If we can't get in . . ." He let out a long exasperated breath. "I don't know. I guess I shoot you now, then go take care of Grandpop if he's still alive, and take off."

The weathervane squeaked loudly overhead.

"Oh hey, that reminds me," I said. "There's a spare key to Egypt's room up on the roof. She told me."

"Up on the roof?" he frowned. "Why the roof?"

"Because Egypt wanted to keep everyone out of her room. She wanted a little privacy; can't blame her for that."

"Why the roof?" he repeated.

"Would you think to look for a key on the roof?"

"No, I guess not. Where is it?"

"Under the eaves. Want me to get it? There's no way for me to escape up there, and I'll come right back."

"You could call to the neighbors for help."

"But you'd just shoot me, so that wouldn't do me any good."

"I'll go with you."

Rats. Still, maybe George had managed to go for help. I had tied only his hands, so he could have run. Except that he was not a young man, and I'd pushed him to the ground, and then he'd been shot and he had bad knees.

Where the hell was Peregrine? Why couldn't old cranky-pants show up when a person needed him? When he came down the stairs earlier, I had been sure he would be my salvation.

Instead, as we started up the spiral stairs, Mason at my back, there were photos of Flora on every other step. Flora dressed as an acrobat, as a wood sprite, as an equestrian. And beside her, in one of the photographs, was Chantelle. Dressed just like her, standing arm in arm.

"Did you notice the photos?" I asked Mason.

He had been stepping on them, apparently not caring.

"*Destornillador, herramienta,* Chantelle," I started muttering. "*Llave inglesa, hilo de plomada!* Chantelle!"

"Stop that, or I'll—"

"She's already here, Mason, look! She's here in the photos!" I picked it up and thrust it at him. He grabbed it.

"What? How—"

While he was distracted I shoved the skylight open and bolted through, then slammed it shut. I raced across the turret roof to the ladder and shimmied down, landing on the flat part of the roof.

Chapter Thirty-two

Mason popped up through the window and shot once, hitting an eave by my ear, splinters raining down all around me.

The weathervane spun wildly.

Mason started down the ladder. While his back was turned to me I threw myself at him, slamming his gun hand as hard as I could against the metal rung.

He dropped the gun and we both lunged for it, rolling on the roof. Suddenly there was another presence with us.

"Get off the roof!"

Finally Peregrine decides to show up, I thought, as Mason and I struggled, both of us with our hands on the gun. Mason didn't seem to notice the ghostly voice, intent as he was on wresting the gun from me.

We were locked together, rolling on the slanted section of the roof, while he tried to use sheer force to turn the muzzle of the gun toward me.

There was no way he would miss this time.

I concentrated every ounce of strength on keeping the gun at bay. But the muzzle turned toward me, millimeter by millimeter. My strength was almost gone; I was outmuscled.

Suddenly Peregrine was right in our faces.

"What is the meaning of this?" he yelled. *"And who is that man bleeding in my hallway?"*

"Ahhhh!" Mason screamed, rearing back and letting go of the gun.

Without thinking about it, I fired. Mason looked stunned, and a bloom of red appeared on the shoulder of his shirt.

"Mason, I'm sorry," I said, inanely apologizing to the man trying to kill me. "I'll get help, wait—"

But Peregrine wasn't waiting. He was berating Mason, putting his ghostly face right into Mason's, giving him a dressing-down. "Leave me in peace! Leave me my *photographs*! They're all I have left! *Leave me my Flora!*"

Mason backed away, crawling on the slippery roof tiles, making a whimpering sound.

"Mason, be careful, you're going too far—"

One foot fell over the edge of the roof. There was nothing for him to hold on to; he splayed, belly-down, on the shingles, trying to keep from slipping farther. He looked behind him, surprise registering on his face.

Then he held out his uninjured hand to me. "Help me! Please!"

I looked around for something to hold on to. If I tried to help him up, would I be able to? Or would he pull me over the edge with him?

"Wait, Mason. Don't move, let me—"

I whipped off my leather belt, attached it to the base of the weathervane, then held on to it with one hand while reaching to Mason with the other.

He reached up for me, and grasped my hand. I tried to pull him up, hoping he didn't pull my arm out of its socket. The gun was still in my pocket and I tried to calculate how quickly I could get to it, once Mason was up and safe and, no doubt, newly homicidal.

I heard someone on the turret roof and twisted around to look.

"Landon!" I yelled.

No ladder for him. Swearing a blue streak, he leaped off the turret, clambered up one side of the roof until he was at the peak, near the weathervane.

He held on to the belt and with his much longer arms was able to easily reach Mason's wrist, and pull him up far enough for Mason to get purchase on the roof tiles.

I let go, relief surging through me. My shoulder ached. I grabbed the gun and kept it trained on Mason, who was now splayed on the tiles far enough up to be out of danger.

"I swear, you really *are* like a bad penny," I said, breathless. "What are you doing here?"

"You said you found the weathervane so I assumed, correctly, that you would want to install it right away. You didn't return my texts so I thought I'd come over, see if you needed a little backup."

"Maybe Chantelle wasn't the only mind reader in your family."

He gave a humorless laugh. "Could I ask you a question?"

"Sure."

"Did you shoot the old man downstairs?"

I heard sirens in the distance and started to laugh in exhaustion. "Didn't George tell you?"

"He seems to have passed out, but he's alive. I called nine-one-one. Is he another culprit, then? I left him tied up, just in case."

"No, this is Mason's—"

At that moment Mason lunged at the gun in my hand. Landon launched himself at Mason, and the three of us rolled down the steep roof again. I nearly panicked when I felt my feet slip over the edge.

Landon grabbed my arm with one hand and an eave with another.

Mason kept rolling. He caught the rain gutter, and our eyes locked for an instant before he lost his grip and disappeared.

His bloodcurdling scream blended with the deafening sirens of emergency vehicles.

I squeezed my eyes shut. I was still hanging half over the edge, dangling four stories above the sidewalk. Only Landon's white-knuckled grip kept me from sharing Mason's fate.

"I don't think I can . . ." I gasped. Upper body strength wasn't my strong suit.

"None of that, now, General," Landon said. "Hang on. We'll do this slowly but surely."

Inch by inch, he hoisted me up as I used every last bit of my energy to scrabble on the tiles until I was high enough that I could collapse, sprawl on my back, and catch my breath.

"Thanks for the hand," I said, panting and blinking as I gazed up at the sun.

"Anytime," Landon whispered, rolling over and leaning over me. He ran his fingers along my forehead, and his hand cupped my cheek, as though to be sure I was okay. "You truly are the most astonishing woman, Mel Turner."

"Okay, let's go over this again," said Annette. I was sitting on the bumper of an ambulance with a blanket wrapped around my shoulders. An EMT was trying to get me to drink a cup of juice and Annette Crawford was peppering me with questions, but all I wanted to do was sleep. Adrenaline crash.

Also, I was desperately trying not to look toward the spot on the sidewalk where Mason Flynt had landed. The first responders had put up some plastic barriers and there were so many people standing around that I wouldn't have been able to observe anything, anyway, but I still didn't want to take the chance of seeing something I couldn't later *unsee*. It was enough to have his final scream echoing through my head.

"When Chantelle came in to do the reading of the house, she took each family member in a separate room for privacy and gave them each a reading," I said. "Andrew had to pay a lot extra for all of that."

"Why would he have done that?" Annette asked.

"I think it was Stephanie's idea. She thought Chantelle would be able to give them all special guidance from beyond. She couldn't have known what would come of it all."

"I hear Chantelle was pretty sought after," said Annette.

I nodded. "Very exclusive. Anyway, I guess she really was able to read Mason's mind, or maybe he just got himself worked up and let something slip."

"I don't suppose we'll ever know that for sure."

"I think you're right." I sipped my juice. It helped. "Meanwhile, Egypt, the computer whiz, had done some Internet work for Andrew, then stayed on as caretaker here and met Chantelle. Then she hacked into the company's computers and got hard-and-fast proof of the embezzlement. Chantelle then pressured Mason into supporting her bid to become a spokesperson for Tempus, Ltd."

"She was smart enough to think of her future, rather than focusing on the immediate payoff of blackmail."

"But then Mason panicked when he realized his father had called in yet another psychic."

"Who?"

"Mel Turner, at your service."

"You're a psychic?" Annette asked, raising her eyebrow. "I thought you could just see ghosts, sometimes."

"True, but I guess it's a kind of psychic ability."

"Some might even say psychosis," she said with a smile.

"Cute." I hugged the blanket a little tighter around my shoulders.

"And Mason went to Chantelle's on the day of her death to try to get her to call things off, to keep you out of Crosswinds. They had words, and he just lost it. Or . . . he clearly evaded the security cameras, so maybe he went there with the express intent of killing her. Another thing we'll probably never know for sure."

I nodded. "And then today, George seems to have figured out Mason was the one embezzling funds. I remember when I was at the Tempus offices, he told Lacey that her brother was handling the books for the audit."

"George said you knocked him down."

"My bad. He was pretty antipsychic in that moment, so I thought he was the killer. How is he?"

"He'll live. The gunshot wound isn't serious, and he's a pretty tough old bird. He was yelling at the paramedics to 'wrap him up so he could go home.'"

I smiled. "I'm glad. He's got a very dysfunctional family, but I'm glad he's not seriously hurt. Maybe they'll all pull together now, learn to work together."

Annette snorted in a pretty good impression of George Flynt. "And pigs will fly."

"Anyway, I managed to convince Mason that George had a heart attack, and then got him to go up on the roof."

"And what were you doing on the roof?"

"Looking for a key to Egypt's room"—I yawned—

"so I could go in and wipe the computers of all the embezzling info."

One eyebrow went up. "How were you going to manage that?"

"I was playing it by ear. As it happens, once out on the roof Peregrine joined us, and we rolled around a lot, and then . . ." I cleared my throat and drank a little more juice. "And then Landon came and rescued me and Mason, and then Mason lunged at us again, and then he fell off the roof."

"And somewhere in there you shot him."

I nodded, but couldn't speak.

"I'm going to assume it was self-defense?" she said very gently.

"Yeah," I croaked. "I don't even . . . What scares me is that I don't even really remember doing it. We were struggling for the weapon, and the ghost appeared and scared Mason, and I shot him. Just like that."

"It happens that way sometimes. The instinct for self-preservation is strong."

I nodded.

"We'll have to do a little more investigation, Mel, but I'm going to guess it will be declared self-defense. He forced you upstairs at gunpoint, and George Flynt and Landon Demetrius both attest to that."

"Good."

"You okay?"

I nodded.

"There are people you can talk to, you know. It might not be a bad idea. You've seen a lot; sometimes this sort of thing haunts a person. No pun intended."

"Thanks, Annette. Right now I'd just like to go home and sleep, if that's possible."

"You've got it."

Chapter Thirty-three

Graham flew in the next day. We had dinner plans.

All day, going from one job to another, I practiced: "Graham, you are a wonderful man, you deserve better. Graham, I don't think I want to have children. Graham, I've met someone and even though nothing happened it feels as though something could and that isn't right."

As bad as I was at relationships, I was worse at *ending* one. At least when my marriage broke up I had good reason to despise my husband, so I could stomp around and call him names and be righteously indignant. But the last thing I wanted to do was hurt Graham. And yet, that was exactly what I was going to do. There was no way around it.

I offered to bring takeout to his place so we could speak in private. I picked up Ethiopian from one of his favorite restaurants and had it waiting for him when he arrived from the airport.

We ate and shared some wine, and dinner conversation mostly revolved around my chasing ghosts and nearly tumbling off the roof. I tried to downplay what happened at Crosswinds, since I still hadn't quite wrapped my mind around the fact that I had shot a man, no matter how much he might have deserved it. And I couldn't forget that sickening moment when I watched Mason slip over the edge of the roof, the terror in his eyes, his horrific scream, and the awful knowledge that his body had slammed into the pavement four stories below.

At the time I had been so intent on not sharing his fate that I hadn't dwelled on it, but the image kept coming back to me. Haunting me.

Mostly, I enjoyed making Graham laugh by recounting the phantom food fight at the Mermaid Cove apartment.

I was trying to work up my courage to begin The Talk when Graham said, "So, I have some big news."

"Really? What is it?"

"I've been offered a great job. In Paris."

"Paris?" I echoed. "Paris, France?"

"No, Paris, Texas. *Of course* Paris, France."

He brought a small robin's egg blue box out of his pocket and placed it on the table between us. Tiffany's.

"Oh, no, no no no no," I said. "Graham . . ."

He cocked his head. "I thought you'd be thrilled. You've been wanting to move to Paris ever since you got divorced."

"Yes, but . . ." It's true I'd been talking about running away to Paris ever since my marriage ended. Those fantasies had gotten me through some dark days, and the promise of that shining city propelled me forward, kept me sane. But now . . . I thought about Turner Construction and saving old houses and keeping my crew employed. And Dad, who wasn't getting any younger. And

Caleb, who would be going off to college soon. And Dog, who I couldn't bear to leave, or to rip away from his current home. And Stan and Luz and . . .

A trip to Paris was one thing, but did I really want to *move* there?

The fact was that I had changed. Without my fully realizing it, I had moved on in my life not by traipsing off to Paris, but by staying in the Bay Area and reinventing myself, throwing myself into work I loved with people I loved, caring for others and being cared for. I didn't want to move to Paris.

I didn't want to move to Paris. Wow.

"You okay?" Graham was asking. "I have to say, in my mind this discussion went a whole different way."

"I know. I'm sorry. I'm really sorry, Graham. You're wonderful, and you had every right to think I would want to move to Paris with you. But . . . I don't."

He fixed me with a grim look. "You don't want to move to Paris, or you don't want to move to Paris with *me*?"

"I care deeply for you, Graham. I do. But I'm not ready for marriage, much less children. And the truth is, I'm not sure I ever will be. I don't know that I want that anymore. Even though my marriage to Daniel wasn't ideal, I already experienced that with him: I was a wife and a mother, and I loved some parts of it—like Caleb, obviously. But now Caleb's about to go off to college, and I'm pretty happy with myself, with my weird dresses and my crew and my strange life . . . and even with talking to ghosts. I just realized, just right this second, that this is what I want. I want the life I have."

"Without me?"

I took a deep breath. "I think we want different things. You're fabulous, a really good person, and gorgeous and sweet and loyal. And you deserve to have someone meet you halfway."

He blew out a long breath and ran a hand through his hair. "Is this about that Landon character? The one who kept you from falling off the roof?"

"Why would you think that?"

"From the way you speak about him."

"I'd be lying if I said I didn't feel anything for him. But that's not what this is about. It really is what I said: You and I want different things out of life. Don't you want children?"

He nodded.

"I'm not sure I do at this point. And that's a pretty huge issue for any couple."

He nodded slowly and started carrying our dishes to the sink. Silence reigned for several minutes. Finally, Graham let out a long breath and said, "I tell you what. I'm going to take the gig in Paris, and maybe you'll come for a visit. I'm not willing to give up on this. On *us*. Not yet. We'll see what happens when you taste a *pain au chocolat* fresh from the *boulangerie*."

I smiled. "You really are an amazing man, Graham Donovan."

"And don't you forget it."

The next night, Luz and I found a miraculous parking space on California Street, not far from where I'd been last time. I had given Luz the short version of what happened with Graham and made her promise not to ask me about it for the interim. For the moment, it was all I could do to hold it together enough to deal with the ghosts in my life; my romantic prospects were going to have to wait.

"Okay, my friend, are you going to tell me why we're here?" Luz demanded. "This is supposed to help me get over my guilt about spurning my dead grandmother? 'Cause I probably have better things to do."

"You ever go to camp when you were little?"

She raised one eyebrow at me. "Where I come from, we spent the summers dodging bullets. Picking four-leaf clovers and singing 'Kumbaya' at camp wasn't an option."

"So you never heard the campfire story about the hitchhiking ghost?"

"I have a feeling I'm not going to like this story," she said as she craned her neck to look in the backseat.

There was no one there. Yet.

"So usually, a hitchhiking ghost asks for a ride home. Then when the Good Samaritan pulls up to the address the ghost gave him or her, they find an abandoned house, or some elderly mother who tells them her daughter died ten years ago in a car accident. Something like that."

"That is so frickin' sad," said Luz.

I nodded.

"So . . . are we looking for said hitchhiker?" she asked.

I nodded. "Flora Summerton, the daughter from Crosswinds. She ran away and became a missionary in Hawaii, but tried to come back to visit her father on his deathbed. But she was struck and killed by a cable car right along here somewhere, so she never made it home."

"Is her father waiting for her? He's the one haunting Crosswinds?"

I nodded. "I think they're both seeking reconciliation. They won't be able to rest until—"

I was cut off by a banging on the window. Luz and I jumped, and she rolled her passenger-side window down.

It was Deputy Doofus.

"Yes?" Luz said, her tone polite but not particularly friendly.

"Hi," I said, looking around Luz at the rent-a-cop. "So nice to see you again."

"You guys wanna move it along?"

"No." Luz raised her window and turned her attention back to me. "As you were saying, her father's still waiting for her?"

I nodded. "Sometimes she appears here, walking in the middle of the street. I guess a lot of people have seen her over the years, and some have tried to help her get home, but they've never managed. She always disappears before they get there."

"And you think we can help her?"

"I hope so." I brought out the envelope full of her photos, including one with Chantelle. "I'm hoping that Chantelle can help us, maybe talk to her from the other side."

Luz perused the photos, then gave me a look.

"As always," I continued, "I don't claim to know what I'm doing. But it seems worth a try, don't you think? I was thinking that with you, me, and Chantelle, Flora might not slip away this time."

"Chantelle's dead, right?"

"Yep."

"Oookay, just wanted to be sure I was clear on this concept. So it's you, me, and a dead woman looking for yet another dead woman. Sort of like freaky girls' night out?"

"Something like that."

"I don't—"

"There she is," I said quietly. "See, in the middle of the street?"

Luz opened her door and stood.

"Get out of my way," she told the security guard. "Flora?" she called.

Flora turned around.

"Hey," said Luz, clearing her throat. "We'll, uh, give you a ride."

A cable car passed in front of Flora. When it passed, she had disappeared.

"Get in, Luz," I said. "This is how it happened last time."

Luz got in. And when we looked back, Flora was with us.

I started driving. We had pretty much the same conversation as last time, with Flora asking us to take her home, and me telling her I knew the way. Luz's eyes were huge but she hung in there, turning around and addressing the ghost directly.

Luz passed the photos into the backseat.

"These are beautiful photos," Luz said.

The ghost looked shocked. "Papa took these. I wanted adventure, and he said this way I would live a thousand lives. I look very . . . young."

Luz nodded. "Hey, Flora, you know how you always disappear when you get near home? Because it's probably pretty overwhelming and scary. How about this time, you and I go in together?"

Luz, straight-talking spirit social worker.

I pulled up to the stop sign where Flora had disappeared last time, and looked back.

She was still staring at the photos. One finger brushed over Chantelle's face.

"Do you know who that is?" I asked.

She nodded. "We've been introduced."

"Stay with us this time, Flora," I said, taking my cue from Luz. Might as well call a spade a spade, to the dead as well as to the living. "Don't disappear. Your father's waiting for you."

She looked up, sadness in those big eyes. When I pulled up in front of Crosswinds, Flora was still in the backseat.

Luz climbed out and opened the back door.

"Let me take you in, Flora," Luz said, reaching out to her. After a moment's hesitation, the ghost put her hand in Luz's. "Let me take you home."

And hand in hand, they walked up the steps of Crosswinds, where Peregrine waited.

Chapter Thirty-four

Six weeks later, Andrew and I stood in the foyer of Crosswinds.

Sleek, sterile surfaces had given way to one paneled wall with ornate moldings and a large bookcase. I had replaced the modern fireplace surround with the one I'd found at Uncle J's, featuring carved cupids; antique crystal chandeliers now hung from decorative plaster medallions overhead.

Crosswinds was now a surreal mélange of old and new, but the odd blend worked, somehow.

"The buyers loved the idea of the secret passage," Andrew said. "The wife's an amateur photographer, and the husband's a real history buff."

"That's great, Andrew. I'm so pleased."

"They want to keep Turner Construction on the job a while longer, to finish things up and make everything consistent."

"I'd be honored. Please give them my contact information."

He nodded, sadly, taking another long look around

the room. I could hear far-off strains of a Strauss waltz, but decided not to mention it. After all the havoc, the Flynts had lowered the price on Crosswinds to a mere twenty-two million, and Karla had signed a lovely couple who would be moving in soon with their children and large extended family. They seemed positively sanguine about the strange goings-on in the house, which now consisted of occasional orchestra music and, every once in a while, a photograph of Flora Summerton appearing out of thin air.

George Flynt had recovered from what was, after all, a simple flesh wound and shock; Egypt was still nursing a broken leg, but her concussion had healed. George had hired her to work on the computer systems at Tempus, Ltd., reinforcing the firewall to prevent future hacking. George thanked me for my help that terrible day, and offered me free enrollment in a Tempus antiaging program. I thanked him but declined; I would take my aging as it came. I could use all the maturity I could get.

Landon Demetrius, for his part, was enjoying teaching at UC Berkeley and had decided to relocate permanently. He had hired Brittany Humm to find him a great house in the area, and was intent on teaching me to waltz. It wasn't going well, even when I agreed to take off my steel-toed work boots.

"How is Stephanie?" I asked Andrew.

He shrugged. "I guess . . . Well, it's simply devastating when something like this happens. Obviously. She doesn't leave the house much. But she's on a retreat now, at Green Gulch Farm. That helps. And believe it or not, Lacey went with her. They're . . . newly close."

"That's good."

"You know . . . Mason was always such a good boy. Such a sweet boy. He had some rough teenage years and

had to be put on medication, but somehow we thought ..."
His voice grew faint and husky. "I guess we all thought he
was over the worst of it."

"I'm so sorry, Andrew." That was all I could think to
say. What on earth does someone say to a parent who
has lost a child? Especially when that child was hell-bent
on the destruction of others, including your contractor,
and your own father? Words were woefully inadequate.

"Well," he said in a forced upbeat tone indicating he
was more than ready to change the subject. "I'm off to
work. Nice to see you again, Mel."

"You too, Andrew. Please give my best to your family."

"Oh!" he said, turning back and taking something out
of his briefcase. "I almost forgot. I found this the other
day and Karla told me you might want it. Can't imagine
what for, but ..."

He trailed off with a shrug and handed me an old
sepia-toned photo.

It was Peregrine and Flora Summerton, standing on
the roof of the turret, by the newly installed widow's
walk. The skyline behind them was modern-day, and included the Golden Gate Bridge.

Wind whipped their hair, and they both smiled into
the camera.

"Good morning," Aidan said as he joined us. "Lily . . . stunning as always. I do like that color on you. It's as joyful as the first rays of dawn."

"Thank you," I said, blushing and avoiding his eyes. The dress was orangey-gold cotton with a pink embroidered neckline and hem, circa 1962, and I had chosen it this morning precisely because it reminded me of a sunrise. "Aren't you just the sweet talker?"

You catch more flies with honey than with vinegar, my mama used to tell me. Did this mean I was the fly and Aidan the fly catcher?

"Is everything all right?" Aidan asked. "Am I sensing trouble? Beyond the norm, I mean."

"Dude, Lily just got *served*," Conrad said.

"Served? I fear we aren't speaking of breakfast."

"A lawsuit," I clarified.

"Ah. What a shame. What ever happened?"

"Oscar head-butted a customer."

"That's . . . unusual." Aidan had given me Oscar and knew him well. "Was this person badly injured?"

"I wasn't there when it happened, but according to Bronwyn and Maya, the customer seemed fine. But now she's claiming she sustained 'serious and debilitating neck and back injuries that hinder her in the completion of her work and significantly reduce her quality of life,'" I said, quoting from the document.

"That sounds most distressing. Might I offer my services in finding a resolution?"

"*No.* No, thank you." The only thing worse than being slapped with a slip-and-fall lawsuit—the boogeyman of every small-business owner—was being even more beholden to Aidan Rhodes than I already was. Besides . . . I wasn't sure what he meant by "finding a resolution." Aidan was one powerful witch. Autumn Jennings might very well wind up walking around looking like a frog.

"You're sure?" Aidan asked. "These personal injury lawsuits can get nasty—and expensive, even if you win. As much as I hate to say it, you may have some liability here. Is it even legal to have a pig in the city limits?"

"Don't worry about it; I've got it handled," I said, not wishing to discuss the matter any further with him. "Was there some reason in particular you stopped by?"

Aidan grinned, sending sparkling rays of light dancing in the morning breeze. He really was the most astonishing man.

"I was hoping we might have a moment to talk," he said. "About business."

My stomach clenched. Time to face the music. I did owe him, after all. "Of course. Come on in."

The door to Aunt Cora's Closet tinkled as we went inside, and Bronwyn fluttered out from the back room, cradling Oscar to her ample chest. She was dressed in billows of purple gauze, and a garland of wildflowers crowned her frizzy brown hair. Bronwyn was a fifty-something Wiccan, and one of the first—and very best—friends I had made upon my arrival in the City by the Bay not so very long ago.

"Hello, Aidan! So wonderful to see you again!" she gushed.

"Bronwyn, you light up this shop like fireworks on the Fourth of July."

"Oh, you do go on." She waved her hand but gave him a flirtatious smile. "But, Lily! Our little Oscar-oo is very upset, poor thing! I think it has something to do with the woman with the motorcycle helmet who was just here—what was that about? He's never reacted this way to *Sailor's* helmet. . . ."

"She was serving Lily with legal papers," said Aidan.

"*Legal* papers?" Bronwyn asked as Oscar hid his snout under her arm. "For what?"

"Remember when Oscar head-butted Autumn Jennings a couple of weeks ago?" I said.

Oscar snorted when I said "butt."

"Of course, naughty little, tiny piggy-pig-pig," Bronwyn said in a crooning baby voice. "But I have to say she really was bothering all of us. But . . . she's *suing* you? Seriously?"

I nodded. "I'm afraid so."

"Well, now, that's just bad karma," Bronwyn said with a frown.

"You said she wasn't hurt, though, right?"

"She was fine!" Bronwyn insisted. "She fell into the rack of swing dresses. You know how poufy those dresses are—there's enough crinoline in the skirts to cushion an NFL linebacker, and Amber Jennings is, what, a hundred pounds, soaking wet? I saw her just the other day when I brought her some of my special caramel-cherry-spice mate tea and homemade corn-cherry scones. Come to think of it, when I arrived she was up on a ladder, and she certainly didn't seem to have any back or neck injuries. She was a little under the weather, but it was a cold or the flu."

"When was this?"

"Day before yesterday, I think. . . . I thought I should make the effort, since you weren't even here when it happened. I just wanted to tell her I was sorry. Plus, to be honest, I was curious to check out her store, after what she said about our merchandise. Very nice inventory, but if you ask me not nearly as warm and inviting as Aunt Cora's Closet. The whole place was too snooty for my taste, by half. And expensive! Too rich for my blood."

"Did anything happen while you were there? Did she say anything in particular?"

Bronwyn frowned in thought, then shook her head. "Nothing at all. She didn't seem particularly bowled over by my gift basket, but she accepted it. But like I say, she told me she was a little under the weather, so maybe that accounts for her mood. She did have a very sweet dog, and I always say a pet lover is never irredeemable."

"Okay, thanks," I said, blowing out a breath. "If you think of anything else, please let me know. Aidan and I are going to talk in the back for a moment."

"I'll keep an eye on things," Bronwyn said, lugging Oscar over to her herbal stand for a treat. Oscar was a miniature pig, but he was still a porker.

In the back room Aidan and I sat down at my old jade green linoleum table. I bided my time and waited for Aidan to speak first. In witch circles simply asking "What may I help you with?" can open up a dangerous can of worms.

"I have to leave town for a little while," he said.

"Really?" Even though I knew perfectly well that he

had lived elsewhere in the past, including when he'd worked with the father who had abandoned me, in my mind Aidan was so associated with San Francisco that it was hard to imagine him anywhere else. "How long do you think you'll be gone?"

"And here I was rather hoping you would beg me to stay," he said in a quiet voice, his gaze holding mine.

"Far be it from me to dictate to the likes of Aidan Rhodes."

He smiled. "In any case, I need a favor."

Uh-oh.

"While I'm gone I need you to fill in for me and adjudicate a few issues. Nothing too strenuous."

"Beg pardon?"

He handed me a heavy well-worn leather satchel tied with a black ribbon. "You're always so curious about what I do for the local witchcraft community. Now's your chance to find out."

"I never said I wanted to find out. I'm really perfectly happy being in the dark."

Aidan smiled. "Why do I find that hard to believe? In any event, find out, you shall."

I sighed. As curious as I was about Aidan's world, I hesitated to be drawn into it. However, I was in his debt and the bill had come due. "Fine. I'm going to need more information, though. What-all is involved in 'adjudicating issues'?"

He shrugged. "Little of this, a little of that. Mostly it means keeping an eye on things, making sure nothing gets out of hand. Handling disputes, assisting with certifications ... valuable job skills that really beef up the résumé—you'll see."

"Uh-huh," I said, skeptical. At the moment I didn't need a more impressive résumé. I needed a lawyer. "What kind of certifications?"

"Fortune-tellers and necromancers must be licensed in the city and county of San Francisco. Surely your good friend Inspector Romero has mentioned this at some point."

"He has, but since I'm neither a fortune-teller nor a necromancer I didn't pay much attention. So that's what you do? Help people fill out forms down at City Hall? Surely—"

"It's all terribly glamorous, isn't it? Resolving petty squabbles, unraveling paperwork snafus . . . The excitement never ends," he said with another smile. "But it's necessary work, and you're more than qualified to handle it while I'm gone. You'll find everything you need in there."

I opened the satchel and took a peek. Inside were what appeared to be hundreds of signed notes written on ancient parchment, a business card with the mayor's personal cell phone number written on the back in pencil, and a jangly key ring. I pulled out the keys: one was an old-fashioned skeleton key, but the others were modern and, I assumed, unlocked his office at the recently rebuilt wax museum. "Aidan, what are . . . ?"

I looked up but Aidan was gone, his departure marked by a slight sway of the curtains. Letting out a loud sigh of exasperation, I grumbled, "I swear, that man moves like a vampire."

"Vampire?" Bronwyn poked her head through the curtains, Oscar still in her arms. "Are we worried about *vampires* now?"

"No, no, of course not," I assured her as I closed the satchel and stashed it under the workroom's green Formica-topped table. "Sorry. Just talking to myself."

"Oh, thank the Goddess!" said Bronwyn, and set Oscar down. Whenever Aidan was around, Oscar became excited to the point of agitation, and his little hooves clicked on the wooden planks of the floor as he hopped around. "Never a dull moment at Aunt Cora's Closet.

Anyway, Maya's here, so I'm going to take off unless you
think you'll need me this afternoon."

"A hot date?"

"Even better—I'm picking up my grandkids after day
camp and surprising them with a matinee at the Metreon.
Then we're going to go back to my place to make pizza
and popcorn and tell scary stories with all the lights out!"

"They're lucky to have you, Bronwyn."

"*I'm* the lucky one."

"By all means, go have fun," I said as we ducked back
through the curtains to the shop. "I'll be here for the rest
of the day. Hi, Maya, how are you?"

"Doing well. Thanks," Maya said as she shrugged off
her backpack, a soy chai latte in one hand. She leaned
down to pet Oscar and slipped him a bite of her crois-
sant. "I think I aced my final exam."

"That's great!" I said. "Not that we're one bit surprised, mind you."

"Certainly not," Bronwyn said. "Maya, you're a natural born scholar."

"Nah," she said, though clearly pleased at our compli-
ments. "I just study hard."

"If only that was all it took," I said, remembering my
recent struggles with algebra. I had refrained from using
magic to help me pass the GED, but just barely. The
temptation to cheat—just a little—had been nearly over-
powering.

"Oh! Guess what," said Bronwyn as she filled her large
woven basket with her knitting, several jars of herbs, and
assorted snacks. "I have the most wonderful news."

"What?" asked Maya.

"You remember my friend Charles?"

"Charles Gosnold?" I asked.

"That's the one!"

Maya and I exchanged glances, and I barely managed

to refrain from rolling my eyes. Privately, I referred to him as Charles the Charlatan. Although he claimed to be a clairvoyant, he was about as sensitive to the world beyond the veil as a rhinoceros, and even less graceful when it came to interacting with humans. I couldn't imagine why Bronwyn would consider him a friend, except that she was so bighearted that she saw the good in just about everyone. Except, perhaps, vampires.

Seeing the good in others, especially when it's not apparent, was a lesson I struggled to put into practice.

"Well, you'll never believe this, but for my birthday Charles has arranged for the Welcome coven to spend the night at the Rodchester House of Spirits!"

"The house of what, now?" I asked.

"The Rodchester House of Spirits. It's a haunted house in the South Bay," Maya explained.

"Haunted?"

"*Allegedly* haunted," Maya said.

"*Wonderfully* haunted!" Bronwyn insisted. "You mean you haven't been, Lily?"

I shook my head. I hadn't lived in the Bay Area very long and hadn't managed to visit many tourist attractions. And in any case, haunted houses weren't high on my list of places to see. I had enough of that in my regular life.

"I went years ago," said Maya. "My auntie got a kick out of it, but Mom wasn't thrilled. I remember a staircase that went nowhere, and a door that opened onto a wall ..."

Bronwyn nodded enthusiastically. "And six kitchens and *hundreds* of rooms."

"Why on earth did this Rodchester person need six kitchens?" I asked.

"She didn't, really," Maya said. "According to legend, the Widow Rodchester kept building, adding onto her house because she was afraid to stop."

"*Exactly.*" Bronwyn nodded. "Sally Rodchester's husband made his fortune manufacturing the famous Rod-chester rifles, the ones that were said to have 'won the West'—which meant, essentially, killing the people who used to live here. After both her husband and her baby died young, Sally consulted a medium who told her the souls of those killed with Rodchester rifles were angry. The only way she could stave off further bad luck was by continually adding onto her house. Which, by the way, was already huge."

"How would adding onto her house appease disgruntled spirits?" I asked.

"I can't remember the rationale, exactly . . ." said Bronwyn.

"My guess is the medium's brother was a carpenter," said Maya. "But then, I'm a cynic."

"Oh, silly! But can you believe we get to spend the *night* there?" Bronwyn may have been in her fifties, but when she got excited about something she glowed like a little girl. And spending the night in a haunted Victorian mansion was just the sort of thing to excite her sense of wonder. "What a magnificent birthday present!"

"Bronwyn, that sounds. . . ." *Dangerous,* I thought. My life hadn't been characterized by the love and kindness my dear friend had known, so I tended to see things in a more complex light. ". . . interesting. How did this even come up?"

"I happened to see a brochure for it the other day, and thought to myself, I haven't been there in *ages*. I mentioned it to Charles, and he surprised me with the arrangements! We're going to form the circle, and call down the moon . . . Oh! And mix cocktails!"

Cocktails. Of course.

"What could possibly go wrong?" said Maya, smiling but shaking her head. "The Welcome coven, cocktails, and the spirits of angry gunshot victims?"

"You two will join us, won't you?" Bronwyn asked.

"I say this with the greatest of respect and affection, my friend," said Maya, "but: No. Freaking. Way. How 'bout I take you out to lunch for your birthday? Empanadas?"

"Well, I'm disappointed you won't be there, but I accept your offer of lunch with pleasure. Lily? How about you? This sounds right up your alley."

"Bronwyn," I began, "I really don't think this is a good idea."

"Why not?" Bronwyn looked crestfallen.

"It just . . . seems like a bad idea, that's all," I said, unable to articulate the peril I sensed lurking on the dark horizon of my consciousness, elusive but no less real. But then, as I had just been telling Aidan, I wasn't a fortune-teller. I was probably just put off by the idea of a haunted house. "Won't you rethink it?"

"But everything's all arranged. The whole coven's going! Please say you'll come! I know it's late notice, but they had a cancellation, which is how we got in. It's next Saturday!"

Traipsing around haunted tourist venues on a lark wasn't my idea of a good time. I dealt with enough supernatural weirdness and danger as it was. But could I let my friend—and her coven—go into a potentially hazardous situation without me?

I rubbed the back of my neck. It was barely noon, and I'd already been served with a piggy lawsuit, burdened with Aidan's bureaucratic responsibilities, and now faced the prospect of chaperoning Bronwyn's coven overnight in a haunted mansion.

As my mother used to say: Don't some days just starch your drawers?